MENDED BY ASHES

AMY
ENGLE

This is a work of fiction. Names, characters, places, and incidents either are the product of the author's imagination or are used fictitiously. Any resemblance to actual persons, living or dead, events, or locales is entirely coincidental.

Printed in the United States of America

Cover by Zybrena Porter

ACKNOWLEDGMENTS

Back in 2012, a childhood friend expressed interest in going to see “Les Miserables” with me. I hadn’t seen Brittany in years, so of course I was excited to see her. I distinctly remember the sense of awe I felt during the opening sequence when Jean Valjean and the other prisoners performed feats of almost-super human strength as they pulled a ship into the dry dock. It was then that I had my first inspiration for “Mended by Ashes.” I got to thinking about all the hardships humans go through and how they can either break us or make us stronger. Everything else in this story grew out of that one concept.

Fast-forward a few years to 2018. I hadn’t directly spoken to Brittany since we saw “Les Miserables” in 2012. When she found out I was publishing books, she wanted to meet and catch up. After sharing what we’ve experienced, I realized what an awesome woman Brittany is. She has always had a special place in my heart since she was a friend to me in years when I really wasn’t a loveable person. But her story reminded me so much of my main character. And so I’d like to dedicate “Mended by Ashes” Brittany Regalado for her determination and strength of character. May you be like the majestic Phoenix and continue rising out of the ashes.

Chapter 1

The ladder buckled beneath Myx. She returned her hands to the runs. Clutching tightly, she leaned forward until she had re-stabilized against the shelf of boxed goods. Myx knew her efforts were useless, but she felt like she had to try for it anyways.

A shimmering yellow wisp floated gently just inches from her grasp, almost taunting her as it drifted back and forth along the faded ceiling panels.

Of course, the wisps weren't actually sentient. At least, that was the determination of the Institute scientists that researched the colored radiation. However, Myx was positive that this one was mocking her as it repeatedly evaded her touch. The pale gold energy phased through the ceiling for a moment before reappearing in the air vent. It then drifted further out of reach to the middle of the store.

Her attention was redirected to the media broadcast across the shop. There was rarely anything good on that time of the evening; Myx only played it to have background noise as she stocked the shelves with jarred and canned goods.

The broadcast was set on a segment selling domesticated, miniature beasts. Kaefh would never let her adopt a spindly, six-legged zowen or a furry little gnarfsul. However, Myx was hopeful to convince her foster mother by explaining that a pet would brighten up their infinitely dull life.

Warmth filled Myx's clenched fingers as the straw-colored wisp passed along the edge of her thumb where it clung to the ladder. Startled, her outstretched hand returned to the rungs, attempting to grasp the bit of radiation that hadn't been absorbed by her skin. The sudden motion caused the ladder to rotate away from the shelves that supported it. Myx gasped as she landed on the back of her shoulder.

The impact didn't hurt as much as it should have been. A mild chill flew up her arm, resting on the injury. The mysterious radiation numbed the pain of her fall.

"What a waste of a good wisp!" Myx groaned as she stood to her feet. She had been hoping that the energy would make her pink tourmaline eyes brighter or her pitch-colored hair silkier. Instead, it healed the inflamed muscles that had been damaged while acquiring it.

While she righted the stocking ladder, President Naichom's sigil filled the broadcast's screen—a grey figure absorbing half a dozen multi-colored wisps of radiation. The Tarasi Anthem began its five-minute overture, giving the citizens a chance to finish their affairs and gather to watch the transmission.

"Kaefh!" Myx called toward the back room. "The President's Estate is making an announcement!" She moved to the payment counter. As she swiped the top of the screen with her index finger, the anthem volume increased.

Smearing green-powdered hands down her apron, Kaefh joined her foster daughter by the broadcast screen. Despite having been cooking in the kitchen, her stark white hair was neatly tied into a perfectly clean high knot on her head. "Did you finish putting out the kelbrino berries?" She skimmed the store with her discerning, yellow-brown sinhalite eyes.

"Not yet," Myx admitted, trying unsuccessfully to use a gentle tone. She was about to make an excuse, but Kaefh would have replied that catching wisps wasn't a productive use of Myx's time. "I'll be sure to after the President's broadcast."

Kaefh pulled a comb from her apron and motioned for Myx to kneel before attacking the gnarly hair. "What does Naichom have to say now?" She tied the thick black strands into a pair of girlish tails over Myx's shoulders and continued, "Perhaps that there's a meat shortage and that we're all to eat artificially processed protein until they can raise more heshes to slaughter." Kaefh secured a white bow-clip to Myx's bangs and returned the comb to her apron.

Myx examined herself in the shop window's reflection. She looked at least three years younger—not at all like an eighteen year old. Tugging at the ties, she loosened the pressure digging into her skull.

"Where is your sister?" Kaefh demanded, taking a seat on her stool by the register. "She better not be at the Radiation Springs again. If that girl walks into this store with hair shining and eyes glistening, I'm going to suspend her allowance." The foster mother reached up and grabbed Myx's chin, examining her eyes. "You're looking rather wilted, Myx. I'm proud that you don't squander our hard-earned money on useless beauty treatments."

A quick nod was all Myx needed to do to get out of Kaefh's hold. Yes, it would have definitely been a horrid idea to tell Kaefh that she had wasted time that afternoon pursuing a wisp.

Myx turned back to the broadcast, which was still blaring the Tarasi anthem. As she waited for the song to end, she continued examining her reflected image in the window. Kaefh had been correct. Her pink tourmaline irises were getting duller by the day.

The tails of her pitch-colored hair lightly brushed her hunched shoulders as she shook her head. She could use an hour in a Radiation Spring to add a bit of sparkle to her appearance. But sadly, the energy waves would do nothing to make her petite frame more plump and attractive.

As the anthem concluded, the front door chimed and a hooded figure came racing in. “Oh, good! I didn’t miss the announcement.” Sievly stood by Myx, tightening the collar of her coat around her neck, despite the humid air.

“Where did you go after school?” Kaefh inquired, squinting at her youngest foster child.

“Quiet a moment, mama.” Sievly pointed at the broadcast. She pulled her blonde waves out of her buttoned-up white coat as she joined Myx beside the broadcast. “I’m sure this is important.”

It was not the President that made the announcement; Naichom always preferred to send a political Intern to speak to the press due to her “exceptionally hectic schedule.”

This particular young man was in his late-teens, just a bit older than Myx. “My dear fellow Tarasi, on behalf of President Naichom, it’s most regrettable that as of this morning, we are at war with our neighbors, the Hathak.”

He continued prattling on about the details of the War Declaration—about how the inhabitants of the southern hemisphere profaned the uses of the sacred wisps. But Myx didn’t care to hear the history lesson. The news broadcast had regularly reminded the Tarasi of the growing conflict with the Hathak. However, many had begun to speculate that the next war would never begin since it hadn’t been renewed in nearly thirty years.

All Myx could focus on was her sister’s smiling face. “What are you so happy about, Sievly?”

Undo the clasps of her coat, Sievly showed off the Charm pinned to her shirt lapel. It matched her green malachite eyes. “I have been selected to be an Intern at the President’s Estate!”

Myx was truly thrilled for her foster sister; fifteen years old were rarely instated as Interns. But Sievly’s natural beauty combined with her pleasant demeanor made her an obvious selection for the prestigious role. And yet, Myx couldn’t help feel jealous since she herself didn’t even know if she would even get into the Institute, let alone qualify to be an Intern.

Sievly flipped her waist-length blonde waves over her other shoulder and pointed at the man on the broadcast. “I’ll be the broadcast liaison for the next year at Naichom’s Estate. Starting tomorrow, I'm going to have that guy's job. Those I interviewed with wanted me to announce the War Declaration, but that guy had already been promised that he could finish his Internship with this historical broadcast."

"I knew you'd amount to something when I took you in!" Kaefh beamed, embracing Sievly. "Just be wary of those politician men. You know how I worry about your virtue, dear."

When Kaefh turned her attention to balancing her budget receipts, Sievly discreetly passed Myx an envelope. Grabbing the watering can, Myx headed to the store front under the pretense of caring for the plants.

Her fingers paused on the envelope's silver wax seal. It contained the sigil of the Institute—a ten-pointed star within a thick ring. Myx's future depended on if she had been accepted into one of the government's trade schools. But she couldn't bring herself to rip the wax just yet. Living in ignorance a couple moments longer was preferable to learning that she didn't make it in.

Putting the letter in her back pants pocket, she leaned down and tilted the watering can over the red pauriz flowers.

Above her head, radiation wisps danced in the wind. Well, they didn't actually dance—according to the scientists. But the way they moved about in the violet rays of Star Lyrwen reminded many of dancing.

Despite the beautiful afternoon, there was a noticeable level of tension in the streets. Tarasi civilians huddled in groups, gossiping about the War Declaration. Others shouted at their families that they were leaving the planet until the war was over as they rushed about carting haphazardly packed luggage with clothing sticking out the seams.

Pressure on her shoulder tore Myx's attention away from the street. Bishing stood over her, a somber look on his face.

"Just when we thought there might not be another War Declaration, it happens." She straightened and wiped wet fingers on her half-apron. "I guess the war will create some much-needed jobs. Maybe you'll be commissioned to—" When he looked away, Myx knew there was something difficult he wanted to tell her. "What's going on, Bish?"

He pulled a paper out of his jacket pocket and put it in her hands.

Myx unfolded it. "A recruitment flier? The War Declaration happened five minutes ago! How do you already have one?"

She looked him over. An old accident had left Bishing without a tongue, making communication rather difficult. It was from before Myx had met him, so she didn't know what maimed Bish. But she had spent the past several months studying his body language and hand signs to better understand him.

"You're just going to leave? Money's tight, so you're gonna sign up to be a soldier? They might not even want you." Myx regretted the words the moment they left her mouth.

Bishing met her gaze. His grey, smoky quartz eyes became strangely cold. Dark blonde brows furrowed together, indicating that it had been a difficult decision for him to make. He took the flier back put it in his jacket.

It might have been a decision he had struggled with for years. The Tarasi went to war with the Hathak about every other decade, depending on the tempers of the President and Emperor. Joining the military was often on the minds of both civilizations as they prepared for their next disagreement.

Nevertheless, that didn't mean Bish had to squander his artistic talent by dying in the war.

Myx suppressed a sigh. "Bishing, I know there aren't many commercial painting jobs these days. But there are plenty of other things you can do." She cursed the wisdom in her own words. There she was, worried about her own career just as much as her friend was. "But I suppose I can't blame you for seizing your future when I myself am too frightened about my own." Myx handed him the still-sealed letter. "It's from the Institute. Can you read it for me?"

Bishing tore the wax from the envelope. Since his face didn't brighten, Myx knew it wasn't good news.

"Then it looks like I don't have any prospects either." She laughed to herself. "There are no opportunities here in Capitaras. I know that I could stay and help Kaefh with the store. But that's not something I can do forever. I wonder if I should come with you."

He bit his bottom lip—his way of telling her that he didn't approve of her decision but wouldn't do anything to deter Myx. He affectionately tugged at one of her pitch-black hair tails.

"Now the problem is: how do we pull this off without being stopped by Kaefh?"

She began brainstorming. However, that wasn't exactly something she was talented at. After a moment of her mind wandering, she gaped as Bishing stepped into the store.

Even with the door closed behind him, Kaefh's displeased voice boomed through the glass. Bishing wasn't exactly the elderly woman's favorite person. However, the exact particulars about her abhorrence were a mystery to the rest of the household.

Myx took advantage of Bish's distraction and climbed up the drain pipe to her bedroom.

Chapter 2

"She's barely an adult, you perverted little pedophile!" Kaefh screeched at Bishing, her voice travelling through the floor of Myx's bedroom. "I don't like you hanging around here. She is much better off without—" Her foster mother's voice continued, bellowing indistinctly.

Ignoring Kaefh's usual rant at Bishing, Myx skimmed the couple belongings she had, deciding which she should bring with her. There were too many memories in the room—trinkets and gifts from the various foster sisters she'd received over the years. However, many of those involved painful remembrances; several of the girls had left suddenly, determined to find their own way in life rather than remain under Kaefh's loving-but-restrictive rules.

She didn't want to risk the military confiscating her few treasures, so Myx merely stuffed her bag with clothes, leaving the other items scattered across her bed.

As she sat in her window sill, the door opened with a soft creak.

Sievly didn't look surprised to see Myx half-hanging out onto the small balcony. "Leaving, huh? I suppose I knew you would also abandon me one day." Her voice had the right blend of disappointment, hope, and understanding. Not only was she gifted with physical beauty, but she was a talented manipulator; Sievly would be a great addition to the President's Estate. "Can you tell me what happened before you go?"

"I didn't get into the Institute," Myx explained, flinging her legs back into the room.

Sievly joined her on the wide sill. Despite being a couple inches taller, the younger girl put her head on her big sister's shoulder. "The Institute isn't your only option. Kaefh was going to leave you the store when she passed away. It could be a nice, comfortable life for you."

Myx stroked Sievly's long blonde curls. "It might have been comfortable staying here. But I need some excitement in my life." She paused as she recalled all the speeches given by foster sisters who had left Kaefh's protection. No, Myx wasn't like the others. They had been talented, but she had no skills to depend on. "I won't know if I can care for myself unless I leave here."

Sitting up, Sievly lost control of her emotions. Her green malachite eyes burned with indignation. "You can barely lift the pallets of uckaira bread! How do you expect to do well in the army?"

Not wanting to say anymore, Myx simply kissed her on the forehead.

"Wait." Sievly wiped at her tears as she grabbed a pouch of paper and pens from a shelf. "Promise you'll keep in touch?" She placed the writing materials in the pack with Myx's clothes. "Good-bye, sweet sister. Please return to us someday."

Nodding, Myx embraced Sievly, the bright green Intern Charm digging into her collar bone.

She eased herself over the railing. Although she'd never had the rebellious nature of her former sisters, she had seen enough of them leave the house that way that she knew the best foot- and hand-holds. Kaefh used to threaten about sealing the balcony windows shut every time a girl left. But she was soon distracted by a new foster daughter and forgot her promise, never getting around to it.

Bishing waited for Myx in the back alley. His left cheek was red and slightly swollen, likely from Kaefh's raging rant. Although the woman was only five feet tall and barely eighty pounds, she knew how to put force into her strikes.

However, that didn't appear to be what was bothering him. The pleading look in his grey, smoky quartz eyes suggested that he wanted her to reconsider before they left.

Myx shook her head and handed him her satchel.

Sievly's warning rang through her ears as she took off down the alley. Myx had very little strength herself, as well as a lack of hand-eye coordination. What made her think that the military could use her? Like Bishing's gaze had implied, it wasn't too late for her to change her mind.

Looking at the shops they passed, Myx tried to picture herself in each occupation. Could she be a law clerk, organizing case files and scheduling appointments? Or would she do better working with young children and sharpening the skills of the next generation? Perhaps being a mail-carrier was her true calling, delivering letters and packages? No, she couldn't see herself in any of those vocations for the rest of her life.

An explosion shook careers from her head. Was the Hathak attacking already? Myx ducked for cover inside a store front. Curiosity took over her mind and she sneaked a peak around the corner.

Across the road, a red-headed man stepped through the shards of a broken window. Black powder covered his torso. The man paused briefly, scratching at the red-orange scruff on his chin and causing the soot to smear across his face. He nodded as he chose his path through the crowded streets of Capitaras.

Bishing took off after the crazed, ash-covered ginger. Myx knew that Bish wouldn't want her to follow. She did so anyways, enjoying the emotional high from yet another act of rebellion.

The fleeing man nodded at every woman he passed, unaware of the scowls their gentlemen partners gave him. He only seemed vaguely aware that he was being chased by Bishing, since he let himself be repeatedly distracted by the female pedestrians.

"Hello, beautiful," the stranger shouted across the street at a young Institute woman. "Ah! Is that an Agriculture Charm I see on your lapel?"

Bishing moved to intercept the man, but was stopped by an incoming transport.

The red-headed man moved closer to the pretty Institute worker. "So, do you enjoy planting things? Has a man ever planted anything inside you?"

He was face-down on the walkway a moment later. The man went limp as Bish tried to raise him to his feet. Myx approached, slightly out of breath and confused as to what was happening.

"I know that pick-up lines have been over-used for centuries," the soot-covered man said, wriggling in Bishing's grasp. "But I enjoy them! And so will my lady-love—when I find her."

"Don't hurt him, Bish!" Myx gasped as her companion raised a fist.

Bishing's pale grey eyes widen as he saw Myx approach. He released the man and moved to keep her back. The stranger took advantage of the distraction and ran off again. After a couple yards, he looked over his shoulder. Something made him stop in his tracks before he returned to Bishing.

He pushed past him and held out his hand. "Hello, miss. I'm Rauno. Can I have the pleasure of knowing your name?"

Bishing knocked Rauno's hand away. Dark blonde curls fell past his ears and into his face as he placed himself defensively in front of Myx. His breathing came out hard as he panted for air. And yet he still maintained a formidable stance as he rose over the ginger man.

"Hello." She stepped around Bish and took Rauno's hand. "I'm Myx."

"Ah! What a beautiful name for a beautiful young lady!" Rauno brushed soot from his clothes, seemingly embarrassed at his appearance. "By any chance are you unattached?" Rauno looked Bishing up and down. "Please don't tell me that this quiet fellow is your husband; he looks old enough to be your father."

Myx put a calming hand on her friend's shoulder. "This is Bishing. Sadly, he can't speak. There was an accident that left him without a tongue. But, no, I'm not married; I just turned eighteen."

"That's the perfect age to marry, my dear," Rauno replied with a respectful nod.

"I'm terribly sorry, but you seem a bit old for me as well," Myx said as nicely as she could manage, hoping she didn't offend him. "You're what, in your mid 30's?"

"Why yes, I'm getting a bit up there in age." Rauno smiled down at her, his emerald green eyes sparkling as though he had just emerged from a Radiation Spring. "But that's all the more reason for me to find a bride. Any chance you have an older sister or young aunt that is in need of a husband?" He turned his attention to Bishing. Rauno didn't seem at all upset that he had recently been tackled by the quiet man. "Or perhaps you know someone that you can send my way? A cousin or a niece, maybe?"

Changing the subject, Myx asked, "So what caused the explosion?"

"I was brewing a love potion and I grabbed the wrong oil." Pulling open his jacket, Rauno showed her the dozens of vials sewed into the lining. He removed a plastic pack of deep blue gel and squeezed it onto a burn across his hand. "I keep doing that—making mistakes. Oh, well. I left the landlord enough money to cover the renovation expenses, if that's what your friend is concerned about."

Bishing's face didn't change as he continued to stare down the stranger.

Rauno shrugged and smiled. "It's time to start over. I think I'll get the potion right the next time I attempt it."

"Speaking of starting over, that's what Bishing and I are doing." Myx ignored Bishing's low, protesting groan. "We're joining the army—today actually. Would you like to join us? I'm sure there will be plenty of eligible young ladies in the military that you can ask to marry you."

Rauno was quiet as he scratched at the orange hairs on his chin. "I bet the police will be after me because of the explosion. They gave me a stern warning after the last incident. I guess I broke my promise and owe them a week in a prison cell. That's a good enough reason to seek sanctuary with the military since I won't meet any respectable women in jail."

Myx blinked at him. “You what now?”

He chuckled softly to himself before growing serious. “But first I need to get cleaned up. My future bride would never fall in love with me if she saw me in these scorched clothes.” Rauno had begun to walk away, but paused before asking, “May I treat you to the Radiation Spring, Myx?”

It had been nearly a year since she had been in one, so of course she was interested. As she accepted his offer, Myx hoped the energy waves would give her enough stamina to follow through with her resolution to join the Tarasi military.

Chapter 3

"That is the most attractive group of vagabonds I've ever seen," Myx whispered to Bishing. She smiled nervously at the homeless people when they noticed her staring.

Colored waves of energy flitted out of the walls of Radiation Spring. Some were absorbed by the poor wretches camped out in front of the door that were unable to afford admittance. Other wisps floated to the darkening sky, rising like steam from a boiling pot as. And many bits of radiation simply sank back into the ground from whence they came.

Bishing made a gesture with his hands that suggested that Myx should pay closer attention to their situation.

He didn't seem to care for Rauno. However, Bish hadn't object when the scorched man offered to pay for all of their admittance to the Radiation Spring. Still, he kept a close watch on their new "friend."

Polite as always, Bishing held the door open for Myx. Rauno pushed past her, his mouth hanging open as he surveyed the sparkling lady attendants inside. Bishing's scowl lessened when the first wave of wisps hit him. Myx put a comforting hand on Bish's arm and gestured towards their red-headed host.

As they waited in line at the Spring lobby, Rauno chatted excitedly about speculation on the various effects of each shade. "Scientists have tried to identify which colors of the spectrum have what effect, but first they need to discern how to separate the bands. Personally, I think most in the field only study radiation so that they can sit in it all day and enjoy the rejuvenation. They—" He trailed off as he eyed a pair of attractive women in sleek robes.

After smack to the back of the head from Bishing, Rauno continued prattling on about the theories of his former Institute colleagues. He didn't seem to hold a grudge against Bish for the repeated physical assaults.

Myx tried to pay attention while Rauno explained his research, but she didn't have enough scientific background knowledge to follow his reasoning. The best she could understand was that many believed that the radiation was triggering an evolutionary response in their DNA. Rauno use to study the differences between people's genes now and when their ancestors had settled the planet. He was skimpy on the details of why he left the Institute. However, Myx suspected that it might have been due to some kind of sexual harassment issue.

"Radiation study," Rauno continued, directing them to a different reception line, "was one of the great dividers between the Tarasi and the Hathak back in the days of early colonization. The First Hathak Empress worked to harness the power of the wisps to make humans stronger. All the while, the Tarasi President wished to find ways to make his people's life easier and to rejuvenate them from the stresses of everyday life."

"That's interesting," Myx replied, fighting the urge to tell him that she already knew that.

Rauno continued on, unaware that he was beginning to bore his young companion. "As to their current intentions, I have no idea. It's been a couple years since I've been affiliated with the Institute."

A group of patrons was led out of the lobby, deeper into the Spring. With the room emptier, Myx was able to get a better look at building's interior. Radiation shot out of vents in the floor, the colored energy fanning out as though it was water spewing from a fountain. The wisps and threads then flitted through the crowds of patrons and attendants.

As Myx was admiring the mottled discoloration along the brick walls, a group of attendants approached and began fussing over her appearance.

"See these split ends? Her hair looks like the back end of my pet rinchys."

"And those jagged nails! You'd think that she dug ditches for a living."

"Ah, those poor eyes; they've almost reverted back to plain, mud brown."

They murmured to each other about how they'd never seen such a wretched-looking young woman and that she needed to be put in the epicenter of the Spring. Two of the women linked arms with her and pulled her into a tunnel. The third walked behind them, picking at Myx's pitch-black hair tails with glossy, lacquered fingernails.

Myx did her best to remain pleasant as the strangers continued commenting on how horrible her appearance was. Embarrassment was not an uncommon feeling for her, but she hated how it made her face hot and flushed.

"Thank you for your concern," she squeaked, unused to so much attention. "I hope the radiation makes me as lovely as all of you."

The attendants feigned modesty.

"Oh, it's all due to the radiation!"

"I'm usually such a mess."

"You can be even lovelier than us if you could come to the Spring every day!"

The two clutching Myx's arms stopped and let go of her. They turned and faced the third girl. Envy flashed in their eyes.

"What?" the last girl asked, looking confused. "Is that not true?"

Myx gawked in astonishment as a fight broke out among the three attendants. They each accused the others of being ugly, declaring herself to be the most beautiful of them all. With their attention off her, Myx sprinted out of sight and entered the nearest alcove.

Warm, moist air surrounded Myx as she walked down a long, twisting corridor. The tunnel ended at the edge of a small stream. Barrels of clean white towels sat to the side of the room, as well as long benches covered in lidded boxes. Radiation mingled with the water, causing the currents to look like rippling rainbows.

After stripping down to her smallclothes, Myx waded in. The water was the perfect temperature as the waves tugged against her. Thick wisps the length of her arm passed through her torso, giving Myx a rush of euphoria.

A woman's head emerged through the river's surface. She barely glanced at Myx with purple tanzanite eyes as she moved to a towel barrel. Myx couldn't help but stare at the six-foot-tall, towering woman. Radiated water dripped from her tanned, muscular form. She hastily arranged her dark brown hair into a long, simple braid over her shoulder.

"Here are your clothes, Alycee," a perky attendant said to the woman, holding out a lidded box.

Alycee closed the space between her and the girl in an instant. She grabbed the attendant by the jaw, causing the girl to drop the box onto the damp ground. "You tell anyone else my name and yours won't be relevant anymore. Do you understand?"

The attendant nodded, tears welling in her terrified, red ruby eyes. The girl fled the cave the moment Alycee released her.

"That was rude," Myx commented, not sure why she felt compelled to scold a stranger. She tugged the ties off her hair tails and placed the bands around her wrist. "Don't bother threatening me. I got the message loud and clear: you don't want people knowing your name. I promise not to tell anyone."

Collecting her clothes box, Alycee didn't take her stark purple irises off Myx. The woman dressed cautiously.

"Not that it matters, but I probably won't be alive long," Myx mused as she walked further into the radiation-infused water. She used her fingers to get out the tangles of her pitch-colored hair. "My friends and I are joining the army. We very well might die during the first battle we are in."

Alycee paused with her shirt halfway down her abdomen. "Then why go?"

Myx shrugged, fixing her gaze on the cracks along the rock wall. Wisps flitted out gently before mingling with the other threads of energy.

"I suppose because I'd rather die having an adventure than live a long, boring life." Myx dunked her head under the stream's warm surface. When she came back up, Alycee stood at the edge of the water.

"Hmm. I wouldn't have pegged you as a soldier." Alycee looked her up and down. "It'll take a bit of work for you to become combat-ready."

"I'm not scared of hard work," Myx corrected, not sure why she felt the need to explain her motives to this woman. She twisted the water out of her black hair, noting that it felt a little silkier than it had before. "My foster mother has made me do my fair share of it." She narrowed her pink tourmaline eyes at the muscular woman, wondering if she had just met Tarasi a militant. "Why do you care anyways?"

Squeezing water from her braid, Alycee replied, "I was thinking about joining myself." The woman's voice was oddly defensive as she continued, "It seems to be a popular mind-set due to the War Declaration this afternoon."

Unsure of how to reply, Myx resumed her washing. Buoys containing soap cubes bobbed up and down across the river's surface. She removed one and lathered herself up. The skin cleanser tingled as colorful, radiation-infused liquid passed over it. Dropping below the water's surface, Myx swam the length of the river to where it became increasingly shallow.

Alycee held out a towel for her. "Still, I think I should come with you—to make sure that you don't tell people who I am."

Myx didn't understand what that had to do with anything. Not moving out of the stream, she tried to work out why Alycee would feel the need to come with her. Myx didn't benefit from revealing the woman's identity. Still, she wondered if Alycee was only agreeing to come with her because she was lonely and in need of some friendship; these days, companionship was difficult to find and people tended to hold close to the few kind fellows they met.

She lethargically waded out of the water. Accepting the towel from Alycee, Myx said, "I'd be happy if you joined me."

When both women finished dressing, they headed back to the lobby. The trio of attendants was being restrained as their bloodied finger nails furiously extended towards the others. Alycee gave them a stern look and they settled enough to let them pass by peacefully.

Rauno and Bishing lounged on a pair of pastel blue couches tucked to the side of the lobby. The scientist seemed to be in the middle of a lecture on the different affects of wisps during intercourse. All the while, Bish appeared to be scanning the patrons as he attempted to ignore Rauno.

Bishing darted off his resting place and charged towards Myx the moment he laid eyes on her.

Myx held up a hand in greeting. "I made another new friend, Bish. What a great day this is turning out to be! Well, I suppose it's not all great—you know, with the War Declaration and all. But—"

The towering stranger put a hand on Myx's shoulder to stop her rambling. "Greetings, gentlemen. My name is Alycee. I wish to join this young woman in her quest to become a soldier. If you don't like it, that is unfortunate. But I won't change my mind." When they didn't protest, she added, "I hope you don't go around spewing my name; I'd like to remain as unknown as possible."

Looking the woman over, Bishing's face tightened.

His lack of civility confused Myx. If anything, he should be grateful that she had added new friends to their group; there were more people to keep an eye on and protect her in the military. She made a mental note to talk him about it at another time.

"Well, we should probably get going," Myx said, hoping to diffuse the tension.

As she reached the main lobby, she froze.

Kaefh walked through the glass doors of the Radiation Spring. Although she was a foot shorter than most of the patrons, she still was able to spot her foster daughrter. "There you are! Myx, come here this instant!" She moved through the gathered attendants. Her white top knot was barely visible above the crowd's shoulders. "What are you doing running away from home with this monster? There's nothing but pain and heart-ache with him."

For a moment, she nearly believed Kaefh. Reasons why she shouldn't join the military flew through her mind. But then she remembered why she was throwing caution to the wind and seizing her future.

Myx turned to her newest companion. "Any chance you have a transport?"

Alycee nodded, heading to a side exit. "Down the street."

Kaefh ran to the nearest attendant. "Help! That man is stealing my daughter!"

Bishing grabbed Myx's hand and hauled her along after Alycee and Rauno. They didn't make it far before sirens rang in the distance.

Chapter 4

Myx's face slammed into the transport's side window as Alycee veered left. Fumbling with the restraints, she attempted to secure her body before her newest companion's driving killed her.

Sirens grew louder as a pair of police squads appeared, making Alycee's maneuvering even more frantic as they fled the Radiation Spring. Myx was still moist from her dip in the stream, so she slipped around in the smooth seat; the belts squeezed her joints uncomfortably as she was tossed about.

"We can't stay in Capitaras," Rauno commented as he opened his jacket. The lining had dozens of unlabeled vials sewn inside it. He pulled out a thin, glass container and tossed it out his half-open window.

Thick smoke billowed behind them, allowing the vehicle to tuck into an alley unnoticed. The sirens diminished as the pursuers sped away from their hiding place.

Alycee's driving skills were hindered even further as she strapped a leather sheath around her right thigh. She often took her attention from the controls to tighten a strap or check the contents of the dozens of pouches along and within the material.

"Can't that wait?" Myx asked, clutching at her restraints as Alycee barely missed hit a pair of pedestrians.

"I have been driving since before you were born," the menacing woman said, this time purposely swerving to make the vehicle jerk. Alycee removed a small blade from one of the pouches and palmed it in her left hand. "I know what I'm doing."

Myx wondered if Alycee was telling the truth. The other woman was perhaps a dozen years older than her. It didn't seem likely that she had learned to drive as a child. And yet, she couldn't help feeling like Alycee hadn't exactly had a traditional childhood. So she nodded and kept her mouth shut as they weaved in and out of incoming vehicles.

Rauno's fingers skimmed through the chemicals. His facial expressions altered depending on what was in each vial. "They'll find us anywhere we hide in the capital. But there should be a recruitment center in the next metropolis over."

"The police will suspect we fled Capitaras," Alycee replied, turning her vehicle into a junk yard. "We should stay here."

The scientist continued fussing with the vials in his vest, seemingly to check that nothing was broken. "Or maybe they'll think we stayed because leaving is such an obvious choice for kidnappers. If so, we should flee to a different part of Tarasi."

Bishing leaned back in his chair. He folded his arms into each other, clearly still unhappy at having picked up strangers.

All three stared each other down before turning to Myx with expectant looks.

"What? It's up to me?" Since when was she allowed to be in charge? It felt both satisfying and frightening to have the others turn to her for advice. Myx would need to make the right decision so that they'll continue trusting her. She thought a moment before saying, "Sorry, Alycee, but I think Rauno's suggestion makes more sense."

Alycee didn't look pleased, but she started up the transport once again. "Who am I to argue with future militants?" she scoffed, sarcasm thick in her tone.

The ship groaned as the intimidating woman steered it towards the highway.

"You wanted to stick with us for a little while, but you're going to have to stay longer than expected." Myx put a sympathetic hand on her shoulder. "I appreciate your help, though."

Scowling, Alycee shrugged off her touch. "I'm regretting this already."

They sat in awkward silence for several hours as they sped in out of traffic. Myx tried on several occasions to spark up a conversation, but they all averted their attention out their windows.

At the edge of Capitaras, a hotel appeared suddenly to the left and Alycee cranked the controls to make the turn.

Pieces of the hotel's disintegrating roof flew off in the wind. Deep slashes in the peeling paint looked as though a wild animal had clawed its way across the rickety building. As Myx opened her transport door, she was greeted with a pungent, musty odor similar to wet cofarsen pups.

Rauno removed coins from various pockets sewn into his jacket. "You couldn't choose a hotel with a little more class? I can't imagine any scenarios where I find my future bride in this dump."

"I can't imagine any scenarios where you find a bride at all," Alycee retorted, her purple tanzanite eyes glaring at the lanky man. She then reminded him, "You wanted to leave Capitaras. This is the best chance we have. Checking into pleasanter lodgings would only draw the attention of the authorities."

The four checked into a single room and began to settle into the cramped quarters.

Bishing made several signs with his hands.

Myx translated, "We should hunker down here for a day or two until the police give up their search."

The others agreed, but they didn't seem thrilled by the idea.

As they waited out the clock, Bishing helped Alycee sharpen a set of large knives. Myx had wanted to help, but Bish shook his head.

Instead, Myx was pressured into helping Rauno replenish his supply of chemicals. She squeezed the complimentary toiletries into thin glass vials as she listened to the researcher's lectures on what he had learned about radiation during his Institute days. The technical words fell on her uninterested ears as Myx fixated her gaze on the mold-colored stains along the chipped plaster walls.

Rauno held up a small jar. "You know, I've got a couple chemicals that greatly enhance one's beauty when combined with radiation. I should have given them to you when we were at the Spring. We could venture to another one tomorrow to try it out."

Myx looked uncertainly at the jar. "Try?"

"Oh, yes. It's still experimental, but it should safe. I suppose radiation isn't really a necessity for this experiment." Rauno scooped out a creamy dollop with a finger and moved towards Myx.

Bishing was between them in an instant, grabbing Rauno's wrist and twisting it back. He wiped the ointment onto the scientist's jacket, took the jar from the other hand, and moved to the restroom. The sound of rushing water echoed in their tiny room, followed by a gurgling flush. Bish returned to the common area and handed the wet-but-empty jar back to Rauno. Without another look, he resumed sharpening an axe for Alycee.

"I think he simply fears having competition for your affection," Rauno mused as he filled the empty jar with thufgal cream.

Myx ignored him. She plopped onto the bed and turned on a broadcast. It wasn't an interesting show, so she swiped her hand along the bottom of the screen. Hoping to find an update on the war, she continued flipping through the segments.

"There's something that I don't quite understand," Alycee mused, not looking up from the blade she whetted against a stone.

"I imagine that many things confuse those who prefer more physical interests than the expanding of one's mind," Rauno replied as he tucked vials into his jacket. His tone had more arrogant than insulting, not intending to offend the woman. "What is it that you wish to know?"

Alycee ignored Rauno and turned to Myx. "Why are the police so interested in stopping us? They should be focused on protecting Tarasi from the Hathak, not tracking down a single teenager." She stood and moved toward the bed, her hand still clutching her knife. "You are eighteen and can make your own decisions. Why are you so important?"

Myx didn't know how to answer. "I'm not sure why. My foster mother is a very forceful woman." She felt herself starting to ramble, but she couldn't stop. "Kaefh has lost nearly a dozen foster children over the years and I guess she never thought I'd leave like the other girls."

Bishing moved to her side put a comforting hand on her back.

Alycee shrugged, returned to her seat, and began returning the sharpened blades to her thigh pouches without another word.

Turning her attention back to the broadcast, Myx calmed herself by searching for a diverting segment. She hadn't realized how hard it would be to run away from home. A flitting sensation moved through her insides, growing as her anxiety swelled.

As she swiped, something familiar caused her to flip back to the previous channel.

Looking even more radiant than usual, Sievly stood behind a podium. Her long, blonde curls shimmered in the fading purple light of Star Lyrwen as she addressed the press. "...pleased by the reaction of the Tarasi civilization. Military recruitment has increased by nearly 500%. President Naichom appreciates the enthusiasm of our new troops."

Rauno stepped in front of the broadcast screen. "Who is this golden goddess of a woman?"

Sievly's voice continued, the girl unaware that there were likely millions of men acting similar to Rauno. "Within the week, we plan on launching a counter-strike when we've prepared our recruits. In the meantime, the reserve forces have been called in and will act as a shield against the Hathak's next strike."

Seeing her foster sister brought on a fresh wave of regret. Myx continued watching the broadcast as Sievly gracefully answered the press's questions.

"That's my foster sister," Myx replied, joining him at the wall.

"Does she have a boyfriend?" Rauno asked, not taking his eyes off her.

"Stop thinking like that about her! Sievly is only fifteen!"

Rauno smirked, smoothing his red, scraggly beard. "If she is meant to be my future bride, I could wait three more years for her."

Myx had an overwhelming urge to snatch one of Alycee's scattered blades and hack Rauno to pieces. Her breath ragged and face burning hot, she reached for a small knife mere inches from her grasp.

Alycee snatched Myx's hand and firmly put it back in her lap. "A fifteen year old is allowed to be one of Naichom's Interns? Hmm. And I suppose that answers my question about the police; relatives of the Estate's Presidential Force are fiercely protected. I apologize for my earlier outburst."

A fresh wave of guilt overcame Myx. And then she had a solution to their problem. She removed the pouch of paper and pens Sievly had given her and began a letter. It was the least she could do to clarify any confusion for her family and the police.

She wrote about her new friends—of course, she omitted their names to protect Alycee and Rauno. And since Myx didn't want the police staking out the recruitment centers to find her, she didn't tell Kaefh that she was signing up for the army. Instead, she simply said that her band of companions would be travelling on a journey of self-discovery; it wasn't that much of a lie after all.

Sirens sounded outside as Myx put the final touches on her letters. She placed the pages on the bedside table and went about collecting her things.

"That's not a good idea," Alycee interjected, clasping the correspondence.

Bishing seized the woman's arm. He took back the wrinkled papers and placed them on the bed-side table.

"Don't worry," Myx assured Alycee. She nearly gave in as the six-foot tall woman stared her down with her intense, purple tanzanite eyes. But Myx had been made the leader when they turned to her for decisions. So she defended her position. "I didn't put anything about the military in them. And I definitely didn't mention your names."

Rauno barged out of the bathroom, mixing multiple vials together in an ice bucket. "This should confuse the police for a bit."

He set the smoking container by the door before moving to the broadcast screen. Over the scuffed floor boards, Rauno emptied another vial and lit a match. The ground caught fire and almost instantly crumbled into the room below them.

The scientist gestured at the hole. "Ladies first."

Pulling on her pack, Alycee said, "I'm very concerned by the amount of explosives that you keep on your person." The woman gave him a wary glance before jumping through the opening. She landed with a hard thud on the couch in the room below. Alycee did a quick scan of her new surroundings before motioning for the rest to follow.

Myx awkwardly leaped next and stepped aside for the men to descend.

In the corner, a frightened couple huddled together as pieces of their ceiling continued to rain into their room. They hid their faces and mumbled prayers as they clutched each other.

"Thank you for your hospitality," Myx said in her sweetest voice, but it sounded ominous and off-putting. "We'll be leaving now. Sorry for the mess," she apologized as Rauno once again set the floor on fire.

Chapter 5

"We lost them once; we can lose them again." Alycee pulled hard on the transport controls and they spun last second into a side street.

Behind them, police vehicles collided with the nearby walls and light poles. Sparks flew from the exposed wiring, igniting the nearby awnings over a local bakery. Fleeing citizens blocked the path of several other pursuing transports.

In the back seat, Rauno mixed together various liquids from the vials sewed into his jacket. Bishing then strategically tossed the explosives into the road, making wide craters in the asphalt. All of which was difficult to do with Alycee's erratic driving. However, they soon adjusted into an effective groove as they fled the police.

Myx had been concerned about endangering the lives of nearby pedestrians, but luckily Bish had exceptional aim. To be on the safe side, she pulled up a map of the city and navigated their path to less populated areas of Capitaras.

Her initial feeling at being followed by the police was that of terror. And yet, the more they fled, the more that diminished. Now Myx enjoyed the rush of adventure and camaraderie that she had been craving. It was the most exhilarated she had ever been and her body ached for more.

"There's a launch ramp three blocks north," Myx told Alycee, bracing herself against her window. "Turn left up here."

But Myx wished she hadn't said that as Alycee obeyed; a blockade appeared ahead.

Alycee fiddled with the controls as she directed her transport towards a business building. The front right tire went up the structure, followed by the other three, jostling the passengers in the process. For several moments, they were perpendicular to the ground as they drove along the wall. The police stared as the fugitives passed the blockade.

"Where can I get me one of these, Alycee?" Rauno chuckled, covering a spilling vial with his thumb. "I bet my future bride would love a ride in it." As the vehicle lurched back to the street, Rauno added, "Oh, yeah, this probably isn't the right time for this conversation. We can talk about it later."

The launch ramp soon became visible, rising above the shorter buildings by it. The wide expanse of concrete ended at the edge of a cliff overlooking Lake Vista.

“Are you sure this is a good idea?” Rauno asked, clutching his stomach. He seemed to have lost all interest in combining his jarred elixirs. “I’ve heard of awful accidents that occurred during failed launches. It’d rather not—”

Bishing put a hand over Rauno’s mouth and checked the straps of his chest restraints with the other. Alycee followed his lead and made sure that she and Myx were secure; she motioned for Myx to let go of the controls while she prepared for the upcoming drop. No one else said a word as they approached the ramp.

Myx had never been launched before. She was both frightened and excited as Alycee’s transport zoomed off the slope.

And then they began to fall.

Rauno screamed in between shouting obscenities; he clutched at his jacket to prevent the precious glass vials from flying out.

Alycee’s hands messed with the controls until there was a thud. A pair of wings unfolded on the sides of the transport, preventing them from falling any longer. Instead, they glided with the winds.

Myx turned her head to check on the men.

“Oh, that wasn’t as bad as I thought,” Rauno said, wiping sweat from his brow.

Bishing shook his head and rolled his grey, smoky quartz eyes. He cradled the air and swung his arms gently before tapping his left ring finger.

“What?” Rauno slicked back his frazzled red hair and looked to Myx for translation.

“He says that you’re a baby and that’s why you can’t find a wife,” she explained with a sigh. Myx frowned at her friend. “That’s not very nice, Bish. I think you owe Rauno an apology.”

But there wasn’t time for all that; a dozen police vehicles launched off the ramp after them.

“Well now they know that we’re leaving Capitaras,” Rauno groaned, sweat continuing to drip down his pale forehead. His emerald eyes went wild as he asked, “What are we going to do, Myx? I’d love to help you on your journey to freedom, but I’m confident that I don’t want to continue my wife-search in prison.”

“You won’t have to,” Alycee smirked, nodding at the horizon.

White lightning cracked through dark clouds, followed shortly by the boom of thunder. Pockets of radiation wisps were visible throughout the tempest, moving lazily despite the sturdy gusts. It would have been considered a pretty sight if not for being pursued by the authorities.

"Hit that blue button of there, Myx," Alycee instructed, pointed across the console. "It'll activate my crude-version of a cloaking device. We can't hide if they are close by, but that will keep them from spotting us at a distance." She released her restraints and spun to face the men in the back. "I'm taking us back to Capitaras. If you want to leave, you're welcome to once we get there. But I now feel a responsibility to Myx. So I'm sticking with her whatever she wishes to do. What do you have to say?"

Rauno scratched his chin. "Gee, you sure seem to get into a bit of trouble. But I guess I do, too. But it only makes sense to stick with a woman such as yourself. Alycee, you're a very capable woman; I feel safe when I'm around you—that is, when we aren't shooting off ramps. Do you mind if I tag along?"

"You're pretty competent as well." Alycee's purple tanzanite irises had a hint of amusement for a moment before returning to her normal, emotionless stare. "You may stay so long as you stop flirting with me. Do we have a deal?"

Bishing tapped Rauno on the shoulder and made a circle along his chest with his fist. Myx explained that Bish was sorry. She added that he hoped they could start to get along—even though he hadn't exactly expressed that. The silent man's gaze suggested that he didn't care for her addition, but he didn't contradict her.

For safe measure, Alycee circled the storm for several hours before returning to the Tarasi capital. However, their determination to remain civil ended as they fussed over what kind of food they wanted to get for dinner.

"I can't believe you left the rations back at the hotel!" Alycee shouted at Rauno.

Despite the harsh tone directed at him, the scientist's words were gentle as he replied, "I was too busy melting the floor so that we could escape. Bishing or Myx should have grabbed them.

Bish signed something that Myx didn't care to translate. Besides, she was too busy apologizing or suggesting places to eat. But none cared for her ideas.

Rauno kept insisting to get fried aplidos and Bishing repeatedly made exaggerated X's with his arms to show his disgust for that meal. Alycee offered that they get fylith stew while Myx told them that she was in the mood for pab and ohgam sandwiches.

They were so distracted with their grumblings that they barely saw the man in the road before their transport ran him over.

"I vote that Alycee shouldn't drive anymore!" Rauno screeched, opening his door.

"You didn't see him either," Alycee snapped, following him out of the transport. She put her ear to the stranger's chest and then began puffing air into his mouth. Pausing in the middle of the resuscitation, she added, "Besides, it's my vehicle. No one else has permission to drive it."

Myx sat on the opposite side of the unconscious man. She didn't know what to do, but she had often seen actor doctors check eyelids in broadcasts. The dark blue irises shrank against the dilated pupils. Sitting back on her heels with a sigh, Myx mused, "I don't think he's from this planet. His eyes are weird; they aren't gem-colored."

Bishing gently pushed her aside. He ripped fabric off the man's pant leg and pressed it against a bloody gash in his thigh.

"His name is Voumatir," Rauno said after finding the man's identification card. He pursed his lips as he searched through the wallet. "I can't pronounce his home planet. Strribiaeheun, I think. Never heard of it. Do you think we should take this foreigner to the hospital?"

Nodding in reply, they each took one of Voumatir's limbs and gently lifted him. They paused a moment as a melodic humming escaped his mouth. But he didn't awaken. After exchanging confused looks, the four continued hefting him to the transport.

"We should call an ambulance." Myx continued her examination of him, fascinated by his finger nails; the short, soft nubs were a clear, pinkish hue instead of hard and slate grey. It was strange to see an adult without the physical effects of long-term radiation exposure. At least he had a muscular frame, despite lacking the strength boost that the wisps granted over time. "I wonder if the doctors at the hospital know how to treat aliens."

"No! We can't take him there. That would just attract unwanted attention from the police," Alycee explained, getting into the pilot's seat. "We will just leave him near the hospital entrance. Someone is bound to find him sooner or later."

The alien ceased his humming and gasped awake. "Ah! My leg feels like it's been sawed in half!"

"Hello. I'm Myx. We, uh, saw you get hit by a vehicle." She hoped that the fact that the man was losing a lot of blood would help make her lie seem believable to the injured man. Myx pressed his shoulder down when he tried to sit up. "We're taking you to the hospital. You should be better in no time. Just try to relax."

"Oh, I'm very relaxed!" Voumatir muttered with a giggle. He ran a hand through his ruffled, bright blonde hair. "I dreamt that I had been kissed by an angel. Which one of you is my guardian savior?"

Alycee's transport turned abruptly before any of the others could tell the man who had given him mouth-to-mouth resuscitation. As they recovered, there was another jolt in the other direction. The warrior woman coughed loudly when Rauno opened his mouth to say something; the researcher surprisingly picked up on Alycee's hint.

"I'm just glad that I wore my body armor today," Voumatir said, unphased by the frantic driving. "Otherwise, I might have lost my leg!"

Rauno raised an eyebrow at Voumatir. "You just happened to be wearing armor?"

"With this whole war business, I thought I'd rather be safe than sorry in case there was an attack. So I invested in some protection. I guess I'm pretty lucky that I was paranoid. I don't usually get such serious feelings like that." Voumatir sat up and looked over Alycee. "Thank you for saving my life. I've heard of people having guardian angels, but I didn't realize that mine would be so beautiful. Honestly, I thought the spirit watching over me would be some wrinkly old dude or something. Ha!"

"How droll you are!" Rauno pulled a vial and a white cloth from his jacket and poured out a clear liquid. Deftly, he placed the cloth over Voumatir's mouth and the man fell unconscious once again. "He was starting to bond with Alycee. I can't allow that."

"I appreciate your intervention, Rauno." Alycee pulled her vehicle next to a hospital sign.

They picked up Voumatir and roughly guided his body out of the transport.

Myx removed note materials from her back and scribbled a description of what happened, hoping that the alien knew how to read the Tarasi script.

As she turned to leave, a hand grasped her wrist.

"I don't want to stay here!" Voumatir clutched onto Myx with the astounding strength of someone experiencing an adrenaline high. "Don't leave me. Let me stay with my guardian angel!"

Chapter 6

Myx struggled to get out of Voumatir's grip. She spoke as soothingly as she could manage while also sounding firm and resolute. "It's going to be okay. You'll make a full recovery at the hospital. The doctors in Capitaras are the best on the planet. We wish you happy healing. Now I must leave."

Not giving up, Voumatir pulled on her until he was sitting up. "Oh, I'll be fine! I just need some pain meds—and a perhaps a little time at one of your planet's fantastic Radiation Springs." With a groan, the alien struggled to get to his feet. He swayed a moment before adding, "Maybe we can all go together! Not that my guardian angel needs it; she's already the most beautiful—" He trailed off, and wiped at his pale lips before giggling like a loon.

Bishing came to Myx's side and added his effort to freeing her from the stranger. He firmly pressed several pressure points in Voumatir's forearm, but his grip never faltered.

"I think he's in shock," Myx commented, feeling uncomfortable under his sweaty hand.

Voumatir became lucid suddenly and leaned on Myx. He began walking, pulling her along to the transport as he limped. Ignoring the others, he smiled at Alycee. His plain, blue eyes beamed at her. "What do you say gorgeous? Can I treat you to a day at a Spring? I love those places! I can't wait to have gemstone irises like your guys. How long will that take?" He continued mumbling about other things he enjoyed about their planet.

"I've picked up enough strays for today." Alycee came to Myx's rescue. She held a knife to edge of Voumatir's chest. "Let go of her, or I'll sever all the tendons in your shoulder."

The stranger looked absolutely elated that Alycee was so close to him. He released Myx and latched onto the tall woman. However, their embrace didn't last long. Alycee somehow managed to rearrange his limbs so that he was clutching at the hospital sign for support.

"No! Don't let go," Voumatir begged, reaching for Alycee. He stumbled on his bad leg, but was able to keep himself erect.

"Good day. May we never meet again!"

"Look, I've had a rough day." Voumatir ran a hand through his disheveled, bright yellow hair. "My band just kicked me out of our tour. I don't have anywhere else to go. A fresh start is all that I need. I have a good feeling about you guys; I think we'd make a nice little family."

Myx rubbed her wrist and backed away. In a low voice, she said to Bishing, "I suppose that we don't need to be friends with all the new people we meet."

The fact that the others were walking back to their transport didn't deter Voumatir in the least. "Where are you guys headed? Sorry, I guess that sounds a bit needy." He choked down a sob as he bit his lip. "I'm fine! I'll be alright, I guess. I'm sure that we'll meet again."

Rauno sighed as he removed a bottle from his jacket. He retraced his steps back to the alien. "I hate seeing people in need. I've got some pain killers."

Alycee dashed at Rauno and knocked the pills out of his hands. "Don't treat the alien! Once you do, we'll never get rid of him. If he needs medicine so bad, he can walk into that hospital and get some." She pointed at the emergency room doors before adding, "Besides, we have the police on our tail; I'm sure that he doesn't want to get involved with criminals."

"Criminals?" Voumatir looked them over and shook his head. "I doubt that very much. You seem like decent folks. If you weren't, you wouldn't have brought me to the hospital."

Bishing tapped Myx on the shoulder. He pointed at Alycee and then Voumatir before lacing his fingers together. She couldn't quite figure out what he was trying to say about them, so he drew a heart outline with his index fingers.

"No!" Myx whispered to her friend. "Alycee can't stand him. Why would you even suggest that? They'd make an awful couple!"

"Who would make an awful couple?" Rauno asked, putting the retrieved pills back into their hidden pocket. "I hope you aren't talking about me and Alycee. I'm finally starting to wear her down."

Voumatir fell into Alycee, pretending to pass out. His eyes kept opening to stare at Alycee before quickly shutting again. The poor woman scowled as she attempted to drop the alien to the ground; his hands tangled in her long, brown braid. The stranger pulled her hair gently, causing Alycee's face to align beside his.

"You have such bewitching eyes," Voumatir sighed.

"Bishing thinks those should get together," Myx explained to Rauno.

The scientist frowned. He scratched at his scraggly red hair with a slate grey finger nail. "That's just great! Another ladies' man is the last thing this group needs. I was hoping Alycee would marry me someday. I'm telling you, we should find more women for our merry band so that I can have a wider pool to fish in."

Bishing smacked Rauno over the head; there was no need for Myx to translate. She made no attempt to reprimand him for striking their companion; Rauno really needed to learn to think more carefully before speaking.

They rejoined Alycee to find that Voumatir had somehow taken a seat inside the transport. Unsure of what to do, they let her deal with him.

Hospital staff and pedestrians stopped to gape at the scene.

"Do you need us to call security?" an elderly woman asked.

One of her friends added, "There's a strapping nurse over there that can assist you with your problem."

Myx smiled kindly at the ladies. "That won't be necessary. They are just having a lovers' spat. It'll be cleared up soon. But thank you so much for your concern! Have a lovely day." She wasn't a gifted liar, but the women seemed to believe her.

The group waved goodbye as they passed, explaining to Alycee and Voumatir how important clear communication was in a relationship.

Voumatir moved to the navigator's position of the transport, carefully placing Myx's bag behind the seat. "Perhaps a kiss is all I need to feel better. What do you say, gorgeous?" He extended his bloody leg across the console. "Will my guardian angel use her magic lips to heal my wound?"

"I'd rather kiss a corpse!" Alycee snatched his foot and pulled.

He jerked backwards but remained in the seat. "If you're worrying about what I can contribute, that's not a problem. I can play multiple instruments and I have excellent people skills. I'm also willing to do some cleaning and assist with cooking. Oh, and I'm told that I'm good at making people feel better when they're sad. My former buddy and I—"

"This isn't an interview." With a huff, Alycee removed a small, pronged object from under her chair. She stabbed the points into Voumatir's knee joint and hit the trigger.

His body shook for several moments before going limp.

Not being careful anymore, Alycee tugged Voumatir out of the transport and placed him on the ground. "Alright. Who's hungry?" She went back into the pilot's seat. "I really don't care where we go anymore, so long as it's nowhere near here."

The other companions returned as well after giving the unconscious Voumatir one last sympathetic look. None offered suggestions on where to eat as they strapped in.

The alien lay sprawled on the lawn, looking as though he were napping.

"I still think we should take him all the way into the hospital," Myx commented as she retrieved her bag from behind her seat. All her dislike of the man had somehow been replaced with pity. "What if he dies because no one realizes he needs medical attention?"

Alycee took off into traffic, her driving even more erratic than it had been during the police chase. "We did the most we could do. Remember: we are on the run."

Bishing made a series of hand motions, pointing at each person of the group. He swirled his wrist around the inside of the transport before pretending to spoon food into his mouth. With one last gesture, he held up a single index finger and waited in that position until Myx understood his signs.

"Oh, Bish knows a place he thinks we'd all like." Myx squished towards the window as he moved to the navigation grid. "It's some kind of buffet-style restaurant. How does that sound?"

They all agreed—their moods improving despite the fact that they just left an alien unconscious on the ground after hitting him with their transport and electrocuting him.

Chapter 7

The recruitment center was the epitome of bureaucracy. Bathed in the dimming violet light of the setting Star Lyrwen, the building was full of counters and cubicles, with people rushing every which way. Signs indentified each station. Confused-looking recruits wandered to various stations, only to be sent elsewhere by the recruiters.

Bishing moved to the desk under the sign saying, "START HERE." He mimed a writing motion and the unpleasant-looking woman behind the counter handed him a clipboard. Once they all obtained their paperwork, the group moved to the sitting area to fill in their information.

"Since we are wanted fugitives," Rauno whispered, "should we make up aliases? I'd like to be called Yorcen; I'll be a twenty-five year old banker who dreams of the glory of battle."

Alycee sniggered. "Yeah, like you'd pass for twenty-five! You're in your mid-thirties."

Myx shook her head. "Fill it out like normal, Rauno. The military is in such a need of recruits that they probably won't care if there's a warrant out for you—not that the police know your identities. Besides, if they ask about it, we can explain what happened and we'll be off the hook."

"Just so you know, I'm thirty-four," Rauno pouted, turning back to his forms. "People my age play teenagers on broadcasts!"

They ignored his sulking as they spent the next hour completing the paperwork. They returned to the "START HERE" desk, but the woman referred them to the counter labeled, "PHOTOS." However, that employee sent them to the "PHYSICALS" station before being allowed to have their ID pictures taken. The group was then informed that they would need to take a lie-detection test before any of that could occur.

Alycee smoothed stray strands from her long, brown braid, the closest gesture to anxiety she had yet to display. "I guess we have no choice but to tell them about the mix-up." She rested her gaze on Myx. "Don't be afraid to tell them what happened."

Nodding, Myx followed after the technician. He opened a door and then closed it as soon as she had entered. Alone in the stark room, she took deep breaths as a meter-long scanner zoomed around her body. It emitted a pale orange light as it whirled about. She jumped as a deep voice spoke to her.

"Now, Myx. Tell us why you're here."

She looked about, but saw no one. There wasn't so much as a camera on her, so how did they see her?

"Um, so this all started when…" She felt like a blubbering gyseerif monkey as she ranted about how she yearned for adventure and immediately met her new companions. Thankfully, she got away with not revealing the whole Voumatir situation. Myx ended her explanation by insisting that it wasn't Bishing's fault for taking her away from Kaefh; it had been her decision.

The orange-light scanner ceased moving about her and retreated back to the ceiling from where it hang. The disembodied voice thanked her for her information and told her that she may leave.

Returning to the seating area, she found the other three waiting.

"You were gone so long," Rauno said, wrapping her in his arms. "We were worried that they had sent you home."

Bishing separated them and placed himself in front of Myx.

"It's alright, Bish," she assured him. Myx joined Alycee, who seemed uncommonly fidgety. "What's wrong?"

Alycee shook her head and smiled, making Myx more suspicious; in the two days that she had known the towering woman, Alycee had not smiled once.

"I'm glad to see that you'll still be traveling with us," Alycee explained, clearly hiding something. It must have been the lack of sleep they had endured that kept the stern woman from better controlling her emotions. "If you were returned to Capitaras, I'd have gone on my own way. I don't care for the—"

She was interrupted as their names were called to various desks.

Over the next several hours, they took turns getting rest in between stations throughout the early morning.

Myx stared at the clock on the far wall and sipped her kagin tea. A second cup steamed on the nearby table, its sweet scent enhanced by a passing leaf-green wisp. She waited for the minute hand to reach the next hour before waking Rauno. When he didn't open his eyes, Myx pressed the cup in her hand against his cheek.

Rauno moaned as he awoke. He yawned and took the offered cup and rubbed his eyes. "We should have waited a couple of hours before coming here; we could have then joined with a little more dignity."

Ignoring the other cup of tea, Myx put her head on Bish's shoulder. She closed her eyes, but sleep wouldn't come. "I don't think so. I had an interesting chat with one of the recruiters. She said that this is the slowest it's been since the War Declaration." Myx was startled as Rauno shook her arm.

The scientist whipped his head about, the hot beverage spilling down the sides of the cup and running down his fingers.

"I know what you're going to ask," Myx replied, shoving him away. She leaned back onto Bishing's shoulder and nestled her head until she found a comfortable position. "No, the recruiter wasn't very pretty. Now let me get some sleep."

It felt like only a moment later when someone stroked her forehead.

"I already told you," Myx mumbled, covering her face. Through her laced fingers, she said, "The woman was ugly."

"I am not Rauno," Alycee's voice said. "It's morning. Bishing brought us breakfast."

The four sat in lethargic silence as they swallowed a fruity povric sauce and some hard leuquist cheese. As they completed their meager meal, an announcement called them to the final station.

A square-shaped woman stapled packets together as she said in a monotone voice, "Myx, Bishing, Rauno, and Alycee. You're paperwork has been processed. Congratulations. You are officially members on the Tarasi military." She handed each of them their packets. "Read through these materials for information on your first assignment."

As they made their way to the hangar, Rauno whispered to Myx, "You were correct. She's absolutely hideous. Thank you for not introducing me earlier."

Myx nearly commented that that wasn't the woman she had talked to the previous night. But that only would have re-sparked his interest in finding her informant. Instead she directed the group's attention to finding the ship they were assigned to.

"The Louse? Who names their ship after lice?" Alycee asked as she approached the hull. "Why not something more heroic like—"

Myx held out a hand to silence her as she reached the top of the ramp. She turned her gaze back to her female companion. "Alycee, please don't do anything rash. There's someone inside—well, I mean. I don't understand how but—" Unable to form the thoughts in her head, she stepped aside and let Alycee through.

Voumatir sat across the way, chatting with an elderly woman. He noticed them and stood. "It's so good to see you guys! Can you believe they put us on the same team?"

"You're here?" Alycee asked with a frown. She broke their gaze and moved around him to the other side of the passengers' seat. Her face completely devoid of emotion, she waved her companions over and strapped herself in.

"My communicator fell out of my pocket when I was in your transport," Voumatir explained, his plain blue eyes beaming at her. "Tracking it, I barely caught up to you in time to see you enter the recruitment center. I then had to settle my affairs before I could join the military with you." The alien blocked Myx's path to the seats and whispered, "Would you mind taking Rauno and Bishing over that way, Myx? I'd like some alone time with Alycee."

Alycee glared at him. "You know our names?"

"Why yes, I do." Voumatir gave her a smoldering grin. He crossed to their side of the transport and sat beside Alycee. "Myx's and Bishing's pictures were all over the news at the hospital. The police had a difficult time identifying Rauno, but someone saw him fleeing an explosion with them the other evening."

Rauno removed a black vial from his jacket, pursed his lips and shook his head before putting it back. "What about Alycee? How do you know her name?"

Voumatir smirked, a hint of mischief evident in his face. "That was easy. I got a good look at the license plate as you guys took off." He tucked a strand of dark brown hair behind Alycee's ear. "It's a pleasure to see you again, my guardian angel. I know we got off on the wrong foot. But I'm determined to change your view of me as we prepare for a career in the esteemed Tarasi militia."

Myx stepped aside to let them get reacquainted. Motioning at Bishing and Rauno, she found the three of them seats by a window. Alycee unbuckled and moved towards them. But seeing that there wasn't a fourth chair for her, she found an empty seat across from them.

Voumatir sat beside Alycee once again. "What an interesting assortment of recruits we have here. It feels almost as though you and I have been placed in the rejects' ship."

Alycee stood to find a different seat, but all the others were now full. With a huff, she slumped down next to Voumatir, into the last chair. "That's very rude of you to say. But what do you mean by rejects?"

He motioned at Bishing. "For starters, there's that mute over there. The poor thing is going to have a difficult time communicating with anyone except Myx—a talentless teenager with no prospects." Voumatir paused before adding, "I say that with all the respect in the world, of course; I'm sure that you are a very charming young lady."

Rauno cleared his throat. "And what is wrong about me? Too handsome to be a soldier?"

Voumatir looked over the ginger man. "Based on what I've seen, you're a misogynist that is only joining the army in hopes of getting lucky. As I've travelled the galaxy, I've seen hundreds of men like you—nothing special in the least. Still, there must be something wonderful about each of you if Alycee is your friend."

Rauno looked like he wanted to reply, but an attractive flight attendant walked past him and he became distracted. "Sky-waitress! I get nervous when I fly. Can I hold your hand?"

Compared to Alycee's driving, the launch was surprisingly docile. Myx barely felt the take-off, only being jerked in her restraints for a moment. The engines emitted only the faintest roar as they propelled the recruits to the training station on a small, orbiting moon.

Myx took advantage of the silence to admire the view of space. Below, the planet looked so beautiful with its varied terrain of brown, green, white, and blue all swirled together with the occasional bit of grey from the cities—the Tarasi civilizations in the northern hemisphere and the Hathak barbarians to the south. From orbit, she could see vibrant swirling wisps where the radiation flowed out of the planet's core. Star Lyrwen glowed brightly in the distance, its violet rays bathing the nearby planets.

The moon grew bigger as they approached. Landing had only been slightly more jostling that the launch. Recruits staggered under the new gravity field, trying to regain their balance as they filed into the hangar.

Rauno didn't seem to notice the women of the group. He studied his surroundings, looking as nervous as Myx felt.

Bishing tapped on Rauno's shoulder and made an hourglass shape with his hands.

The scientist was growing increasingly adept in understanding Bish's gestures, but it still took him a moment to catch on. With a contented sigh, he scrambled after a trio of ladies. "Can I borrow a kiss from one of you goddesses? I promise that I'll give it back."

Holding up a single finger to Myx, Bishing left for a moment before returning with a map. He moved to Alycee and showed her something on it.

Alycee glanced over her shoulder at Voumatir. She squatted behind a group of other recruits that was heading towards the opposite end of the hangar. The alien looked confused when he realized that Alycee was gone. Bishing pointed animatedly at the cluster that Alycee was hiding in.

Voumatir smoothed down his bright yellow hair and took off after her, whistling a merry tune.

"Why'd you do that?" Myx asked Bishing, raising an eyebrow.

He shrugged before lounging against the wall.

"Oh, I get it. You miss our alone time, huh?" She punched him playfully on the arm. "I know you don't care for our new companions. But part of having an adventure is meeting new people."

Still, Myx didn't think that Bishing should encourage Voumatir's affection towards Alycee. The warrior woman seemed overly agitated at the alien's attention. And there was something about Voumatir that didn't quite sit right with Myx—she just couldn't quite identify what was wrong with him.

Distracting her from her train-of-thought, Bishing pulled out another map and pointed at the section marked "Residential." They started heading that way when blue lights on the ground began flashing.

A voice chimed over the intercom. "Good afternoon, recruits. Thank you for choosing the Tarasi militia as your career. Please follow the lights to the training area to begin preparations for your new life."

Chapter 8

The recruits followed the blinking blue lights cautiously, unsure of what was happening. The training center was mostly a series of plain, grey halls that eventually emptied into a large room, full of equipment and screens. The lights trailed past rows of exercise machines, firing ranges, and weapon displays before ending at a dozen kiosks.

"Anyone else freaked out that we're being directed by computers," Myx asked no one in particular. She was the first to approach a kiosk; it prompted her to sign in.

There was no verbal reply, but the level of tension increased as each of the recruits followed her lead. Several murmured to their companions, expressing their confusion about where all the training center staff were. Overall, most of the recruits seemed uncomfortable in their current situation.

Alycee joined Myx and Bishing. She signed in and grunted, "I finally got away from him. That darn alien! I'm not going to get any peace and quiet until this blasted war ends." Stepping away from the kiosk, she crossed arms over her chest and scowled.

Voumatir snuck up behind Alycee and put his hands on her waist. "Hey, angel! I nearly lost you there for a second."

"Get off me!" Alycee kicked her heel upward.

"Ah, that could cause some serious harm, toots," Voumatir chuckled as he jumped away.

Rauno voice boomed nearby. The crowd parted to show him backing away from a large, overly-muscular man. "Hold on, sir. I didn't realize that the woman was attached." He raised his hands in the air and continued retreating from the silver-hair stranger. Rauno ducked behind Alycee and Voumatir. "Perhaps you should have her wear a ceremonious ring on her left hand to indicate that she belongs to someone. I don't mean any trouble. Oh, come on, sir! Let the misunderstanding slide."

The commotion gathered the attention of other recruits. They came closer to inspect the altercation.

"He said that I was his true love," a dim-witted looking woman commented.

Her friend nodded and added, "That man has been flirting with every woman he meets—no matter how old or how young."

Another woman chimed in. "He asked me, 'If nothing lasts forever, will you be my nothing?' And when I told him to leave me alone, he said that the only thing that my eyes hadn't told him was my name."

A thin, spindly man looked offended as his lady friends continued accusing Rauno. "That man should be shot out an air-lock for sexual harassment. He can't go around and distress the women. It's hard enough acknowledging that we are finally at war with the Hathak, but he's acting as though it was no big deal."

Alycee stepped forward. "I know that he can be obnoxious, but I won't allow such violent behavior on a poor man born without the benefit of shame. Threatening to kill an annoying man is far more severe than his inappropriate comments."

The crowd began to protest, but quieted under Alycee's stern gaze.

"If he bothers you so much, all you need to do to divert his attention is to decline his advances."

Rauno sniffed and wiped at his eyes as he sobbed, "Oh, Alycee! I didn't know that you cared so much about me! I shan't back down and let that Voumatir alien win your heart." He flung his arms around the towering woman until most of the gawkers dispersed.

"I'd rather eat brapvil pet teats for the rest of life rather than return your affection."

That seemed to have enough of an impact to make Rauno back off. Still, other recruits weren't satisfied with Alycee's words. They became agitated as the confusion of their situation grew.

A chime rang and the antsy recruits settled down.

The voice addressed them again. "Thank you for gathering so promptly. For the remainder of the day, feel free to peruse any of the thousands of the instructional videos we have, or work at the various machines. Happy training!"

Several recruits enthusiastically ran towards the different stations, while others browsed before reluctantly choosing an activity.

Myx waited to see what her friends decided to do. Alycee apathetically pounded at a punching bag until Voumatir started bugging her. Then she smashed her fists into it with greater vigor.

Despite his earlier brush with danger, Rauno walked about the room is search of the prettiest girl in their faction. After a few moments, he followed a attractive blonde to the firing range. He had removed a vial from his jacket pockets and was explaining something to the group of ladies.

“Aren’t you going to do anything, Voumatir?” Myx flicked him playfully in the arm.

“Na! There’s nothing better for me to do other than gaze at that beautiful woman as she pretends to beat the crap out of me.” Voumatir blew a kiss at Alycee. “I’ll wear her down in time.”

Myx rolled her eyes, hoping that she’d soon make more male friends that weren’t so obsessed with uninterested women.

Bishing tapped Myx on the shoulder and nodded at the instructional videos. She followed after him and settled down on the floor. Together, they began learning the basics of self-defense, beginning with the history of prominent martial arts. Myx wondered why they needed to know where each originated back on Earth and how they were adapted throughout the centuries. It felt a little like a waste of time, but she kept her mouth shut about her complaints.

An hour passed. Most of the recruits grew bored with their original tasks and moved to other stations. Some gave up working after merely a couple minutes, though, and stood about while spreading gossip about the War Declaration.

Rauno had remained with the pretty blonde. She and her friends took turns throwing darts at him, but that didn’t deter the scientist.

Somehow, he took it as flirting and continued with his advances. “Thank you for helping me develop my reflexes, ladies!” Rauno’s gasped as one nicked his ear. He smiled, a hint of mischievous amusement in his emerald green eyes. “Oh, you like it rough, do you?”

Growing increasingly bored of the history lessons, Myx moved to a different screen and looked through its files. Finally, she had discovered descriptions of basic self-defense forms. She motioned for Bishing to join her. Myx had a difficult time, often tripping over her feet or falling into Bishing. It was hard work, but her dear companion was very patient and helped correct her form.

“Hasn’t anyone wondered where all the militants are?” Alycee asked, joining Myx and Bishing. She raised Myx’s fist so that the punch was at shoulder-level.

“Perhaps they need every available soldier on the front lines,” Myx offered with a shrug.

“Or maybe they’re watching to see which are worthy of moving on with their training.” Alycee untwisted her long, brown braid and began retying it. “Then the ones with the greatest potential will get specialized attention. If so, what will happen to those who don’t measure up?”

Bishing pursed his lips and shook his head. He looked at Myx and raised an eyebrow.

"I don't know, Bish." Myx stopped her instructional video and scanned the training area. "I see you've managed to lose Voumatir, Alycee."

"Yeah, he's taking a nice little nap in the corner," the towering woman replied with a grin, gesturing across the room. "He got really sleepy after his face collided with my knuckles. I don't think he'll be awake anytime soon."

Myx stared over Alycee's shoulder. "I wouldn't be so sure about that."

"Morning, toots!" Voumatir snuck a kiss on the back of Alycee's neck. "Thanks for helping me sleep. I didn't get much shut-eye the other night." He rubbed the swollen skin across his left cheek. "I really needed some rest."

Alycee groaned, her tanned face growing a faint shade of red. "What's it going to take to get rid of you?"

Rauno joined them, several shallow cuts across his cheeks. He didn't seem to mind as blood dripped to his chin. "I met the most wonderful ladies! I think one of them is definitely my future wife."

Myx grabbed his jaw and inspected the slices. Although she had no official medical training, she at least knew how to treat small wounds. Minor injuries had been common throughout her childhood as Kaefh learned to cook for the various foster daughters she brought into her home.

"I'm just not sure which to go after," Rauno mused, letting Myx treat his cuts. "If I make a mistake, the others wouldn't consider being courted by me. It's such a difficult decision."

"Good man!" Voumatir slapped Rauno on the back. "Go after your love, never ceasing until she is yours." He turned back to the rest of the group. "I shall never relent in my pursuit of my exquisite guardian angel!"

Bishing pushed Voumatir away, getting between the two of them. He glared and swept his hand in front of him before clenching the air.

"What is he saying?"

Myx carefully thought through her memory of Bishing's gestures and looks before translating. "He doesn't care that you're infatuated with Alycee. But he thinks you should back off a bit." She hesitated before adding, "You're being too needy, Voumatir; that's very off-putting to women."

Voumatir was about to respond when a loud blaring echoed in the room. The recruits stopped their respective tasks and stared at blinking orange streaks along the ceiling

The voice spoke to them again, gently and yet urgently saying, “Recruits, please follow the lights back to the hangar and enter the ships in an orderly fashion. Quickly! The Hathak are coming.”

Chapter 9

There was nothing orderly about the chaos the ensued. Without the flashing lights to guide them, the recruits ran wild through the hallways, shouting where the dead ends were.

Myx did her best to keep up with her friends, but she wasn't in as good of shape as the rest of them.

People slammed past her as they fled, not caring who they trampled to get back to the hangar. A particularly gruff man knocked her over, causing Myx lost sight of Alycee and the others.

She called out, but her voice was lost in the chaos.

Someone put a hand on her shoulder. "After all we've been through to keep you in our group," Rauno said, "it'd be a shame to lose you now." He took her hand in his and escorted her through the crowds.

Bishing was ahead, craning his neck every which way. He signed at Alycee and Voumatir. However, they seemed confused as they stared blankly at him.

Raising her hand, Myx hoped Bish would catch sight of her. Alycee was the first to notice since she dashed forward, nearly knocking over everyone in her path. She took Myx's other hand and pulled her along without a word.

Ahead, several had stopped dead and were turning back.

Shots ricocheted off the walls.

Before Myx knew what was happening, Bishing grabbed her away from Alycee, shoved her into a storage closet, and locked the door.

Myx pounded on the handle, trying to get out. "Bishing! What are you doing?"

Outside, people cried out in fear as the blasts continued to sound. Myx stopped trying to get out and listened carefully to what happened. Thuds added to the noise. She could discern the voices of her friends, but their words were indistinguishable.

She felt as though she should be afraid. Less than a day into her military career, she was already in combat. But fear was replaced with rage at the thought of missing out on the action.

Finding a small, metal spade, Myx began hacking at the door handle. Her weak arms quickly grew tired, but she didn't give up. The racket she made from attacking the locks drowned out the noise in the hallways.

When she paused to take a break, she noticed that things were beginning to settle down outside. Myx remained silent a moment, listening until there were hardly any shots or thuds.

The door handle jiggled and Myx stepped away. She glanced through the closet, looking for something to hide behind, but there was nothing. Myx readied herself to fight, unsure if the recruits or the invaders had won the battle.

She held her tool in front of her and did her best to look formidable.

The handle stopped twisting before the panel shook with a bang. There was a deep clunk and the door burst open.

Alycee stepped through billowing smoke. Her long, brown braid swung across her broad shoulder. The warrior woman raised an eyebrow at Myx huffing in amusement. "You're a lot fiercer than we gave you credit for." She took Myx's hand once again and pulled her outside the closet.

"What happened?" Myx asked as Alycee dragged her down the hall. She tried not to look too closely at the dozens of corpses strewn across the floor. But she kept the spade handy just in case someone came at her.

"I thought it was pretty obvious: the Hathak attacked us." Alycee rounded a corner and paused as she surveyed the recruits huddled where the walls ended. With a sigh, she roughly positioned Myx in the middle of their male friends and said, "Watch her. I'm going to scout ahead."

Bishing wrapped one arm around Myx's back while the other held up a pistol.

Myx bent down to grab a gun off a Hathak corpse, but Bishing put a hand on hers. He shook his head and mimed shooting a gun at Rauno and Voumatir.

"Please don't tell me that he's saying that we're all going to die?" Rauno asked, nervously clutching his own stolen firearm. "If we aren't more positive, I don't know if I'll be able to go on."

Voumatir shook his head. "Nah, he doesn't want Myx to have a gun because he's afraid we might all succumb to friendly fire." He playfully elbowed Rauno. "Cheer up, man! This is the kind of adventure that you guys have all been craving. Besides, Alycee seems to know what she's doing." His dull, alien eyes examined the hallway. "By the way, does anyone happen to know what she's up to do?"

They all shook their heads. Alycee seemed to prefer her privacy, never revealing information unless it was relevant.

Myx surveyed the wounds of their group. Many were strangers, but she still felt compelled to help them in any way that she could. "If there are any scraps of your clothes that aren't bloodied, rip them off. I need bandages."

Most of the men gave up their sweaty shirts, while others simply used her spade to rip off the sleeves or the bottom hems of their pants.

However, Rauno refused. "You have no idea what I have sewn into my clothing. They might save our lives or very well explode and kill us all if mishandled. I think we can all agree that we don't want that. So I'll keep my clothes for the time being."

"Fine," Myx consented, ripping the fabric of her shirt sleeves. "But do you happen to have any antiseptic I can borrow?"

Rauno nodded and began rummaging through his various secret pockets.

Treating minor cuts and bruises was nothing compared to the human tissues leaking blood. For some unknown reason, the stench didn't bother Myx as much as it did some of the others. But she found it alarming just how quickly it pumped out of her comrades.

A young man a couple years older than her clutched at his wound, but the red river kept flowing from his arm. He groaned, his hands shaking and pushing her away. She tucked his hands below his hips and continued her treatment. However, as Myx tied strips of cloth around the gash, the man slumped to the ground.

"Move on, Myx," Voumatir prompted, pulling her hands away from the boy. "It's called triage. He can't be helped, so you need to treat the next most severe injury." He surveyed the rest of the group and pointed at a middle-aged man. "He should be looked at next."

"You seem to know an awful lot about war for an alien musician," Rauno commented, narrowing his eyes at him.

"Your planet isn't the only one at war, scientist," Voumatir snapped, sounding defensive.

Myx told herself to be confident as she wrapped the knee of the middle-aged man. She took deep breaths to keep the fear of failure at bay.

They continued tending to the wounded for what felt like an hour before Alycee finally rejoined them. A second group of injured recruits trailed after her. None seemed to be seriously wounded.The towering woman held a finger to her mouth and then waved for them to follow her down the next corridor.

Those who remained conscious walked in silence, stopping carefully at every intersection before continuing on to the hangar.

Bodies covered the floors, blood dripping along the grey tiles and collecting in mingled pools. Upon closer inspection, Myx realized that several of the bodies were still breathing, with exception of the occasional corpse whose head had been bashed in or throat slit.

Myx yearned to help them in some way. She was about to stop to assist them when she realized that Alycee likely wouldn't let them stop until they were safe.

Voumatir pointed at one of the nicer, faster-looking ships in the hangar. "I vote we take that one."

Alycee nodded and led them through bodies.

Other recruits chose different ships and began carrying as many barely-conscious bodies as they could to their cargo bays.

And of course, Myx was stopped by Bishing when she tried to help.

"I have to do something, Bish! We are all comrades now. What if it was me lying unconscious, about to be taken by the enemy?" She paused and let him process what she had said. Myx could feel her face get hot in rage as she added, "Wouldn't you want a stranger to come save me? If it were you lying there, I'd do everything in my limited ability to save your life."

Before Bishing could respond, one of the nearby ships exploded.

Rauno raised his hands in exasperation and shouted, "It wasn't me! I promise!"

A vessel appeared at the edge of the hangar, painted with swirling Hathak markings. Bishing threw Myx over his shoulder and loaded her into the ship like a sack of perith spuds. Alycee and Voumatir rushed to the cockpit and began the take off sequence.

Several ships nearly rammed into each other as they all launched at once. Alycee's erratic driving came in handy as she narrowly missed hitting the others. Out in the vacuum of space, they were met with other enemy spacecraft. Alycee continued to maneuver through them, dodging the incoming stun waves.

Rauno found the weapon controls and returned fire. "How do you like that?" He targeted the shooters and let the energy beams fly. "Myx, any chance you can take a video of me? I'd like to show my future bride how heroic I am."

"I don't think this is the time for that, Rauno," Myx replied, joining him at the consul. She mimicked his movements, but missed every time. "How do you set the targets?"

"Okay, sweetie, I know you want to help, but you're wasting charges."

Bishing turned her chair away from the gun controls and motioned for her to stand.

"I was just getting the hang of it," Myx pouted, moving out of the way. She stood behind the pair of them, watching their movements in case she had another chance to prove that she could be useful.

Rauno blasted his third Hathak ship. "Fear my virile manhood, you Hathak—"

Bishing sent a fist at Rauno's arm before he could finish him comment.

"I'm an army man now," Rauno whined. "I should be allowed to flaunt my masculinity at those I dominate." He cried in pain as Bishing responded with second, harder punch. "Fine. I'll enjoy my victory in silence, like you will for the rest of your life."

It took Myx a moment to realize that Rauno was mocking Bish's lack of communication abilities. She wanted to scold the scientist, but Bishing countered the comment perfectly by miming scissors with his fingers.

Rauno shut his mouth and crossed his legs as he returned to blasting the Hathak ships.

Myx joined Voumatir at the front of the ship. "Is there anything I can do to help?"

Voumatir was busy setting their navigation back to Capitaras. "Why don't you go check on the people in the cargo hold?" His voice was sweet, not at all condescending like Alycee and Rauno.

She did just that. Myx made sure to grasp the railings so as not to fall when the ship jerked during Alycee's evasion tactics.

Down in the hold, the recruits were still strapped in. Myx was still sorry that they didn't have more time to get them all. In total, they only saved eight—not including those that made it to other vessels. Carefully, Myx checked the straps to make sure they were all secure. She also tended to their minor injuries with her remaining clothe scraps.

A little disappointed in herself, Myx wished that she was more talented. She should have tried harder to develop productive life skills. Kaefh had scolded her enough for her sloth-like behavior.

But the nagging only made her more determined to slack off. Now that she was older, she was seeing the effect of her laziness.

There was a loud bang outside the cargo hold, followed by a hiss. Orange lines formed on the wall, making a lumpy square.

The wall fell away and Hathak soldiers stormed in.

Chapter 10

Myx yelped as she was tossed into a cell after Bishing. He steadied her as the door slammed shut.

Rows of cells lined the bowels of the enemy ship. Several of the injured recruits tried to explain to their captors about their wounds, but were still roughly deposited into their cages. Red smeared along the floor and walls as the bloody bandages slammed against the glistening metal.

"Don't worry, toots!" Voumatir assured Alycee. "We'll get out of here soon."

"Will you shut up?" Alycee snapped. From their shared cell down the way, there was a metallic ringing as she kicked at the bars. "You can't let me down because I have no expectations from you!"

Myx shuddered in the cold, stale air, growing bored of their childish bickering.

Rauno was in the cell on the other side of Myx. He seemed to be in better spirits as he flirted shamelessly with a young lady. "It's alright, my sweetheart. These Hathak barbarians can't possibly keep a beautiful thing like you locked up. I'm sure they'll release you right away. Just you see!"

The girl instantly began shouting, "Guards! Please! Move me to another cell."

"Okay, okay. I'll stop. That line would work on the love of my life." Rauno sat in the corner of his cage and folded his arms as he pouted about once again being rejected.

Time passed—no one was sure how long they sat in their cells. Myx wished there was a window to keep her distracted from what was happening. But as radiation wisps began to glide through the ship's hull, Myx realized that they had returned to the planet.

Bishing put a comforting arm around Myx and stroked her hair. He made gestures that sparked memories of happier times, attempting to cheer her up. All it did was remind her that she was a weak, unskilled girl that was going to die after her short, naive attempt to be an independent woman and find adventure.

She took Bishing's wrist and removed his hand. "Don't treat me like a child anymore. I'm a soldier now; I can comfort myself."

He met her gaze, his smoky quartz eyes looking ashamed.

Myx was about to apologize for her outburst, but was cut off as the ship landed. She fell forward onto her face and Bish didn't move to help her up. As disorienting as it had been, she felt as though a measure of equality was forming between them. It was time that she began acting more like the adult she was meant to be.

She watched the doors warily, but no one entered. The entire cargo hold began to vibrate with a reverberating tapping. After a loud clank, the floors of the cells opened and the recruits tumbled onto a bank of sand.

Righting herself, Myx patted the dust from her clothes. She turned her head away from the other recruits to see a hundred Hathak soldiers with their weapons poised in their direction. A dozen men and women less formerly attired stood behind the uniformed figures; these were more relaxed in how they spoke casually to each other.

A tall man with salt and pepper hair walked between the guards and prisoners. His olive skin glistened in the light of the rising purple sun. As he passed Myx, she made eye contact with him; a pair of turquoise irises held her gaze.

"Greetings, Tarasi soldiers. My name is Warden Parnuss." He paused, taking time to look more prisoners in the eye before continuing. "At my war camp, you will do everything you are told to—without question or hesitation. If you can manage that, you will have a pleasant stay here."

The non-uniformed men and women behind the guards stepped forward, looking more serious than they had when the Tarasi had been dumped in the sand before them.

Parnuss gestured at these individuals. "These fine Hathak patriots will be your Handlers. Only a select few will have the honor of their tutelage during their stay. The rest will merely have to live with your own common sense to help you get use to how things are run."

The Handlers approached their Tarasi prisoners, herding the group into straight rows.

Before stepping aside, the Warden made one last comment, "Ladies and gentlemen, welcome to Camp Hathak."

Analysis of the prisoners began. The Handlers walked up and down the rows of captured recruits, examining the Tarasi's eyes, finger nails, and anything else they felt like. When one found someone they liked, the Handler pointed or waved at them and walked towards the stone structures on the horizon.

Myx felt like livestock as one ran his fingers through her pitch-black hair. To make the humiliation worse, he put his calloused fingers into her mouth to inspect her teeth.

Of all the Handlers, only one passed Myx by—a perky, blonde woman with orange amber irises. The female seemed even picker than all her comrades as she sorted through the prisoners. She stopped in front of Voumatir.

The alien musician didn't meet her gaze. He turned his head and stared purposefully at Alycee.

"Got a girlfriend, do you, handsome?" The woman seemed interested in his plain, blue eyes. She ran her crimson-lacquered finger nails down his arms. Her hands then slid across his mid-back, pulling Voumatir into an embrace. "I'll take the alien." She took a step away from the prisoners and faced the Warden. "If that's alright with you, Parnuss."

"Very well, Heikah," the Warden said dismissively, not bothering to look at her. He nodded at the distant structure. "Now take him inside and find something productive for him to do."

She motioned for Voumatir to follow her. "Alright, handsome. Let's go. Come and tell me your story."

Voumatir gave Alycee a longing, guilty look before taking off after Heikah.

Myx turned her attention to Rauno. The women Handlers seemed to have learned to keep a distance from him.

"Come on, ladies!" Rauno whined, reaching towards one of the females. "None of you searched me thoroughly. I give you permission to put your hands all over my body." He smoothed back his scraggly red hair. "No? None of you are going to be my bride? Just give me one chance, miss!"

One of the male Handlers grabbed Rauno's jacket lapel and yanked him upward. He held his other hand in the scientist's face and clenched it into a fist. "Will it quiet you down if I touch you?"

Rauno's cheeks turned bright pink. "Sir, I'm sure that you are a talented lover. But I'm afraid that I'm only attracted to women."

The Handler cocked his arm back, but stopped at the sound of the Warden's voice.

"I'll take care of him," Parnuss announced to the remaining Handlers. "Choose from among the others."

A beefy, unpleasant-looking man stopped in front of Myx. Close-set, grey hematite eyes bordered a crooked nose that looked as though it had been broken several times. He held out a thick, scarred hand and gestured at Myx. "Hello, my pet. You can call me, 'Gotasun.' Let's get you started on your first day of work."

Bishing seemed to have forgotten Myx's request about treating her like a child since he stepped in front of her and held out his arms.

A small Hathak woman swept Bishing's leg out from him. She sat on his back, pinning him to the ground. Her sharp facial features arranged into a devious grin beneath thin strands of short, light brown hair. "I'm Frezul. I'll claim you as my prisoner. Tell me your name."

All Bishing could manage was a grunt.

"Not a talkative fellow, huh?" Frezul pulled his hair, causing Bishing to reflexively open his mouth. "Hmm. No tongue? Having a mute is going to be quite amusing." The petite woman waved at one of the guards, who then tossed her a pair of handcuffs. She affixed them to Bishing's wrists. "Let's go for a run, mute." Frezul removed a riding crop from her hip and swatted at Bish.

Defiant to a fault, Bishing remained still. The woman smacked him harder, and he still didn't move.

Myx began to protest, but her Handler hauled her over his massive shoulder. She squirmed to get her face out of his long, mud-colored hair. Getting a better view, Myx saw Frezul mount Bishing's back. The female Handler said something into his ear. A moment later, Bish took off running, directed to the left of the distant mountains.

Gotasun dropped Myx to her feet. He motioned for her to walk in front of him towards the stone structures.

Three openings were visible from the sandy path. She was directed into the middle cave.

"It's dark, Gotasun," Myx said, feeling in front of her. "Can I have a light, please?"

Pressure along her back prompted her to walk faster through the shadows. Myx nearly fell over as her toes found a descending staircase. She made slow progress, but she could soon see light up ahead.

The tunneled staircase opened into a wide cavern. Streaks of light shot out of crevices in the ceiling, but most of the dull illumination came from street lamps posed in between a variety of buildings. As they approached the closest structures, Myx could see that each was labeled with looping Hathak script. She did her best to remember where each building was in correlation to the others, but her mind couldn't keep track of it all.

"Things are pretty simple here," Gotasun explained, pulling her along. "Do as your told and don't cause any trouble."

Myx nodded, not wanting to aggravate the bulky man.

The Handler continued, "Like the Warden said, you can have a productive time here, or a miserable one. There are several prisoners who have already been visiting for the past five days. Make sure that you heed their advice as well." He paused before adding, "Oh, and once week, we will have private sessions to see how well you've done."

Being underground felt restrictive and confining. She supposed that was the point since the recruits were now prisoners of the Hathak. The air felt stale and dusty as Myx struggled to inhale enough breath.

"But what kinds of things will I be doing here?" Myx asked, suppressing a cough.

Gotasun stopped in his tracks. "Inquisitive little thing, aren't you, my pet?" He took her past a pair of buildings labeled Laundry and Tailoring. "I'll give you a tip since it's your first day here: Handlers don't like to be asked questions. They prefer to have their prisoners act with blind devotion—following their every word."

Wisps of radiation flitted out another cave opening. As she reached the tunnel, Myx felt a minor rush of energy with every bit that passed through her. The gnawing hunger in the pit of her stomach began to dull. Her aching muscles eased to a more bearable level.

However, the wisps also made a spirit of defiance rise in her. Myx suppressed the urge to argue with Gotasun, saving the energy to help her get through whatever tasks were in her future.

"During the day, you'll do the task that you're assigned," Gotasun explained. "It'll change based on what is needed. You'll have a short recreation hour after dinner, before lights out. I make weekly Reviews during that time, so don't always count on getting to play every evening." He stopped, grabbed her shoulder, and pushed her into an empty elevator.

Gotasun was such a stocky man that there was barely any room in the cramped space for Myx. She scooted into a corner as far as she was allowed, but her arm still brushed against Gotasun's. Thankfully though, it was a quick decent further into the mountain.

When the lift doors opened, she was corralled into a bio-scanner. Lasers zoomed up and down her torso, appendages, and skull, sending information about her anatomy to a computer,

A technician nodded abruptly and Gotasun pulled her away.

The Handler guided her down one more passage to a wide, open room that branched into dozens of smaller tunnels. He walked her to a rock wall, picked up an axe, and placed it in her hand. "See those colorful veins of minerals? Swing the axe to break them up." Without another word, he departed in the direction they had come from.

Myx began smashing the rock wall along with the other prisoners stationed there. Older men and women followed behind her, sorting through the small boulders and sweeping up the rubble.

After mere minutes, her arms ached under the weight of the axe and her hands felt raw. And then a deep purple wisp phased through her and she felt a bit stronger.

Taking a quick break, Myx examined a vein of brightly-colored rocks. The shades reminded her of the wisps that were flitting about. She returned to her work when a brusque overseer barked for her to keep swinging.

Unsure of how long she would be down in the mines, Myx tried to keep her pace even so as not to tire herself out completely. And yet, she also worried about the punishment that Gotasun hinted about. She didn't want to be accused of being lazy, so she increased her pace. But she also secretly hoped that she wouldn't still be at the Camp by the end of the week, meaning Myx wouldn't have to worry about the Review—whatever that was.

"This shouldn't last too long," she whispered to reassure herself. Myx heaved the axe high behind her. "The Tarasi military will find us and take us home."

As the day wore on, Myx found herself no longer believing her own words.

Chapter 11

Myx had thought that counting out axe swings would help pass the time; she was very wrong. It only reminded her of how much work she had done. When she reached 5,000, she was sure that her arms would fall off.

Hours must have passed, but it was impossible to tell how many in the dark mines. Hunger had gnawed at the Myx's stomach, but the discomfort lessened when wisps passed through her. Still, she had only been given a meager, over-baked bread loaf stuffed with a couple shreds poh meat and diced brenju roots; it tasted awful, but it silenced her stomach enough to let her get through her grueling work.

"Can we switch places, mister?" she asked an elderly man. "I've been crushing these rocks for hours. All you've done is pick through them to find the colored pieces. It doesn't seem fair." Myx paused and examined the man's facial expression. "What? Did I say something I shouldn't have?"

"Be careful what you say around here," he replied, his eyes pressed shut. The old man wiped the sweat running down his bald head, leaving streaks of dirt speckled with blue, yellow, and green."You don't want to add to your punishment."

She scoffed. "Mister, I can't imagine a worse punishment than this."

As they continued to work, Myx wondered why the man kept his eyelids closed. She watched him from the corner of her eye for, curiosity being distracting to her task. When she chided herself for being a creepy stalker, Myx noticed the lids open slightly Through the narrow slits, a soft white light glowed.

When he caught her staring, the man said, "The mines are above a hotspot. The concentration of radiation affects the atomic structure of certain minerals. We are here to extract these minerals in order for the scientists to study them. I've been here a week and the wisps have started affecting my body." The man opened his eyes further to expose shimmering, white opal irises. He shut them and the light vanished. "And, please, stop calling me 'mister.' My name is Tieg."

Myx did her best not to be off-put by his glowing eyes. However, she hoped that she would be released before being exposed to enough radiation to make her own irises light up.

She put her axe down, extended her hand, and introduced herself.

He recoiled from her. “Don’t drop your tool! And definitely never touch another prisoner unless it’s a part of your assignment.”

“Sorry.” She hefted the axe back onto her shoulder. Myx suppressed a sigh. Instead, she lowered her voice and said, “I didn’t realize that there were so many weird rules. How am I to know them all?”

“Use your best judgment.” Tieg resumed his task of sorting through the broken stones. He placed the ones with colorful gems into the sack slung across his back. The plain ones were tossed into a wheelbarrow. “Basically, anything that isn’t necessary or anything that hinders the productivity of the Camp is off-limits.”

Myx slammed her axe into the rock wall, full of rage at how she was to simper to the Hathak scum. She wished she could’ve just sat in a cell all day instead of being their slave.

Tieg seemed to sense that she needed a moment alone. He pushed his collection of plain rocks back to the entrance of the mines. Myx turned her head to see him dump the cart into a wide crevice; the clattering stones echoed deep in the caves. She wondered about the purpose of that. Tieg then deposited his bulging sack of colorful stones with a guard, grabbed a new container, and returned to Myx.

“Don’t despair,” Tieg whispered, his voice barely audible. “There are rumors from those who have worked in Warden Parnuss’s office; there’s a chance of being ransomed. They are in contact with several Tarasi officials, trying to return certain prisoners. I don’t know what the criteria are, but it’s enough to give all of us hope of making it home someday.”

That lifted her spirits. Rauno and Alycee had commented that family members of the employees at the President’s Estate were protected. Would that mean that she might be given special treatment? No, probably not. Sievly likely used all of her limited influence to have the police pursue Myx. It was possible that mentioning her circumstance to the Warden would only put more of a target on her back.

Myx turned back to work. But as she lifted the heavy axe, one of the sores on her hands tore open. Blood dripped hot from the wound. Cursing, she walked to the guard post.

“I need to go to the nurse!” Myx shouted over the refining machinery. She held up her injured hand. Sweat and colored dust mixed with the injury. Wisps passed through her, but the energy did nothing to heal the torn flesh; it only seemed to make her bleed more. “Please? Can you tell me where—”

"You want to go to the nurse, huh?" The guard seemed amused about something. His lips turned up into a sinister grin.

She didn't understand what was so funny about her injury. "Look, I can't work so long as I have this bloody blister. My hand can't squeeze the handle. And the axe is too heavy for me to swing with just my other hand."

His amused expression quickly turned sour as he furrowed his brow. But the hostility was almost instantly replaced with a delighted grin. "Alright. You can go see Dolra in the Infirmary. But you're probably better off just staying here and gritting through the pain. If you insist, go down the Main Street until you pass the Studio. It'll be on the left. Good luck."

Myx began heading that way, wondering what the guard meant by his last comment. A rock whizzed past her head as she approached the mine exit.

She turned to see Tieg waving his hands and shaking his head. The nearby machinery was too loud to discern his words. He moved towards her, but a guard stopped him. Myx waved goodbye and headed towards the Infirmary.

Repeating the directions in her head, Myx did her best to remember what she passed along the way.

There was some sort of Mess Hall full of tables and benches, as well as a seating area with couches that looked as though they had been taken from a homeless shelter. Various signs written in looping Hathak script pointed in different directions at corridor intersections. Past a guard station, the prisoner's cells were to the right. The Butcher's was to the right of the Kitchens, and a strange art Studio was the next building further down the street.

A putrid scent filled the air. Myx sniffed and tried to figure out what she was inhaling. It reminded her of Kaefh's cleaning cabinet, but she couldn't differentiate between the smells.

Eventually, Myx made it to the Infirmary. She stepped inside to see a large, high-vaulted room. Dozens of beds lined the sides of the room, intermixed with different kinds of machines. At the far end was a metal wall with a couple dozen hatches across it.

Several timid-looking men and women in white aprons moved from bed to bed, checking on injuries and dispensing medications. They eyed Myx warily but didn't speak to her. They tended patients who seemed oddly familiar. Upon further inspection, Myx realized they were the recruits that she had treated during the attack on the training center.

"Excuse me," Myx said to one of them. "I was told to see Dolra. Where can I find her?"

The man gasped before nervously looking down the rows of cot.

A stocky, red-faced woman clad in a white nurse uniform shook a meaty fist at one of the patients. "Stop talking that way or I'll lock you in the morgue overnight!" The woman smacked the blanketed patient in the face, her sweaty face scrunched up in agitation. When the patient wouldn't stop squirming, the nurse pinned their wrist to the bed. "Hold still! You need an antibiotic shot!"

Myx realized that she should have listened to the guard. She tried to back out of the Infirmary without Dolra noticing her.

As she went back into the main street, she caught a glimpse of her Handler. Gotasun laughed with a group of Hathak soldiers. Myx didn't want him to think that she was ditching work.

So she put her brave face on decided to take her chances with the vicious nurse.

Chapter 12

"You're so passionate about your work!" The patient being treated by Dolra sounded oddly familiar, despite being muffle through the blankets. "I like that in a woman." When the nurse smacked him again, he chuckled playfully. "Oh! I love it when you're rough with me."

Dolra stuck a needle in the crease of the patient's elbow. "You imbecile! What made you think that turning laundry soap into acid was a good idea? Now you've got chemical burns."

The blanket fell away to reveal Rauno. "If you must know, my dear, I was trying to escape this prison." He winced as Dolra scrubbed the raw burns on his hands and forearms. The scientist let out a disturbingly content sigh as he lay back on his pillow. "Can you really blame me, nightingale?"

"This is a Labor Camp, not a prison," Dolra corrected, tossing aside her wash rags. She put her fists on her wide hips and added, "And I've asked you to stop calling me that."

Rauno grinned like a fool, whatever drug coursing through his veins clearly starting to take effect. "Yes, but that's what you are to me. I have a good feeling about us." He noticed Myx awkwardly waiting for the nurse. "Myx! Isn't this Infirmary wonderful! It's run by the most competent nurse I've ever had—no offense intended towards your care-taking skills. Sure, Dolra is playing hard-to-get now. But the more I'm here, the more I'll wear her down."

Another patient across the room called to Dolra for help.

When the nurse was gone, Myx moved to Rauno's bed. She wrinkled her nose as the smell of burnt hair and disinfectants filled her nostrils. "So how did you try to escape?"

"Oh, they've got all sorts of chemicals in the laundry," Rauno laughed, picking at the edges of the burns. "I swiped something from the janitor's closest when they tried to assign me to cleaning the prisoner's cells; I got out of that right away by feigning incompetence."

Myx grabbed a piece of gauze from the bed-side table and pressed it against the bloody blister on her hand. "How so?"

Rauno's grin widened as he remembered what he did. "I mixed furnisher polish and drain cleaners with the mop water. I then washed the floors using a coal brush. They sent me straight to the Laundry after I spilled the dirty, polish water in the halls." He blinked in rapid succession before shaking his head. "Remind me to tell you about all the fun I had with bleach—when I'm more lucid."

She gasped as she realized that she had smelt his handiwork on the way to the Infirmary. Concerned about Rauno's experiments, she asked, "Aren't you afraid of getting into trouble? My Handler said there would be punishments for those who act out."

He settled into his sheets once again and yawned. "None of the Handlers wanted me. The ladies seemed unphased by my sweet talk—for some unknown reason. They must all be married and don't want to risk having an affair with a prisoner. The men didn't want me because I don't respond to male intimidation tactics."

"I wondered if you were being open about the touching in order to keep them from realizing what you have sewn into your jacket."

"You're sharper than we've given you credit for, Myx."

Uncomfortable with praise, Myx turned the subject back to the Handlers. "I saw that Bishing was claimed by that petite Frezul woman. And that perky blonde took Voumatir."

"Oh, yes!" Rauno chuckled, staring off at a blank place on the wall. "That's Heikah. She's beautiful, isn't she?" He continued picking at his burnt flesh, clearly not in pain from the injury. "Frezul's pretty scary, though. She was riding Bishing around the Camp earlier, like he was some kind of bold knayl steed."

"What about Alycee?" Myx asked, trying to avoid a conversation that would upset her further. "Did any of the Handlers want her?"

He lounged back in his cot. "Alycee didn't get one; she's too intimidating. Voumatir's Handler doesn't seem to have much of a backbone, but she's quite attractive. Maybe he'll redirect his energy towards Heikah instead of Alycee. But I can't see that Handler overpowering Voumatir; she seems like a bit of a pushover."

"All right, gossip time is over." Dolra pushed Rauno's bed towards one of the hatches on the far wall. She entered a code and the door swung outward.

Thick waves of colored radiation wafted through the opening.

After rolling the cot inside the chamber, Dolra pulled a small plastic jar out of her apron and handed it to Rauno. "Rub this on your burns and go to sleep. I'll check on you in the morning." She slammed the hatch closed, cutting off his response. The nurse stepped away from the chamber and eyed Myx with sharp, red jasper eyes.

“I was working in the mines and my hand tore open.” Myx removed the gauze from her bloody palm and held it up to the nurse.

“Sit.” Dolra pointed at the bed at the end of the row. She pulled out another jar from her apron, set it aside, and began roughly cleaning Myx’s wound. “This blister is absolutely nothing. Why are you bothering me with this?”

“Well, this is my first day and I’m not exactly use to hard labor.” Myx pushed back the tears as her flesh was scrubbed raw. “Do you have to be so rough?”

“I’m supposed to make you better so that you can continue working. It’s not my job to coddle you.” Dolra put a clear, sticky substance on the cut and the bleeding ceased. “If you wanted to be spoiled, you shouldn’t have joined the Tarasi military.”

Myx wanted to talk back to the abrasive woman, but she feared that any more conflict with Dolra would only make her situation worse. She bit her lip to keep her from replying. However, the nurse seemed to be expecting some sort of response, so Myx solemnly nodded her head.

“Take this.” Dolra handed her a similar jar that she had given Rauno. She turned her attention to checking Myx’s vitals. “Rub some of that into the wound; it will help you heal faster. Combined with the radiation, that salve can cure any tissue damage overnight.”

Doing as she was told, Myx used her fingers to gingerly spread the salve over the torn skin. She cried out as it stun, burning as though the wound had opened over and over again.

“Can I have some pain killers, please?” Myx asked, taking a shuddering breath.

“Who do I look like? Your mother?” Dolra swept away sweaty clumps of dark brown hair from her forehead. “Serves you right for being careless. Next time, you’ll wear protective gloves, huh, missy?”

Myx wiped away a tear with her shoulder, not wanting to touch her face with neither of her bloody, salve-covered hands. “They didn’t give me any gloves. And this salve really stings.”

Dolra smirked and rolled Myx’s cot into her own radiation chamber. “Yeah, I add a pain-inducer to make careless prisoners think twice about injuring themselves in order to get out of work.”

“What! That’s torture! Especially for someone like Rauno who has experienced a lot of trauma.” Myx tried to get out of the bed, but the nurse pinned her shoulders down. She continued to struggle, pleading with Dolra. "You can't do this! It's unethical. Please! I need some pain medicine."

"I can do what I want, missy. And I choose not to numb your pain." Dolra dashed out of the chamber. She hit a button on the exterior and the hatch eased close with a decompressing hiss. Before it sealed shut, the nurse added, "You and that imbecile friend of yours are both in for a rough night."

Chapter 13

Myx had never found pleasure in cursing. And yet, she couldn't help spewing every inappropriate word she knew during her first night in the Hathak Labor Camp.

Not only did her hand sting and throb from Dolra's sadistic slave, but the waves of radiation made her feel refreshed and energetic. She tossed and turned, restless as she was unable to slumber. It hadn't helped that she'd barely gotten any sleep the previous two days.

However, Myx eventually learned that she could reject the revitalization if she focused hard enough, letting the wisps relax her until she eased into a deep sleep.

Still, she occasionally awoke in searing pain. At those times, Myx checked the healing progress of her wound. Her flesh knit back together rapidly, itching as the new skin inched across the open blister. The salve forced her nerves to repeatedly remember the sensation of blood dripping out as the flesh tore.

The wound was completely restored by morning. Not only that, but her stiff muscles were looser and ready for another day of hacking away at colored rocks.

Myx was already awake when the hatch unlocked and opened with a popping hiss. She pushed the bed out of the chamber, her palm only a dull ache as she returned the cot to its place in the Infirmary.

Rauno's hatch was still closed, though.

Peering through the small window, Myx saw that Rauno's burns were healed. He somehow had sustained new injuries, though. Thick, deep scratches covered his upper arms. Myx guessed that his scientific curiosity had gotten the better of him; the researcher likely had hurt himself in order to have more time to study how the radiation worked with the salve—as well another opportunity to connect with his nightingale.

Rauno noticed her watching him and stopped picking at his raw skin. His emerald eyes beamed as though his injuries didn't bother him. He smiled and waved for her to leave.

Her stomach growled, reminding Myx that she wasn't given dinner the previous night.

Myx quietly walked past several occupied beds on her way out of the Infirmary. Wondering why those prisoners weren't allowed in the chambers to heal, she inspected a couple of them. They were minor injuries: a dislocated shoulder, some bruises, a broken nose, and a couple scratches. Others appeared to be completely fine.

She looked at her newly healed hand. It wasn't as bad as some of the others. But her mind moved on when an answer didn't come to her right away. All that she cared about the next moment was getting something to eat.

Using her memories from the previous day, she made it to the Mess Hall. She grabbed a bowl of some lumpy, beige porridge and went about searching for her friends.

Bishing sat between Alycee and Voumatir, most likely playing referee for them; he looked oddly concerned for the woman. However, his efforts seemed to be failing since Voumatir's exuberance was stronger than ever.

"Don't worry, toots!" Voumatir assured Alycee. He leaned forward to see past Bishing's blocking body. "I would never leave you for Heikah. She is so delicate and perky and she means absolutely nothing to me. So when she tells me to work late or help her with her tasks, just know that I'll be thinking of you the entire time."

"She's your Handler," Alycee replied, not meeting his intent gaze. She took a bite of her lukewarm porridge before continuing, "Don't let her hear you speak like that. Heikah might find a reason to punish you for not being completely devoted to her. She seems like she might be a jealous master." Smirking slyly, she added, "Maybe she'll do me a favor and tame your enthusiasm."

Bishing noticed Myx and his face brightened. He must have heard the rule about not touching other prisoners because he made no attempt to hug her.

Myx took a seat across from them. "I haven't had anything to eat since that piece of stale meat pie they gave me for lunch yesterday." She licked a spoonful of porridge and grimaced at the lack of flavor. "How have you guys fared so far?"

Alycee pushed her bowl aside and retied her long braid. "I didn't get a Handler so I've had to learn about the Camp the hard way—asking people. As you know, I hate chitchat."

"My Handler is a young pushover," Voumatir explained, grabbing Alycee's bowl. He scrapped the last bits of her meal from the dish and added it to his own. "I don't think Heikah really knows what she's doing. She had me picking peas at the farm all afternoon. It wasn't too difficult a job."

They all looked at Bishing. He shrugged and mimed chopping something. Myx guessed it was in the Kitchen, but Bishing shook his head. Waving his arms more violently, he suggested that he killed something before chopping it up. They then correctly guessed that Bish had worked at the Butcher's. None of them cared to bring up the subject of his vicious Handler, who seemed a bit like a butcher herself.

"I haven't seen Rauno since we arrived," Alycee commented, glancing around the Mess Hall. "Last I heard, he nearly blew himself up; I knew he would someday."

Voumatir pursed his lips. "That explains why he always smells like lighter fluid."

Myx scratched at the new skin on her palm and explained what happened in the Infirmary. The others listened closely, not interrupting as she repeated all the details Rauno had told her before they were sealed in the radiation chambers.

"But the strange thing is that Rauno had brand new injuries when I saw him this morning. I think he's deliberately hurting himself so that he can spend more time with Dolra."

"This nurse must be quite a beauty." Voumatir quickly turned his smile to a frown when Alycee gave him a reprimanding look. "But she can't be nearly as exquisite as my guardian angel."

"Well, Dolra isn't exactly the most traditionally attractive woman I've met," Myx mused, trying to accurately portray the nurse's comeliness while also not poking fun at her expense. "There must be something amazing about her that Rauno has the wisdom of seeing, even when others can't."

Alycee tossed her braid over her shoulder. "I don't understand why we are talking about this. If Rauno has found a woman that he finds desirable, our opinions don't matter in the least. Let's simply allow him this happiness for the sake of our own sanity."

Myx shook her head. "But it's not healthy, Alycee. What if he keeps hurting himself until he—" She couldn't bring herself to say the words on her mind.

"I think Rauno is stubborn enough to stay alive until he has his bride." Voumatir moved to sit next to Myx, across from Alycee. "He's a very determined fellow and I admire him for that. Let's let him find happiness through his own heart's path."

Someone tapped the table beside Myx. She glanced up to see Tieg.

"It looks like you're ready for another fun day in the mines." White light glowed between the slits of his eyelids. "You best not be late on your second shift—especially after a night in the Infirmary."

Myx said farewell to her friends and wished them a good day.

Tieg led her down the corridors. When there was no one else around, he said, "I tried to warn you. You shouldn't have gone to Dolra yet."

"What do you mean? Sure, it was unpleasant with all the wisps energizing—"

"What! You went into a chamber?" Tieg's eyes went wide, becoming even brighter. He was about to reply, but quickly shut his mouth. Instead, he bowed his head in respect as Gotasun appeared.

"Run along now, Tieg. I need to have a few words with my pet." Gotasun moved beside Myx and patted the top of her head.

Tieg bowed once again and increased his walking speed towards the mines.

"It has come to my attention," Gotasun said, stroking her hair, "that you spent your first night in a raditation chamber. You think you're special, huh, my pet?" He clutched at the pitch black strands and pulled her close. His grey hematite eyes narrowed and his voice took on a new intensity. "This isn't a spa! You can't get fast healing whenever you want. Sometimes you'll need to suck it up and heal the natural way. We aren't equipped to treat every little boo-boo."

"I'm sorry, Gotasun." Myx did her best to be humble and apologetic. "I got hurt and I asked the guard for a nurse. He sent me to Dolra. I didn't ask for special treatment. I—"

He loosened his grip in her hair, but reached his other hand forward and covered her mouth. "Calm yourself, my pet. You're not in trouble for that. All prisoners are allowed one night a week in a chamber. Most wait until after a behavior Review with their Handler."

"Why do they go to the Infirmary after evaluating behavior?" Myx asked, not sure if she was ready to here the answer yet. Her heart began beating wildly as she imagined what he'd say.

"It's where you'll get punishments or rewards, depending on how you've acted. You'll see later this week." Gotasun motioned for her to enter the mine and then followed after. "But know that from now on all injuries will need to be treated at the guard stations. They have basic first aid materials. Do you understand?"

Myx nodded, resisting the urge to ask follow-up questions.

"Now be a good pet—grab an axe and get to work. I'll see you at the end of your shift."

She did as she was told and hefted her tool onto her shoulder. Myx scanned the wide cave in search of Tieg, but she didn't see him. He must have been in one of the branching tunnels, trailing after a different stone crusher.

There were dozens of other questions that she wanted to ask. They'd have to wait since she didn't trust anyone well enough quite yet.

Myx began her arduous task while pondering on the existence of the Labor Camp. She understood the Hathak's motive behind enslaving the Tarasi prisoners for profit. But there was something more going on.

She nearly began her task, but paused as her brain alerted her that she forgot something. Myx felt a twinge in her hand and remembered to locate a pairs of gloves. Prepared for her long day of hacking, she let her arms swing in a simple, rhythmic motion that freed up her brain. Multi-tasking was never her strongest ability. But she felt the need to practice it as she reflected on her queries about the Review system and how awful it might actually be.

Chapter 14

Wisps floated about the mine, brushing against the worn-out workers. Some of the prisoners purposefully heaved their axes backward at the waves of radiation. This was made all the more difficult to do with an overseer watching closely. But many managed to receive vigor from the radiation before smashing their axes at the rock walls.

However, Myx had yet to time her movements correctly. Her arms would miss the colored energy as she lifted the axe over her shoulder.

On several occasions, she was able to adjust her position enough to feel the rejuvenating warmth of a wisp. But the change usually made for an awkward swing, her axe coming forward in an uncomfortable position for her wrist. After several off-balance swings, Myx decided that catching an occasional wisp wasn't worth damaging her joints; there were plenty enough that passed through her throughout the day to keep her rejuvenated.

Despite all that, her second day in the mines wasn't as bad as her first. Myx seemed to be more responsive to the occasional energy boosts provided by the radiation. She didn't tire as easily and her hands felt tougher as they hefted the immense tool.

Myx eyed the other workers. Most had been there a week, since the War Declaration. They hung their heads as they moved about, resigned to their lot in life.

Was the Camp really that horrific that it could squash the determination of a dozen Tarasi in such a short while? Sure, they were being held there against their will and were forced to do back-breaking work. But these people were basically working in a Radiation Spring, getting vigor and rejuvenation all day. From Myx's perspective, the positives and negatives of their situation seemed to even out.

There must have been more about their circumstances than Myx's realized. After all, she had only been there a day and still didn't understand the rules. Still, she felt determined not to let the Camp turn her into a dejected wretch like the others, even if she had to be there a whole week before being rescued.

"How can you smile?" an elderly woman asked Myx. "Can I share in your joy, miss?"

Another woman, a couple years older than Myx, approached them. "I was also wondering that. What's your secret?"

Myx thought back to what she had been pondering. "I just don't want to let my spirit break. I joined the Tarasi military to find adventure and to learn new skills. I don't want to let this set-back kill the only dream I've ever had."

The women's eyes welled up as they took a step closer. They looked as though they wanted to hug her, but stopped before they came too close.

"Come with us later to the Washroom," the older one said in a hushed voice.

"We'll get you all cleaned up," added the other, her eyes brightening.

She had never been vain, but Myx liked to keep a tidy appearance. And she hadn't showered since that night at the hotel when on-the-run from the police. A change of clothes hadn't even been given to her since she had arrived. Thoughts of the Washroom filled her head the rest of the afternoon.

At the end of their shift, the female mine workers led her to a warm, moist room. A river flowed at the far end of the alcove, tucked behind a row of baths carved into the stone floor. The younger of the two ladies opened several small dams, allowing the river water to fill three tubs. The elderly woman motioned for Myx to strip to her sweat-stained smallclothes.

She did so willingly. Although she was a little self-conscious baring so much skin in front of strangers, it felt good to get out of her filthy clothes.

Myx bit her lip as she immersed herself in the ice-cold liquid. Thankfully, her skin warmed as radiation merged with the bathwater. Wisp-infused water made her hair, eyes, and skin glisten with radiance. She knew it was only a temporary effect, but she felt more beautiful than she had ever been before.

Along the side of the Washroom was a strange, glass wall. At first, it appeared to be a mural of an underwater scene. Upon closer inspection, Myx realized that the images moved. Marine life drifted lazily in the river currents, their puckered mouths sucking in tiny bits of plankton as their gills flapped open and closed. Condensation dripped down the barrier and settled into a drain along the floor.

The subject of names was never brought up; neither were any other topics of any kind. Myx didn't understand why the ladies weren't being chatty, but she didn't ask. She leaned back in the water and closed her weary eyelids.

However, her relaxation ended when she heard the other women scamper out of their tubs.

Myx blinked to see the women rummaging through her clothes.

"Nothing!" the younger woman scoffed. "She's got absolutely nothing!"

"She must have been tipped off to leave her valuables in her cell," the older one mused, throwing the material on the floor. "This was a waste of time."

Myx froze, processing what she had heard. The ladies were only nice in order to rob her? As she thought deeper, she supposed that she really couldn't blame them for their behavior. She was just grateful that she had nothing of significance that she could have lost.

After finding a fresh set of bland clothes, Myx dressed and discarded her old ones.

Outside the washroom, Myx was startled to see someone waiting for her.

White light glowed from Tieg's opal eyes as he turned to address her. "I saw you trying to catch wisps today."

Myx groaned, "Don't tell me that's against the rules, too!"

Tieg shook his head. "Not exactly. I simply wanted to warn you about absorbing too much radiation." He was silent a moment, taking a few steps down the hall. "It's impossible to avoid the wisps; they're everywhere on this planet. But don't go chasing after it—if you value your life."

"What do you know?"

Myx was curious now. She hadn't exactly absorbed much radiation in her life—compared to most people she knew. Growing up, many of her more wealthy classmates had revitalizing treatments in the Springs every week; they all seemed fine.

Rubbing his face, Tieg said, "I lied to you yesterday. I said that my eyes were transformed from wisps in the mine. It actually happened the day I was captured."

Myx didn't like being lied to. However, Tieg seemed like a sweet-tempered man. So she felt compelled to forgive him, depending on the details of his explanation. She nodded and waited for him to continue.

"My squad and I were on a routine border patrol," Tieg explained, strolling down the corridor. His opal irises illuminated the dim passage. "I had done the same thing thousands of times during my forty years in the Tarasi military. It was actually supposed to be my last patrol. I planned to retire the next week—well, technically it would be this week."

As she followed Tieg down the street, Myx suppressed the urge to ask him clarifying questions about his tale.

"We stopped to inspect a gap in the motion sensors. The next thing I knew, I was in the back of a transport and on my way here. Although we knew that war with the Hathak was inevitable, none of us thought we'd live to see another battle. The Tarasi had enjoyed peace with them for nearly thirty years; we hoped that the hostility had finally ceased."

Tieg stopped speaking and stared at the Infirmary door.

"What are we doing here?" Myx asked, feeling confused. "Are you hurt, Tieg?"

He wiped beads of sweat from his bald scalp. "No. I'm sorry, but I was asked to escort you here. Your Handler believes that you should take on extra work to make up for all your blunders of yesterday. You will assist Dolra with whatever she tells you." Tieg looked somber as he turned away. "I'll finish my story another time. Just be wary of the effects of the wisps."

Myx froze with her hand on the door handle. After a day of working in the mines, Gotasun also expected her to put up with the abrasive nurse? She didn't know if she could handle all that.

Taking a deep breath, she calmed herself. At least she'll get to see Rauno, provided that he found yet another way to keep himself in the Infirmary.

Sure enough, he was tucked into the far corner. His upper arms had crusty purple scales where there had been scratches that morning. He picked at the skin before pulling the flakes closer to his face to inspect them.

Dolra stood over him, shaking her head and shouting indistinguishable words. As Myx grew closer, she could discern the words the nurse was screaming at Rauno.

"That is the most irresponsible thing I've ever seen! What possessed you to combine chemicals with my salve? Empty your pockets, imbecile! I want all of it. Now!" She began searching Rauno's clothing for his hidden vials.

"Oh, my! Usually I wait for three dates before I let a woman rip my clothes off." He pushed her hands away, blushing.

Dolra turned to Myx. "Help me strap him down!"

Myx gave Rauno an apologetic look as she assisted Dolra in getting his limbs into the restraints.

"You like it rough, nightingale?" Rauno raised an eyebrow at her. "I can get on board with that. But please don't harm me without warning. Should we come up with a safe word or should we just wing it?"

Groaning, Dolra stuck him with a needle. "That'll shut you up for a bit, obnoxious man." She mopped her brow with a handkerchief as she moved away from Rauno. At another station, she grabbed something in a plastic wrapper and tossed it at Myx. "Eat up. I've got a lot of work for you to do this evening."

Myx removed the wrapper from the object to see a plain brown lump shaped into a thick rectangle. She bit into it and swallowed down a piece. "It tastes like chunky rubber."

Dolra seemed to have heard her since she gave Myx a hateful glare. "Hurry up, missy. You're in charge of cleaning up your friend over there. I can't get the antiseptic on the damaged tissues until you carve the scales off him."

"Carve?" Myx was worried about using a knife on her friend. What if she slipped?

She consumed the rest of her protein bar before putting on a pair of white gloves. With anxiety clawing at her newly-filled stomach, she went about de-scaling Rauno.

The scales were harder to get off than she thought. A chunk of regular skin came up with each one that she pried from Rauno's arms. Myx could see the layers of muscles underneath, a blazing pink that disturbingly reminded her of her eye color. Blood dribbled from the broken skin capillaries and drained into the exposed tissues. The whole sight made her retch into a bedpan.

"Harden that stomach of yours," Dolra said, returning to Rauno's bed. She ran her fingers along the inside of his jacket and removed a vile. "If you think this is gross, you're in for a surprise when you see what I have behind chamber hatch number three." The nurse pursed her lips as she continued raiding Rauno's private stash of chemicals. She sniffed the next glass container and grimaced. "What is wrong with this imbecile? It's a wonder he's still alive!"

As Dolra went about relieving Rauno of his jars, Myx continued de-scaling her friend.

Rauno's forearm hair fell out in patches, shedding all over the stark-white sheets. Myx would likely need to clean that up, too. She was just grateful that the nurse had sedated him so that she didn't also have to deal with his squirming.

As she made progress, Myx noticed a change in Rauno's appearance. He seemed a bit younger—like he was in his late twenties instead of mid thirties. His wrinkles were basically gone and his red hair line had filled in a bit. She opened one of his eyelids and inspected his green emerald irises; the color seemed a bit brighter, but still not quite as bright as Tieg's.

It alarmed her how much had changed overnight. Myx grew concerned that Rauno would need to spend another evening in the radiation chamber. And then she remembered that Gotasun said prisoners only get one night a week and her anxiety was appeased.

Dolra deposited the confiscated items in the incinerator and came to inspect Myx's work. She roughly cut away a couple hunks that Myx had missed, but seemed surprisingly happy about her work. Pulling another salve jar from her apron, she handed it to Myx. "Rub this into the tissue tears. The fool of a man is in for another night in the chamber."

"Um, Nurse Dolra? Myx raised her arm in the air as though she were back in school. Blushing under the woman's harsh, red jasper stare, she quickly tucked her hand below her opposite elbow. "My Handler said that prisoners only get one night a week in the chamber. Why does Rauno get two?"

"Nosy little thing, aren't you, missy?" Dolra sighed, her cheeks turning an even ruddier shade of crimson. "He's a liability. Between his escape attempt yesterday and his chemistry experiment this morning, the Warden will want to get rid of him. In the meantime, he's going to have some very painful nights as we get him back to new for the ransom."

Myx began rubbing the salve over Rauno's injuries. "So that's the big secret to getting ransomed? Piss everyone off? That doesn't seem very smart." She ceased her task a moment as she mused, "Then all the prisoners will revolt and hope they'll be sent home."

"Sure, but it's a toss-up. If the Tarasi President decided she didn't want to pay for this imbecile, then the Warden will just have him killed instead." Her jasper red eyes flashed, as if warning her not to keep spouting nonsense about rebelling. With a huff, Dolra took the salve away from Myx. "Now get along to bed, missy. Report back here tomorrow after your mining duties."

She tossed away her gloves, still disgusted by the mess of her friend's arm hair, skin, and blood cells.

As Myx cleaned the area, Dolra's words weighed on her mind. Rauno was going to die. The nurse's comment had seemed so final. Hope whispered that he might be ransomed, but Myx had grown up enough to know that life doesn't always turn out the way that she wanted.

It would be all her fault. If she hadn't hungered for adventure, then none of them would be at the Camp.

Bishing would have signed up earlier at a different recruitment center and would be training to fight the Hathak scum. Perhaps his artistic talent might have been noticed and he'd be designing military propaganda fliers.

Voumatir would likely have found a musical gig on this planet, using his identity as an alien to gain notoriety—at least until his eyes started changes from the wisps.

And Alycee? Well, no one really knew what her life was like before they all met. But Myx was sure that it was glamorous and thrilling. It would at least be more pleasant than toiling in the Labor Camp.

Lastly, Rauno would have eventually found his bride and lived as happily as he desired.

None of that would happen now, and that realization made Myx sick to her stomach. She wasn't sure if it was the long day in the mines, the attempted robbery, the sight of Rauno's mangled flesh, the guilt of dooming her friends, or the combination of it all, but she felt her resolve to stay optimistic begin to fade.

Chapter 15

Blood oozed out of the deep puncture wounds. Myx applied pressure once again, but red seeped through the bandage. The poor woman had passed out from dehydration and fallen onto a pitch fork down at the Farm. She wouldn't be harvesting levas beans for a couple days.

Myx released pressure on the injury with one hand and spread Dolra's salve across it with her other hand. A fresh piece of gauze was placed over it and taped securely. It wasn't the most ideal situation, but her abrasive supervisor forbade her from stitching up such small holes. Although the pitch fork had penetrated all the way to the bone, Dolra insisted that a night in a raditation chamber was all that the woman needed to heal.

After wheeling the patient through an empty hatch, Myx reminded the woman, "You know what to do—try to relax and pray for morning to come quickly." She set the set the timing mechanism and locked the patient in for the night.

At the conclusion of her sixth night in the Infirmary, Myx was beginning to see several differences in herself and the other medical workers—compared to the rest of the prisoners. They had greater stamina, strength, and dexterity. She planned on speaking with her friends about it during the evening meal, but she didn't have the chance.

On the way to the Mess Hall, Gotasun intercepted her. "Hello, my pet. Can you believe we've already had one whole week together?" His grey hematite eyes beamed behind his crooked nose. "Follow me. It's time for your Review."

He led her past the Main Street, away from preliminary buildings. After strolling down a series of passages, Gotasun pointed at a door.

"Welcome to the Reviewery."

Obedient, Myx entered and sat on the chair in the middle of the room. The Handler cleared his throat and raised his eye brows. It took her a moment to realize that the seat wasn't meant for her.

She stood, allowing Gotasun to ease himself onto the chair. He pulled a small screen from his pocket.

"Based on observations from the guards, cameras, other prisoners, and my own interactions with you, I will add or subtract points for good and bad behavior." Gotasun waited for her to nod that she understood what was happening. "Alright. The mine overseer says you worked consistently without stopping too much."

His face scrunched up in thought before he said, "I'll award five points for that. However, you worked slowly. Minus three. Next, you attempted to engage the other prisoners in chit-chat. That'll cost you six points."

Myx gasped. "Wait. I'm losing points for asking someone about the prison? I was just trying to—" She stopped her mouth as she noticed Gotasun making another note on his screen.

This system went on for several minutes. Gotasun didn't add or subtract out loud; he just spewed off minuses and additions. In an attempt to settle her anxiety, Myx kept track of the number in her head.

While he spoke, she also tried to remember all the things she did that lost her points so as not to make the same mistakes again. Many of her infractions seemed fairly minor, but her Handler still took away several points for each. Myx had lost some for asking for more soup at lunch, trying to figure out where the rest of her friends had been taken, leaving the mines early her first day, several for every time she back-talked to Dolra, and for asking Gotasun questions.

She received positive numbers, too, but not many. These mostly came from helping Dolra in the Infirmary for the past six nights. However, for every two points she earned for her assistance, she seemed to lose one for incompetence or some form of so-called "inappropriate" behavior as a medical caretaker.

By the time Gotasun completed his list, Myx was sitting at negative twenty-three.

Myx wanted to ask what that meant, but she feared the response. Instinctively, she shrunk away from him—slowly making her way to the back wall. Gotasun followed her across the room.

"Your magic number today is negative twenty-five." Gotasun put his screen aside and cracked his knuckles. "Put your arms up."

Negative twenty-five? That wasn't right. Did she do the math wrong? No, she couldn't have; they were small numbers. She almost corrected him, but that might've given her even more points.

Taking a deep breath, Myx raised her hands over her head.

A fist came straight at her torso. Reflexively, her hands came down to block him. Gotasun's knuckles raked across her arm. Her body twisted to cover her injuries, but she wasn't fast enough to dodge a second blow to her other side. Myx let out a stifled groan as she bit her lip.

"I told you to put your arms up!"

The Handler's fingers twisted in her hair, causing her to turn towards him.

"That's three. Twenty-two still to go. Keep your hands out of the way or you'll have an even harder time working tomorrow."

He sent a series of jabs to her abdomen. Her flesh stun when the fists landed, but Myx sensed that Gotasun was holding back

If he had delivered his full strength, she would likely be dead in a matter of seconds. Still, the impact of his strikes sent painful jolts up and down her spine. She bit her lip to keep herself from crying out as she endured the physical abuse.

Myx was thrown against the wall, smacked in the face again, and scratched. That last strike felt a little girly, but she resisted the urge to throw that back in her Handler's face.

Instead, Myx focused her energy on gritting through the pain.

Gotasun moved on to more aggressive strikes: elbowing her in the ribs, kicking at her legs, and tossing her to the ground.

And then she went numb. Myx was still fairly ignorant about human physiology, but she figured that her body had gone into shock to spare her nerves more trauma—or something like that; her brain wasn't exactly functioning at its full capacity.

Finally, they reached twenty-five blows. Spitting blood, Myx got on all fours. Before she could stand, a wave of nausea caused her to spew what little she had in her stomach on the floor.

Without another word, Gotasun left the room. Myx waited for something else to happen, but nobody came to help her. Slowly, she got to her feet. Making sluggish progress, she eventually arrived back at the Infirmary.

It had been a week to the day since her first night in the radiation chamber. She hoped one of the other workers would be there—with the exception of Dolra. But everyone was gone for the night. The patients that were not in the chambers were hooked up to machines that monitored their vital signs.

Myx crawled toward an empty radiation chamber. Tieg's warning about the wisps rang in her ears, but she ignored it. She pushed a bed through a hatch and painfully crashed into the lumpy mattress. Rubbing the fast-healing salve into her newly forming bruises, she prepared herself for the stinging and burning like when she had the open sore on her hand.

The sensation that followed was much stronger. Her nerves re-experienced every pain inflicted by Gotasun. She was hesitant to rub anymore into her skin, but she knew that she needed the salve in order to be mended by morning.

Wisps of radiation flowed through her. Cursing Dolra for her pain-inducing ointment, Myx covered her body with the wretched salve and settled in for the worse night of her short life.

Chapter 16

The pop and hiss of the hatch awoke Myx the next morning. Despite some grogginess from lack of sleep, she felt fine. She ran her hands over the skin that used to be injured. Memories of the agonizing evening were still in her fresh on her mind, but the flesh was unmarred.

Myx still hadn't had a chance to process why Gotasun would beat her so severely. Was he simply a sadist who enjoyed watching others suffer? Did he and Dorla have a pact to inflict as much pain as possible to the wretched prisoners?

Hunger gnawed at her stomach, distracting Myx from her contemplations. Stretching, she stood and left the Infirmary.

At the Mess Hall, Myx found her friends in the corner, staring in bleak silence at their meager breakfast. As she sat with them, their eyes bulged out at her, confusion evident across their faces.

"Are you alright?" Alycee asked, sounding oddly concerned.

"Yes, I'm fine." Myx didn't want to complain since it was one of the things that she had been punished for the previous night. "Why do you ask?"

Voumatir scratched at his forearms. "I saw you limping through the street last night. I wanted to come help you, but Heikah wouldn't let me; she said it was another Handler's business. When I attempted to get past her, she tied me to a pole." He presented his hands, showing them the raw, pink skin of his wrists. "I had to stand there for an hour as penitence. Sorry that I couldn't help you, Myx."

Bishing merely offered her the rest of his meal.

Myx put up a hand to refuse him.

"She's perfectly okay, guys," Rauno said in her defense. He knew first-hand what happened to someone after a night in the radiation chamber. The scientist still had minor wounds on his arms, but they didn't seem to bother him as he ate. "Leave her alone."

Someone tapped her on the shoulder. Myx shied away, wondering which prisoner had the nerve to touch her. She turned to see Gotasun standing over the bench.

"Ready to go, my pet?" Gotasun took away her half-eaten meal and tossed it across the table. "You've healed nicely. Dolra has trained you well in the healing arts. Now come along; you've got a full day ahead." He turned to Alycee. "You too, assassin."

Myx eyed Alycee as she trailed after the Handler. Could she really be an assassin? It sort of made sense as Myx thought through everything she knew about Alycee. But why would an assassin agree to join the war with her? She decided to do some investigating the next time she was alone with the woman.

Gotasun took them to one of the Kitchens. "Alright, my pet, let's see if cooking is a better fit than the mines. Remember, you're preparing food for your fellow prisoners. Make sure not to poison anything." He patted her on the head as he left them to their task.

"So things didn't work out at the Tailors, huh?" Myx asked, trying to engage Alycee in conversation. She couldn't bring herself to look at her companion, so she busied herself with reading the instructions on the counter. "I would have traded anything to get that job instead of the mines."

At first, Alycee didn't reply. She simply searched the walk-through freezer to find a bag of raw energy bars. Placing the frozen blocks on a cooking sheet, she said, "The overseer started to get a little free with his hands. When he crossed the line, I stabbed his wrist with a pair of crafting scissors. I guess Warden Parnuss thought that I needed to be somewhere safer, like a Kitchen full of knives."

Myx pursed her lips in thought. That didn't make sense to her. Why did they put someone dangerous like Alycee where she could take any number of sharp objects as weapons? And Gotasun had seemed a little too pleased when he dropped them off. But working in the Kitchen wasn't nearly as painful as slaving away in the mines. What was he up to?

"Well, there's no manager to stab if you get upset," Myx commented, searching through the drawers for a clean towel. "And maybe Warden Parnuss hopes you'll take out your anger on food instead of people."

"Anger?" Alycee pursed her lips as she arranged the bars on the cooking sheet. "No, I'm not angry. I actually don't really mind this place. I've been in much worse."

Myx couldn't imagine a place worse than the Labor Camp. "I suppose I'd feel the same if I didn't have a Handler," she mused, wiping her hands clean. After tossing the towel aside, she read the heating instructions for the energy bars. She moved to the oven and started preheating it. "Still, I can't help but wonder why you like it here? What's so bad back home that made you want to leave it, Alycee?"

The woman stared at Myx, her purple tanzanite eyes questioning if it was safe to speak her secret. "You heard your

Handler call me an 'assassin.' He is only partially correct. I use to be one—until I messed up a contract."

Myx gasped, shocked at the revealed information. Alycee seemed like the kind of woman who didn't make mistakes. She waited to see if her companion would share more.

"Now I'm on the run from the people who had hired me in the first place." Alycee left the completed tray and began flipping through cabinets. She didn't meet Myx's gaze as she continued, "There's a bounty on my head, but I grew sick of moving from place to place. And now I'm in this secure facility, safe from the other assassins that seek reward money for my murder."

Myx put the tray of frozen bars in the oven. Her fingers brushed one of the racks, but she barely felt the heat. She tried to form her next words carefully, but all she could manage to say was, "Do you want to talk about it?"

Alycee shook her head, her long braid swinging over her shoulder. "All I'll say is that I had a moment of weakness and let myself feel empathy for my target. I keep asking myself what my life would be if I hadn't let them go. But it doesn't do any good to dwell on what could have been."

The morning passed by in relative silence. They completed all the steps outlined in the instructions. Myx peeled and chopped vegetables while almost slicing her finger open, boiled rice that came out partially burned, and sloppily packaged up the bland energy bars for distribution. Alycee was patient as she assisted Myx in the more difficult tasks like boiling fhyjr dumplings and tenderizing the nusprin meat.

"I guess I'm bad at this, too," Myx laughed, trying to break the tension. "My foster mother, Kaefh, never let me help her in the kitchen."

Alycee finished brewing the stew, the smell making Myx's mouth water.

They left the final meal preparations for the evening crew—as the instructions specified—and took a place of "treats" to the Common Room. The walls were decorated with thin, paper decorations and the floor had been mopped clean.

"There were rumors of a reception this afternoon," Alycee explained, setting down the treats. "I didn't think them true."

On the scratched, rickety dining table, Myx arranged the goodies with the crispier ones at the bottom and the better-looking ones on top. Alycee stirred a red powder into a jug of water and set out cups. It was the most depressing party set-up Myx had seen, but she supposed it wasn't so bad considering that they were in prison.

"We forgot the napkins," Alycee said suddenly. "I'll be right back."

Myx was preparing to leave when a man appeared.

He wore simple-looking but high-tech armor. A patterned green and gold mask covered his face. "Where is she?" His voice came out muffled and computerized. Unholstering his gun, the masked man aimed it at Myx. "Don't make me ask you again."

Myx assumed he was talking about her cooking companion. She didn't want to give up Alycee; however, she also definitely didn't want to die. As she began speaking, none of her words made any sense—just blubbering. "She's not really—Well, I wouldn't exactly say that—No, she isn't—What I mean is—"

Before anything of importance was said, Alycee burst forward and slammed Myx behind a couch.

Chapter 17

Alycee tossed the napkins in the air. They fell like thick confetti, distracting the masked man. She grabbed the tray of treats and threw it at the assailant's arm, causing him to drop his gun. With the couch in the way, Myx didn't see what happened after her friend dove in for a tackle. There was a series of grunts and thuds, presumably as they fought each other.

Trying to be helpful, Myx recovered the man's gun. She went to aid Alycee, only to find her wrestling with the assailant on the ground. A knife was clutched in the former assassin's hand, but the masked intruder held her wrist a safe distance away.

Myx wished that she had learned how to use guns in their brief training day. She fumbled with the firearm to figure out how to make it shoot. There were so many curves to the weapon and it felt heavy in her grip. As she fingered the barrel, a shot fired, shattering a broadcast screen across the room.

Now that she knew how to make it shoot, Myx aimed it at Alycee's attacker. Her fingers grasped the same area from before.

The bullet barely missed Alycee's ear.

"Stop trying to help me, Myx!" her friend ordered, slamming the man into a table. Alycee reached for the green and gold mask, but the intruder rolled out of her way. Growling, she added, "I'd rather handle this by myself than have you accidentally shoot me."

A shower of bullets pelted the Common Room. Myx turned to see a woman in the doorway wearing a blue mask with orange swirls.

Myx ducked below the couch once again, raised the gun over the top cushions, and began firing. Someone cried out in pain. Slowly, Myx peeked her head to see the stranger clutching her abdomen before slumping unconscious to the floor.

She returned her attention to Alycee.

The former assassin grabbed the tray of treats from the table and crashed it over the man's head. "They've found me," Alycee whispered, a look of horror on her face. "Myx, I'm sorry that I dragged you into this. Find shelter and wait for this to be over."

"I'm tired of everyone thinking I'm helpless!" Myx shook with anger, her cheeks growing hot. "I can do things. I shot that woman, didn't I? I won't let them kill you!"

Alycee seized the masked woman's gun. "Then let's go see if the men are okay."

They made their way down the main street. A thundering crack echoed further down the way by the Infirmary. Smoke billowed from the Laundry and Myx could see a fiery haze on the horizon. Other masked assailants stalked the streets, shooting down any prisoner they came across.

Myx wondered what had happened to the Handlers and guards. Why weren't they intervening as they saw their prisoners being slaughtered?

"Rauno is up ahead," Alycee whispered, pointing at an upturned butcher's cart.

The scientist's thinning ginger hair was barely visible above the barrier. Myx and Alycee joined him to see other prisoners picking the locks of a guard station.

Tieg's white opal eyes glowed brightly, despite the lids being shut.

Alycee tore a piece of clothes from his shirt and wrapped it around his face. "Keep those unnatural lights concealed."

Rauno hefted a stolen rifle over his shoulder. "I'd listen to her, Tieg. We might not understand what she is planning, but it's a safe bet that Alycee knows what she's doing." He lowered his voice. "Besides, she'll pound you into a pulp if you disobey her."

"But I can—" The older man's protest ended as he noticed Alycee's intense glare.

A scuffle outside their cart barrier caught Myx's attention. Carefully, she glanced to the side to see a pair of masked assassins charging the prisoners. Knife points protruded from their chests before they slumped to the ground. Bishing retrieved his bloody blades from the attackers and wiped them on the corpses. Rauno and Tieg took that opportunity of distraction to shoot the other four in the group.

Alycee motioned for the prisoners to enter the now-open guard station.

"Where's Voumatir?" Myx asked, scanning their small group.

"He was moved to the Warden's office today," Rauno explained, wiping soot from his face. The scientist turned his attention to his clothing and felt the interior of the fabric. His hands came out carrying a pair of glass vials. "Maybe Voumatir is safe in there with the Hathak officials?"

"Unless the alien was sent out on errands," Tieg added, his eyes now only glowing faintly through the fabric wrapped about his face. "We won't know for sure until we see him. In the meantime, let's focus on the task at hand."

Despite Tieg's words, Myx couldn't help but worry about Voumatir. He could have been cold and lifeless, lying in a pool of his blood as the assassins stomped over his body.

"We have to go find him," Myx insisted, putting a hand on Alycee's shoulder. "I know that you don't care for Voumatir, but he's our friend. Please! Can you put your prejudice aside and help me find him?"

With a huff, Alycee agreed. "Fine. We'll go rescue the alien."

Rauno chuckled, "Yeah, that's a good way to deter a man's affections: save his life."

Alycee removed several kitchen knives from her clothing and left them in a pile. She placed Tieg in charge of the guard post with the other prisoners.

As they made their way to the Warden's office, Myx raided the corpses of the assassins. When she found a weapon that she liked, Bishing removed it from her grip. She sighed, but didn't make a further attempt to arm herself.

Occasionally, they'd encounter a group of masked assailants. Alycee and Bishing would quickly take them out while Rauno relieved them of their rifles. Myx gathered a nice assortment of knives, but Bishing still wouldn't let her have a gun. Rauno also agreed to keep firearms away from her when Alycee explained that she was nearly shot by Myx in the initial attack.

Myx tried not to sulk since they were probably right about the possibility of friendly fire. So she admired her knives and hoped that cutting people open would simply feel like performing surgery; she was becoming quite proficient at that from helping Dolra in the Infirmary.

Finally reaching the Warden's office, they were met with armed guards. Holding up her hands, Alycee surrendered to them.

"We aren't requesting sanctuary," Alycee explained, putting her pair of guns on the ground. "We simply want to know which way Voumatir went and we'll be on our way. Is that acceptable to you?"

Warden Parnuss stepped through the guards. "Yes, Alycee. Voumatir was here this morning. But I sent him on an errand hours ago; he hasn't returned. Be assured that we are doing our best to rid our Camp of the invaders." The Warden motioned at one of his men. "As we speak, the Handlers are installing stun emitters in the broadcast system. Any minute, they will activate it and everyone in the Camp who is not in my office will fall unconscious. We shall get to the bottom of this travesty as soon as order is restored."

The guards let the prisoners into the office, but they were pushed to the corner—out of the way.

Alycee pulled Myx away from Bishing and Rauno. She lowered her voice and said, “When this is all over, I need you to keep quiet about my past. Can you do that? I have a feeling that things are going to get more complicated from here on out.”

Myx wanted to say yes, but she wasn’t good at lying. However, she would definitely try since her friend’s life was on the line. “You can count on me.”

Chapter 18

"No! Please don't make me!" The young man shuddered below the thin Infirmary bed covers. "I can't go back. Just give me a scalpel and I'll—I'll—"

Myx put a comforting hand on his knee. Using her most soothing, caring voice, she said, "I understand where you're coming from. But you know that I can't do that. You'll have to be brave. Remember the most basic lesson from our planet's history: war doesn't last forever."

"But I can't go back," the boy whined, his face pale as sheet he lay on. "They made me do—"

"It doesn't matter. What matters is that you are healed and are strong enough to return to your work." Myx checked over her shoulder to make sure that Dolra was on the other side of the Infirmary. She hardener her tone and continued, "But let's say I humor you and slip you a scalpel. Let's say that you do the deed you are thinking of doing. Now on the chance that you are unsuccessful, what do you suppose they'll to you then?"

He swallowed hard. "I won't fail to end my life. I can't afford to."

"Oh, you're absolutely correct. If they heal you before your heart stops beating, they'll take you away and lock you in some hole worse than this. Only, they'll eventually give you what you want; however, you'll have to wait until they've made you beg for that sweet release of death with every one of your final breaths."

The young man rubbed where his arm had been shattered. "Has that really happened?"

Myx would have liked to tell the boy that she was making it up, but she had already see three suicide attempts in the past two days. She nodded at a middle-aged woman tied to her bed at the other end of the Infirmary. "You see her? She tried to drown herself. Dolra has been instructed to keep her oxygen levels at the lowest point possible to keep her alive. Every breath is agony for her."

"That's doesn't really prove that—"

"And this morning," Myx interrupted, "I treated electric burns on a former pro-athlete for the fifth time this week. He tried to fry himself, so his Handler is making him re-experience that pain until he's a lump of charcoal. Now, do you promise to do your best to stay alive?"

He nodded, leaping out of his bed and darting at the door.

On top of all the regular work injuries, the Infirmary had been a chaotic mess for the past several days as all those wounded in the attack were tended to. Since the Camp only had twenty radiation chambers, they couldn't heal all fifty-seven of the injured prisoners at once. So most had to wait and let their bodies heal naturally or until their abrasions were the most severe of the remaining patients.

Dolra had done triage to figure out who were the most mortally wounded. All others had to wait their turn. The Warden had been nice enough to not have those trips to the chambers count against their weekly allowance.

Myx had been moved to full-time hospital duty to aid with the excess of patients. For three days, Dolra kept her busy, barely letting Myx get any sleep. She had been give sort of energy-boosting beverage; combined with residual radiation from the chambers, it was meant to give her enough stamina to get through the long shifts.

As the number of patients decreased, Myx was glad that her time in the Infirmary was finally almost at an end. She found herself becoming gruff with the invalids like Dolra was and she didn't like that the nurse was being such a bad influence on her.

The last batch of patients had come out of the chambers that morning. Myx's job that day was to check vitals and clear them to go back to work. She still had four more to do before being released. Gotasun had been vague when mentioning the next workstation that she'd be assigned to. But Myx didn't care where it was—so long as it was away from the Infirmary.

"Did you really need to scare the boy like that?" Voumatir asked, helping her strip the bed. "I could have sworn he was about to piss the bed."

For the past two days, Voumatir had been assigned to be her assistant. Myx was delighted to see that he hadn't been harmed in the assassin attack. She enjoyed getting to know him as they worked. He turned out to be a very interesting alien.

"He wanted to kill himself," Myx explained, tossing the sheets into a hamper. "The fool would have failed and needed to be treated yet again."

"You might want to watch that tone," the alien mused. "You're sounding like Miss Sunshine over there." He nodded at Dolra with a smile, earning him a scowl from the nurse. "I think it's time for me to lighten the mood."

The patient at the adjacent bed perked up. "Will you finish your tale of the bet you lost to your band's drummer?"

Voumatir's plain, blue eyes sparkled as a wisps brushed past his face. "Yes! Now, where was I—Ah! There I stood, on center stage with my trusty guitar, wearing absolutely nothing but the lead-singer's miniskirt. Oh, they laughed about that for weeks. It was the last time I ever mixed tunrejil wine with kyve rum before a performance."

"Sounds like a wild night," Myx commented, hoping that her lack of experience with alcohol didn't make her a boring audience. "What did your fans do?"

"There were some interesting cat-calls throughout the show. Afterwards, I got a few broadcast numbers. I gave them all to the violinist in the band; he went for that kind of crowd." Voumatir broke out in song as he sanitized the bedside machines, most likely remembering better days when music had been his life.

For hours on end, Voumatir entertained the Infirmary inhabitants with stories from when his band was on tour. Often he would even break out it song. It did wonders for the patients' morale.

However, Dolra found his singing to be irritating. "Cease that ruckus," she would shout at the alien.

He would give her an embarrassed look, but continue his song about the wounded prisoners. "*Oh, Zanyava was a-washing in the Laundry when a vile masked man chopped off her fingers. Prudent to a fault, Zanyava collected her digits to be reattached at a later time. Although slightly crooked, she can still create macramé.*"

Zanyava waved at him with both her hands, stitch markings still visible above all ten of her knuckles. "Not that I don't love my song, Voumatir, but it doesn't rhyme."

"I'm not a lyricist, Zan," he replied, taking a bow. "However, I will always try to please my audience."

As Voumatir rose, Dolra pulled at his ear, her red jasper eyes giving him the glare of death. "Stop that nonsense and get back to work, fool."

Voumatir nodded, slicking back his bright yellow hair. "At least 'fool' is a better nickname than 'imbecile.' It's nice to be better than Rauno at something." Despite Dolra's warning, Voumatir continued his impromptu songs as he worked—just in a lower volume. Dancing, he made his way to the various bed stations and spread out clean sheets.

While releasing her next patient, Myx noticed Dolra tapping her foot regardless of her protests at Voumatir's cheeriness. The stocky nurse even had a rhythm to her voice as she gruffly told the next patient that he needed to leave right then. Myx was surprised to see that the abrasive woman had a soft side. Perhaps that was what Rauno saw in her that no one else could see? She decided not to pry into the scientist's affections anymore.

Voumatir's Handler poked her head into the Infirmary. Her orange amber irises glanced Myx up and down, looking skeptical about something. Heikah moved to Voumatir and pointed a red lacquered fingernail at him. "Time to go, handsome."

When Myx had first seen Voumatir's Handler, she seemed unprepared for the role. However, as the days passed, the young woman seemed to grow in ferocity. Myx grew frustrated at her own inability to read people. Was that what made the Hathak so crafty that the Tarasi were incapable of figuring them out? No, there had to be more to it. Either Heikah was trying too hard to be intimidating, or she wasn't nearly as useless as she appeared.

"Hail, Heikah!" Voumatir chanted, straightening to greet his Handler. He raised a hand straight in the air as he added, "How has this fair day occurred for you?"

Heikah tossed her curly tail of golden hair over her shoulder. "I had no idea that you were musical, Voumatir." She performed her habit of looking people up and down, pursing her lips at him while he waited for her next command. "I think your talents are wasted here changing bed pans. Perhaps I can get you reassigned as a Handler entertainer?"

"Really?" Voumatir looked absolutely giddy at the chance to play music again. "Can we go talk to the Warden about that? Oh, please, Heikah? That would just be the best thing ever!"

"Yes, but you mustn't speak when we are with Warden Parnuss," Heikah said, stroking his lean shoulders. "You know how much your cheeriness annoys him." She spun and moved to the Infirmary door.

"As my Handler commands." Voumatir turned to Myx. "As excited as I am about this new opportunity, I'm upset that you'll still be stuck doing these demeaning jobs. Maybe I can get Heikah to tell the Warden that I need an assistant. By any chance do you have some sort of musical training?"

Myx shook her head. "Thanks for the offer, but I'm afraid that I lack that skill as well. But I'm happy that you'll be doing something that you love once again."

Voumatir winked at Myx as he left and saluted to Dolra while passing her on the way out.

Dolra tossed a chart at Myx. "Hey there, missy. Those patients aren't going to release themselves. Even though it's your last day here, I still expect you to get all your work done. Your Handler will be here soon to collect you."

Nodding, Myx went about checking gunshot wounds in a woman's abdomen. The poor thing had been shot seven times in the torso. She was lucky to still be breathing. However, three nights in the radiation chamber hadn't been enough to heal her fully. Myx wrote notes in the woman's chart, recommending yet another night in a chamber due to an infection that began spreading to her chest. She knew it was useless; the Warden would likely let the woman die rather than to waste one more chamber session on her.

In the days since the assassin attack, Myx hadn't seen Gotasun. She woke up, went to the Infirmary, ate all three of her meager meals there, and was then released from her task late at night. Her friends visited on occasion, either on cleaning or delivery duties. But they had little time for conversation due to Dolra's vigilant gaze. It made Voumatir's time as her assistant all the more special as the two of them finally had time to bond.

When Gotasun appeared that afternoon, Myx double-checked the time. Dolra had never released her so early in the day. Sure, she was finishing the release of her final patient, but there were other Infirmary matters to take care of before that evening.

And then she remembered what day it was. Another week had passed as a prisoner of the Hathak Labor Camp.

Gotasun waited by the door, his arms crossed over his wide chest. Myx quickened her pace, not wanting to let time sour his impatience. She scooted her patient along and sprayed disinfectant across the bed.

Dolra took the towel from her. "Someone else can finish up. Go with your Handler."

Nodding, Myx dashed to Gotasun.

"I thought you'd never be done," he groaned, leading her out onto the Main Street.

As they walked, Myx noticed some changes in the man. Although he was still tall and stocky, much of his girth seemed to have melted away. Muscles were more prominent under his skin, which was significantly less flabby than they had been. His gut still stuck out in front of his hips, but not as much.

Even if he had spent the past three days doing nothing but exercise, there was no conceivable way that he'd have lost as much weight as he had. Myx's curiosity flared inside of her. But she suppressed it as she remembered her first Review.

Myx began to turn left, assuming they were heading to the Reviewery. Instead, Gotasun veered left.

"It's not your Review day. Come along." He stopped in front of the Common Room.

To her surprise, no one had cleaned up yet. Dried blood smeared the broken furniture that littered the room. The stale treats lay scattered across the floor, several crushed into the carpet fibers; Vermin nibbled on crumbs. The only sign that anyone had been there the past three days was the bullets missing from their holes across the walls and broadcast screen.

"You've already given your story about what happened, but I need to know for sure." Gotasun pulled a gun on her. "My pet, you've seemed awfully suspicious since the moment I first laid eyes on you."

Myx had a flashback to when the masked assassin attacked. "I don't—" She fought back tears, not wanting to re-experience memories of feeling helpless. Calmly, she tried again. "Are you suggesting that I orchestrated the attack on the Camp?" When Gotasun didn't reply, Myx continued, "All I know is that I almost died! Please believe me."

The Handler holstered his weapon, not taking his fierce, grey hematite eyes off her. "You know more than you've said. I can sense it. The cameras show a greatest concentration of attackers here. That can't be coincidence."

"You know that I lack several basic talents. Lying is among them. So you have to understand that I truly had nothing to with the invaders."

Gotasun didn't seem completely convinced by her response. "Now that you are no longer needed in the Infirmary, I can have some alone time with you to wear you down." He moved close to her—so close that his crooked nose was nearly touching hers.

Myx had made a vow not to reveal what she knew about Alycee. Gotasun had called the towering woman an 'assassin,' but didn't seem to be aware of what that actually meant.

"Until you tell me everything I want to know," her Handler resumed, "you'll be performing the most humiliating, disgusting things I can think of. Reflect on my words in your cell tonight. For tomorrow you shall wish I had kept you in the mines."

Chapter 19

Gotasun had been serious when he promised that he was going to make her do the worse jobs at the Camp. Myx spent the whole next day at the morgue, cremating the bodies of those killed in the assassin attack. The following morning, she rinsed and scrubbed out the sewage tunnels. Working with fish that afternoon hadn't been too bad, but touching the spanic trouts' guts grossed her out more than when she performed surgery at the Infirmary.

And now Myx was trimming Gotasun's nose hairs. It wasn't a difficult task—mostly demeaning. She sensed that he was running out of awful tasks to give her. Myx was quite proud that she was able to endure all of it without spilling Alycee's secret.

"Toes next, my pet." Gotasun held up a pair of nail clippers. "Be careful not to get too deep, though. And then you'll need to pumice the calluses off my heels."

Frezul scowled at Gotasun. "It isn't fair! How come the Warden let you turn your prisoner into your personal slave?" Bishing's Handler folded her arms and pouted like a little girl, despite being middle-aged.

Voumatir's Handler entered, frowning at Myx. Heikah wasn't pleased about the arrangement either. "Why didn't anyone me that we could make our prisoners groom us? Oh! I'm going to have the alien give me a massage and wash my hair. Do I need to get permission from Parnuss or something to get him out of his entertainment business?"

"It's only a temporary situation, ladies," Gotasun said dismissively, changing the broadcast channel in the Handler's Ward. "If your prisoners got into trouble, I'm sure that Warden Parnuss would let you do the same thing."

Myx completed her job on Gotasun's nasal hairs. After spending ten minutes on that task, she was now convinced that the Handler's nose had indeed been broken several times within his life.

Once she was complimented for being "a good little pet" by Gotasun, she took the nail clippers from her Handler and moved to his feet. Pulling off one of his shoes, Myx felt like she was back in the sewage tunnels. She put her face into her shoulder and breathed through the fabric of her shirt to alleviate some of the stink.

Frezul shook her head. "Oh, you know my method: I like to let the punishments build up so that I can deal it all out in one session." The petite woman cracked her tape-wrapped knuckles with a menacing smile.

"Well, I'd rather have someone groom me than entertain me," Heikah snapped, folding her arms across her chest. The young woman continued watching Myx. "Maybe Parnuss will let us switch prisoners? Voumatir can be your personal jester and I can have Myx give me my beauty treatments."

Myx paused, wondering if switching Handlers was an option. Voumatir seemed to be getting through his time in prison with hardly any difficulties. Heikah had a secret mean streak that would come out on occasion, but she was fairly docile compared to Gotasun.

"Keep trimming," her Handler order, tapping his foot against Myx's cheek. "Heikah, why do you waste your time with all that? There's no one here to impress."

"It's a habit, Gotasun." Heikah ran her small fingers through her silky, blonde hair. Red stained lips pulled into a pout yet again. "I'm accustomed to looking exquisite at all times—no matter who is around."

They stopped squabbling as Warden Parnuss entered the room. The Handlers straightened and removed all evidence of complaining from their faces.

"I'd like to remind you," Parnuss said in his deep voice, "to be careful what you say around prisoners. I'd hate for rumors to start about how you all disagree." He turned to Myx and regarded her with his menacing turquoise eyes. "But I'm sure that you won't say anything to your little friends, will you?"

Myx shook her head, trying unsuccessfully to break Parnuss's gaze.

"Good." The Warden smoothed his salt and pepper hair and addressed the Handlers. "Now, Gotasun, I think it's time for the weekly Review, is it not? Frezul and Heikah, check to see how your prisoners are adapting to their new occupations. You are all dismissed."

Having forgotten that a second week had passed, Myx was nervous about getting another beating. Receiving fresh injuries would mean another night in the Infirmary, and she had no desire to return to that place. She made her face a blank slate as Gotasun walked her to the Reviewery.

Although she wasn't looking forward to having her behavior evaluated, Myx felt significantly less afraid this time around. She knew what to expect.

"You've done much better this week, my pet," Gotasun said, looking over his small screen. He didn't bother rattling off the individual offenses and rewards. "All the extra shifts that you worked knocked down all the punishments that you had accrued when you talked back to Dolra." The Handler put aside his screen and turned on her with his grey hematite eyes. "We are only at minus ten for today. Arms up."

Myx let out a sigh, relieved to have so few minuses. She linked her fingers above her head, shut her eyes, and awaited the first strike. To her surprise, it only felt like a smack instead of a punch. Opening her eyes, she met Gotasun's stunned gaze. Perhaps all the time in the Infirmary getting residual radiation from the chambers had toughened her up?

Gotasun shook his head before striking again.

Again, Myx barely felt it. She couldn't help the smirk that found its way to her lips.

The Handler didn't enjoy her response. His face grew crimson and he repeatedly clenched and unclenched his fists. Mumbling something unintelligible, Gotasun went to a cabinet on the far wall. He pulled out a syringe and a wood staff.

Myx eyed both warily. Was he really going to beat her with that rod? And what was in the syringe? She was proud that she had concealed that the assassins were after Alycee for not fulfilling a contract. However, Myx was fairly certain that she wouldn't be able to hide it with truth serum coursing through her vein. But, no. That wasn't very sporting—not like Gotasun at all.

She barely flinched as he injected her with the syringe.

Gotasun tossed the needle away and explained, "If you get a radiation treatment, this serum will make you sick. So, my pet, I recommend healing the natural way this time." Raising the staff, he swung it in a downward arc across her back.

The force of the blow knocked her to her knees. Myx gasped as she landed. She took in a deep breath, only to be met with a rush of pain as she realized that one of her ribs was cracked.

He continued the rest of the punishment with blows to her limbs and torso. Gotasun left enough time for his pet to feel every agonizing strike before he performed the next. The staff failed to break the skin, so she didn't become a bloody mess. But large welts began to form where he had struck her.

She tried to think of home. Memories of Kaefh and Sievly had comforted her at nights when she regretted childishly running away. But now she couldn't imagine it. Snippets of the store and her small room were blurry in her mind as she sought relief from her distress. It was as though she felt that she didn't deserve consolation. Leaving had been a horrible mistake, and she needed to accept her punishment for it.

"And that makes ten, my pet." Gotasun spun his staff up to rest on his shoulder as he strolled to the door, sweat glistening on his smug face.

Myx attempted to rise to her feet, but she fell back to the ground and smashed her jaw.

The Handler summoned a pair of guards as he left.

Her vision grew blurry, so Myx closed her pink tourmaline eyes tight. She was vaguely aware of what was happening as two pairs of thick hands took hold of her limbs. The guards had no respect for her damaged body as they bore her to her cell like a trash sack.

She experienced déjà vu as she once again plummeted to the ground. Myx opened her eyelids just enough to confirm that she was in her cell. Reaching forward, she found that she lacked the strength to even crawl. Her bed lay across the room; it was thin and creaked fiercely all night, but it was far more comfortable than the cold floor. But she was never going to make it up there.

With much effort, she managed to pull down her thin blanket from the cot. She carefully eased the material over her shivering body and prepared for an agonizing night of slow healing.

Chapter 20

Saying that Myx felt like she was on-fire would be an understatement. She found herself missing Dolra's dreaded ointment. Sure, the salve would have made her re-experience every strike over again as the radiation absorbed into her skin, but at least it helped her heal quickly.

Even though Gotasun only hit her with the staff a few times, Myx's injuries kept her recuperating in her cell for three days.

"Please!" Myx shouted at the cell door. "I know I've asked to go to the Infirmary every hour since you locked me in here. But my infection is getting worse. I need antibiotic ointment from—"

"You wanna lose your lunch like you lost your breakfast?" one of the guards asked. He banged on the door for emphasis. "Settle down!"

Upon her arrival at the Camp, Myx had wished to remain in her cell instead of the hard labor that she was forced to endure in the mines. However, she now regretted those thoughts as the long hours lingered on and on without end.

"If I don't get treatment soon, I'll lose my arm to gangrene." She carefully rubbed a welt on her left arm. A nasty green border around it told her that it had become infected. The other bruises made a natural progression from dark purple to puke brown. "Please! I know where Dolra keeps the pain-killers. I can get you some if you let me. All I need is ten minutes."

"Trying to bribe us, are you?" another guard grunted through the door. "That's not gonna work. Just confess to Gotasun what he wants to know. That's all you need to do to leave."

"I don't know anything," Myx replied for the hundredth time. Obviously she hadn't become more adept at lying like she had hoped. She must have had some sort of tell that gave her away, but Myx was unsure of what that was.

Throughout her confinement, she had often contemplated explaining to her Handler why the masked intruders attacked the Camp. There was a bounty on Alycee's head from the time she had worked as an assassin and failed her contract. Revealing this to Gotasun would result in Alycee being killed and the Hathak earning the reward money. However, if it wasn't for Alycee's decision to help Myx escape the police that fateful day, then Myx would be safe at home with her family.

Although Myx didn't know much about the woman, she still felt compelled to keep her secret; Alycee had saved Myx's life several times on the day they were taken from the Tarasi training center, as well as during the attack on the Camp.

Her regular ranting at the guards was about more than just whining. Yes, it helped her vent frustration, but it also served as a way to access her contraband. Myx had discovered early on that she was neglected for longer when she made a fuss. It was as though they were contented by her pleas and didn't feel like they needed to taunt her as much as they did when she remained silent. With the guards satisfied that she was feeling mistreated, Myx took the opportunity to sneak out the treasures from under her washbasin.

When she had worked in the Infirmary, Myx had taken whatever bits of extra paper she found lying around as well as a couple old pens. She knew that she'd get in trouble if any of the guards caught her, but she was grateful to have a little excitement to break up the monotony of her anguishing solitude.

As Myx sat alone in her cell, she scribbled little notes to Sievly and Kaefh about the horrors that she suffered at the hands of the Hathak. She knew that there wasn't really any point to it; her loved ones would never see the letters. But it was something she needed to do to process what was happening to her. Otherwise, Myx was fairly certain that she'd lose her grasp on her sanity.

Keys jangled in the hallway. Myx hastily stashed the papers back to their hiding place. As the door opened, she moved to the back wall and placed her hands behind her head.

Gotasun stepped through the door, swinging a ring of keys around his index finger. "Well, my pet, are you ready to tell me why you're so incredibly suspicious?" He palmed the keys and stashed them in his pocket.

"I still don't understand what you're talking about, Gotasun," Myx replied. Out of the corner of her eye, she saw her contraband pen amongst the tangled sheets. She stepped forward, ensuring that her Handler would keep his gaze on her as she made her way back to the bed. "Could you please explain what's so suspicious about me?"

"For starters, I don't understand why so many people want to take care of you—the mute, the assassin, the mad scientist, the alien. They seem to feel this compulsion to protect you. Even the human-light has show fondness for you. Why? You don't do anything for them at all."

There was some truth in Gotasun's words. Myx had often wondered about that herself. Why did they take an interest in her?

Myx winced as she eased herself onto the bed. "Let me get this straight—you've kept me locked up in here for three days without medical treatment because you're jealous that people love me?"

"That has nothing to do with—"

She knew that she'd pay for her insolence at her next Review, but she couldn't help picking at the logic behind his actions. "I hope you understand that you've done nothing to harm my friendship with Bishing, Alycee, Rauno, and Voumatir by keeping me in my cell. This is only making their concern for me to grow."

Gotasun grinned beneath his crooked nose. "How are you so sure your little buddies want to see you?"

"I know that Rauno has stopped by at least half a dozen times, based on the mixed scent of aftershave, gasoline, and bleach. A dot of blood on the bottom of my meal plates is a greeting from Alycee—an inside-joke from our time together in the Kitchens. Every night, the man in the cell next to mine sings before he goes to bed, which tells me that Voumatir bribed him to serenade me to improve my mood. As for Bishing, I don't have any evidence to prove he's thinking of me, but I know him well enough to know that he has done everything in his power to come see me. I have a feeling that your presence right now has something to do with that."

Myx stared up at her Handler, feeling smug at his open jaw.

"Tell me I'm wrong," she dared him, tilting her head to the side. "Or let me see my friend."

"Look who's become quite the detective." Gotasun stepped forward and knelt so that his gaze was level with hers. He lowered his voice as he said, "You're starting to develop a bit of a mouth, my pet. Who knows what kind of trouble it might get you into?" Straightening, he moved to the door and swung it open. "Okay, mute. You've earned ten minutes with her."

Bishing strode in, his hands behind his back. His face was stoic as nodded for Gotasun to leave. With the Handler gone, his shoulders relaxed. He brought his arms forward, baring a bowl in one hand and a bundle of towels in the other.

"I can't believe they let you see me," Myx sighed, rising to put her arms around his waist. "How did you earn time with me?"

With his hands still full, he was unable to reply. Bishing nodded at the bed before shrugging his shoulders. When Myx let go, he set his load onto the blanket and motioned for her to eat the meal he brought. His face was uncharacteristically blank as he leaned against the wall.

"How is everyone else, Bish?" Myx asked, taking a sip of the cold noodle broth. She couldn't help being amused that the guard had been unsuccessful in his threat to deny her the next meal; in her isolation, she had learned to take pleasure in the little victories life afforded her. "Is Alycee still busy with kitchen duty, keeping to herself?"

Bishing nodded. He made a motion like he was strumming a guitar.

"Voumatir? Is he enjoying his new position as Handler entertainer? I bet Alycee is happy that he's too busy to bother her." Myx felt a wave of anxiety. She hated that she was being punished for keeping Alycee's secret. But the thought that they'd do something much worse to Alycee kept Myx from revealing what really happened the day of the attack.

She waited for him to sign more, but his attention was on the wad of towels. Bishing removed a small lump of plastic sheeting. He picked the edges open to reveal a thick, white ointment. From the consistency and color, it appeared to be antiseptic.

"And Rauno?" Myx held out her arm, showing Bishing the infected welt. "Is he still desperately searching for his bride, or has he finally found her?"

With one hand, Bish rubbed the ointment into Myx's bruise. His calluses felt rough against her tender skin. The other fingers slowly mimed a motion that made her think of the Handlers.

Myx asked him some clarifying questions before realizing what he was saying.

"So Rauno has asked all the prisoner ladies to marry him? Now he's turned his attention to the female Handlers?" She winced as she imagined the responses that he was likely to have received from the Hathak women.

Bishing completed caring for her infection and moved to the washbasin.

"How did you sneak that away from Dolra?" Myx leaned back on her cot, enjoying the soothing sensation of the antiseptic. She chuckled lightly, resting her eyes. "Let me guess: Rauno distracted the nurse with his talk of marriage while Alycee or Voumatir snuck it away."

There was a rustling in front of her face. Myx opened her pink tourmaline eyes to see Bishing standing over her, waving the papers she had stashed under the basin. His calm demeanor disappeared, replaced by a look of rage. He shook the papers again, not bothering with signing his obvious question.

"Those are just my thoughts of the Camp," Myx replied, taking the pages from him. She turned away, not wanting to see the pity that replaced the anger in Bishing's smoky quartz irises. "I should have told you about all of Gotasun's mistreatments. But he somehow knows every time I complain and he adds punishments for each one. And I didn't want you and the others to worry."

Bishing made a punching motion, pointed at himself, and shook his head.

"Yeah, I've been wondering why Frezul doesn't beat you. Perhaps her intimidation tactic is merely verbal abuse."

Myx couldn't bring herself to tell him what she had overheard Frezul telling Gotasun—that the petite Handler liked to save up punishments and dole them all out at once. She knew it was naive to think that they'd be rescued by the Tarasi military before that happened; Myx couldn't help but cling to that foolish hope.

Trying to cheer them both up, Myx asked, "Remember that day when we first met? You were sitting out on a curb, painting children as they ran up and down street." She flipped through her letters, found where she had scribed the memory, and handed him the page.

Nodding, Bishing pointed at Myx and pretended like he was drawing something.

"Yes, you asked if you could paint my face. You offered a serrip melon in exchange for my time. I agreed, even though the poor fruit looked like it had been dropped a couple times. Still, it was crisp and tasted quite refreshing." Myx stopped to think for a moment. "That was, what, about seven, eight months ago? It seems like an eternity now. Did you ever sell that painting?"

He shook his head.

"No, of course not. No one would pay for a portrait of a wretched-looking thing like me."

Bishing waved his arms in an X motion, still shaking his head. He mimed a square and made the sign for love.

"Kept it for yourself, huh?" Myx shook her head, not sure if she should feel disappointed or flattered. "No wonder you never had enough money if you refused to sell all your favorites, Bish."

He clearly didn't want to talk about that any more as he began tidying up her cell. As he picked up an empty plastic bottle, a thought occurred to Myx.

"I know this is usually Rauno's area of expertise, but I think I have an escape plan." She took the bottle from him. Carefully, she rolled her letters into a thick cylinder, slid them inside, and put the cap on. "You work by the river now, right? Do you think you can sneak this past the guards and toss it into the currents?"

Bishing looked at her like she was crazy.

"I'm perfectly serious, Bish. This could work. I've read about it in stories."

He let out a breath and scratched his jaw. After thinking for a moment, he took the bottle back and stashed in it his jacket.

As he was about to leave, Rauno came in without knocking. "Hey, Myx. Sorry, but the Warden wants everyone in the courtyard for an announcement. Do you think you can walk now?"

Myx nodded and let the men ease her off her bed.

It felt weird to be on her feet again, but she was excited to move around. She let them support her as she inched towards the cell door. And then she remembered the Camp rule about touching; she didn't want them to get in trouble for helping her.

"I'm not a cripple!" She weakly pushed at their hands.

As they backed away, she felt a little unstable as her head spun.

To ease their nervous glances, Myx added, "But just to be safe, please stay close."

Chapter 21

Myx shooed off Rauno's and Bishing's attempt to help her as she sat down on the hard bench next to Alycee; she had been purposeful in choosing her spot so as to separate Alycee from the fawning Voumatir.

As they waited for the assembly, Myx discreetly rubbed more antiseptic into her infected bruise.

"You look awful," Alycee commented. She quickly pulled Myx's lengthening black hair into a messy-but-decent ponytail when the guards weren't looking. "Did they give you any hygiene products during your solidarity?"

Myx shook her head. Her face felt flush, either due to embarrassment at being primped like a child or possibly due to the purple heat of the overhead sun. It had been nearly three weeks since being outside. It felt—alien. And yet, the warmth felt nice on her pale white skin, banishing the chill from the Camp's caves.

Alycee's hands moved to her lap for a moment while she looked distractedly around her. When the nearest guards passed, she put the final touches on Myx's hair tail. "We'll have to get you all cleaned up properly when we're done here."

It felt uncharacteristic of Alycee to offer something so womanly. Myx wondered if the former assassin had an ulterior motive for wanting some alone time with her. Or perhaps Alycee simple felt guilty that Myx had been singled out for mistreatment as an example to the other prisoners. Still, questions about the assassin attack had plagued Myx for the past three days and she was impatient to finally get some answers.

Alycee leaned forward and whispered at Rauno, "You have been working in the Warden's office this week. Do you know what Parnuss is going to say?"

Rauno scanned the crowds of prisoners. "No, but he has been in surprisingly good spirits." He shifted nervously on the bench, scratching at his thickening beard. "If he's happy about something, then it's probably bad news for us. But I'm not sure. Personally, I'm hoping they're going to say that we are free to go; I need to continue my quest to find my bride."

Pleasant as always, Voumatir said, "It might be a Hathak holiday or something. Maybe there will be cake." He gave Myx a comforting smile. "We've got to get some fat on this little one."

Bishing let out a loud sigh and sent a palm into his forehead—his usual sign of disbelief.

"I agree with Bish," Myx whispered, noting the stern expressions on the guards' faces. "It seems a little farfetched that they'll give us a party." She wiped a tear from her pink tourmaline eyes. "What if they're going to execute us? I don't want to die."

Fingers brushed against her neck. Myx shied away as she realized that Rauno was rubbing one of his mysterious concoctions onto her skin.

"It'll make you smell better," Rauno insisted, putting his hand back up his shirt. "Which will make you feel better." Once again, he held out wet fingers. He reached for Myx's wrist and massaged a dripping liquid along her lower forearm.

Alycee put a comforting arm around Myx. When guard passed by, she quickly let go, her long braid swinging across her shoulder. After the guard was gone, she said, "We are too valuable to them. I doubt they're going to kill us. Besides, they haven't ransomed anyone yet—not even him." She gave Rauno a stern glare. "Perhaps they are finally going to send one of us home?"

None of them were terribly enthusiastic about that possibility. They sat in silence as the rest of the prisoners arrived.

Even more squads of guards entered and circled the Tarasi, their uniforms glinting under Star Lerwyn's purple blaze. They faces were unexpressive as they scanned their assembled slaves.

Warden Parnuss appeared on the giant screen in the center of the amphitheatre. "Good morning, my esteemed guests. I have splendid news: the war is almost over! The Hathak military is close to defeating the Tarasi armies. We have won the past several battles and have found a way to end the dispute within the next couple of weeks."

He paused as the prisoners began chattering amongst themselves, processing the information.

Myx couldn't believe it. The War Declaration had happened less than a month ago. The Tarasi weren't so powerless as to be defeated that quickly. There was no conceivable way that the Hathak had advanced their military strategy so much quicker than the Tarasi. In all the previous wars, their disputes raged on for years before being reluctantly settled.

She shared skeptical looks with her companions, but they didn't say anything aloud.

"Please," Parnuss continued, his voice displaying mock sympathy. "I know this is shocking to hear, but it's true." He waited once again, until the crowd of prisoners settled down. "Now, you have all been very obedient to your Handlers, guards, and overseers. I'd like to continue having good relations with you all when the Hathak take over the Tarasi civilization. So as long as you all do as you're told, I'm sure that we can find you a suitable occupation in our Empire when the war is officially over."

The prisoners shouted questions at him, but he didn't reply. Guards took a step closer, silencing the crowds so that the Warden could continue his speech.

"Sadly, anyone who chooses to reject their new life will be branded as a dissenter and sent to the maximum security prison. But all those who can accept the Hathak Emperor as their supreme ruler can enjoy the benefits of being under his care."

The screen went dark and Gotasun called for the prisoners' attention. "The Hathak government would like a more accurate account of each of you. Spend this afternoon filling out a biographical survey about yourself. Please be as accurate as you can so that we might know the best position for you. Now get to it!"

There was confusion as prisoners began shouting questions at no one in particular. Handlers appeared, calling for their Tarasi slaves to come to them and fill out their bios.

Myx didn't much mind her situation. Although she had been born a Tarasi, she didn't really feel a sense of patriotism. If the Hathak would provide her with a decent job, she couldn't complain; it was more than the Tarasi government ever did for her.

Still, she harbored ill feelings for the Hathak due to her mistreatment at the Camp—even though she was now a lot more capable than she had been three weeks ago.

Alycee put her lips by Myx's ear. "Don't put real information in your bio."

Myx frowned, confused by what was happening. "What do you mean?"

"You should lie," the former assassin replied, her voice tight and serious. "Except for obvious things like your physical attributes. Don't let them know anything important about you. Use bits and pieces of information that you've heard about other people. Do you understand me?"

Myx looked to Bishing, but he didn't return her gaze. She turned back to her female companion. "Not exactly. I mean, I understand what you want me to do, but not why. What's going on, Alycee?"

Rauno leaned in on her opposite side. "Warden Parnuss is lying." He caught the attention of the nearest guard, a woman with a face like a freckled thrunys. Smiling at her was just the thing to make the guard to turn her attention away. Continuing, he whispered, "Getting us to do the bios is probably just a way for the Hathak to gain information about life in Tarasi."

Alycee nodding her head. "It looks like identity theft. They might be getting ready to send spies into Tarasi using our personal information. Don't give it to them. Lie, Myx!"

"Don't worry!" Voumatir said, uncomfortably close behind her. "Everything is going to be okay. You tell the truth just to be safe, Myx. Otherwise, they might use it to justify beating you half-to-death again. We'd all rather not see you like that anymore."

Pushing Voumatir away, Alycee told her once more, "Hide the truth."

Someone grabbed Myx's ear. "Are you deaf, my pet?" Gotasun asked, his grip tugging her closer to him. "I've been calling your name."

"I'm sorry." Myx whimpered until he let her go. "I'm just so happy that the war is almost over," she replied untruthfully as she followed Gotasun to the computer stations. She had been concealing things from her Handler for the past week and it was starting to feel natural and pleasing. "It'll be nice when we will be part of the same society and are no longer enemies."

Chapter 22

"I am a transgender man who enjoys logic games and making love in loud space ships," Rauno said loudly as he typed his fake biography into the screen. He scratched his thinning, ginger scalp. "My ideal occupation? Hmm. I think that would have to be a minstrel for a pirate band."

"Are you sure it's a good idea to lie?" Myx whispered, looking up from her blank screen. She was beginning to have second thoughts about it.

Rauno lowered his voice. "If they were sincere in using these bios to help get you a good position after the war, then make sure that you paint a good picture for them. That way they will give you your dream job. However, I'm pretty sure that Parnuss was lying; if you don't want to be the victim of identity theft, then you had better stretch the truth."

Myx nodded. Obviously, she should tell the truth on her physical attributes. But with things like her aspirations, interests, and skills, she made herself sound like the most interesting woman in the world. As she wove her falsities, she wondered if she'd enjoy a career in writing.

"Let's see. How much money is in my bank account?" Rauno stroked his chin. "A hundred million is a little high, isn't it?"

"Probably." Myx set hers at five thousand, which was five thousand more than she had for real. Shocked by the question about her romantic relationships, she hoped she wasn't blushing as she came up with a nice fantasy about dating a broadcast reporter.

Rauno finished his bio quickly and went in search for female prisoners. "Excuse me, miss. I was just wondering what you put as your relationship status?"

Bishing followed after the researcher, protecting what women he could by pulling Rauno away if he got particularly creepy. Myx couldn't hear which of Rauno's pick up lines earned him a kick to the groin, but it did little to subdue him. When he continued pursuing the fleeing woman, Bish waved over a guard to intervene. Limping, Rauno was firmly escorted on his way to his afternoon job.

Signing something that Myx didn't quite see, Bishing took off after Rauno.

Heikah tapped Voumatir on the shoulder. "Vou, it's time to set up for the evening show." The Handler smiled at him, a strange twinkle in her orange amber eyes.

"I've got a real treat planned for everyone today." Voumatir held up a single finger at her, indicating that he needed a moment. He leaned over and kissed Alycee on the cheek quickly before reporting to the disapproving Heikah.

Alycee wiped her face with her sleeve, grimacing as she approached Myx. "Alright, let's get you all cleaned up." She held her up as they walked. On their way to the Washroom, one of the guards told them to stop touching. To which she replied, "If I don't hold her up, she'll faint. Do you want to carry her to the Infirmary?"

The man stepped closer, but then promptly moved back as he waved the air in front of his face. "There's no need to get Dolra involved," he replied, shaking his head at the smell. The guard motioned for them to continue on their way.

Steam dispersed the colored radiation in the Washroom. Although there were more wisps here compared to the rest of the Camp, it wasn't nearly as much as the Infirmary chambers or the mines. Still, there were enough to rejuvenate the worn out prisoners after their arduous work days.

Myx had rarely been able to make it to the Washroom in her three week stay at the Camp since Gotasun and Dolra kept her employed for such long hours. She couldn't remember getting to wash up in the irradiated waters more than twice a week; normally all she was allowed was a couple towels and a pitcher of water for the basin in her cell. It was nice to finally be allowed time for a long soak.

However, the room reminded Myx of the two prisoner women who had tried to steal from her the second day at Camp. She had kept a close watch on what little she had earned over the weeks, not sure who else might try to take advantage of her trusting nature. Myx hated that she now searched for people's motives when she met someone new. Life had been simpler when she still had her innocent view of the world. But she made an honest effort not to let the mistrust creeping into her heart harden her against her friends.

She eyed the strange glass wall to the right of the room. Strong currents swished about leaves and debris, knocking them into the algae-covered rocks lying on the stone riverbed. Besdrens and ylkas swam in coordinated groups, going about their fish lives as though the humans weren't on the other side of the barrier. Water dripped down the translucent pane as moisture condensed against it.

Alycee and Myx were completely alone in the warm, moist room as they stripped to their smallclothes. Wrapping frail towels around their ribs, they stepped further into the cave.

"Why don't you like Voumatir?" Myx asked Alycee after being set down into one of the larger rock tubs. Radiation passed through her body, invigorating her sore muscles. "You two would make such a great couple."

Alycee was quiet a moment as she turned on the spout. She tossed in a soap cube with the steaming water and eased herself behind Myx. "There's something I don't like about him. I can't quite put my finger on what bothers me, though. He almost seems too likeable. I've never been able to rely on a charmer."

As Myx wiped her arms with a sudsy rag, she pondered what their lives would be like after the war.

Eventually, Alycee would realize what a great guy Voumatir was and would allow him to court her. They'd then have beautiful, strong babies and form a band of mercenary musicians as they traveled the universe for the rest of their blissful lives.

In the meantime, Rauno would continue searching for his perfect bride, enjoying the thrill of the hunt more than actually finding a woman to settle down with.

As for Bishing and Myx, they would open an art gallery together. Bish would have the opportunity to pursue his love of painting. All the while, Myx would manage the business side of things, hoping not to run their company into bankruptcy.

"Have you heard Voumatir play his music?" Myx asked Alycee, leaning forward. She groaned as the former assassin scrubbed her back. She clutched the undershirt to her chest. "It's quite beautiful. Maybe we can see if the Handlers would let us attend one of his shows? We could offer our services of carrying trays of food around their entertainment room."

"Being a good musician doesn't mean that he'd be good in a relationship." Alycee paused and chuckled. "Besides, if I dated him, I'd have a lot less time to look after you."

Alycee finished scrubbing Myx's back and moved on to washing her hair. She poured warm water over her head, causing the pitch black hair to flip across her face. What the former assassin said next was gurgled from the water in Myx's ears.

Something hot and sticky sprayed across her backside. Myx stuck her fingers in her ears to clear out the bath water. Rubbing her hands together, she washed off the ear wax.

Her hands came out of the water, the remaining droplets tinted a reddish pink color. She looked down to see ribbons of red flowing through the bath. Myx turned to see Alycee slumped over, her head hanging over the lip of the stone tub.

Blood poured from the cut across Alycee's neck, her purple tanzanite eyes wide in shock. She was still awake for another moment before she slunk to the bottom of the water.

Pulling the shaking woman into her arms, Myx whispered, "Alycee? Come on. Stay with me. No, you can't die!" Blood continued to flow over her hands as she foolishly hoped she could prevent it from all pouring out. "Please. Alycee, I need you! Don't—"

Alycee's body went limp and the red ceased pumping out of her throat.

Myx shuddered as something hot dripped down onto her shoulder. Gasping, Myx looked up to see a masked man standing over her, gripping a knife bathed in Alycee's blood.

Chapter 23

Myx waited for the assassin to kill her. She turned her attention back to Alycee, not wanting to watch him as he plunged down his knife. Shivering in her thin smallclothes, Myx held her friend close and pressed her pink tourmaline eyes shut. But the blade did not touch her. She opened a single lid to see the masked man sever the long, brown braid from Alycee's corpse.

The dim light reflected off the golden geometric pattern on his mask. Then the red-armored figure simply began to walk away from his bloody deed.

Furious, Myx threw a soap cube at him. "Why? Why did she have to die?" She stood to confront him, banishing all thoughts that what she was doing was insane. "Answer me, you miserable wretch!"

The man stopped and faced her. In a computerized voice, he said, "She failed to kill the Hathak Emperor. Alycee was supposed to do it a fashion that appeared like a natural death. Instead, she left him marred and grotesque. So the government discovered the truth. This whole war is her fault."

That didn't make sense. The Tarasi and Hathak had been feuding for centuries. Once a generation, the governments found something to justify a War Declaration. Perhaps Alycee's failure in killing the Hathak Emperor might have sparked it, but the war would have begun despite her mistake. Even if the masked assassin had been correct in his reasoning, there was still a flaw: the Tarasi and Hathak would have eventually decided on something else to fight about next.

The blood on Myx's bare arm illuminated as radiation passed through it. The skin tingled and went numb. Her vision shifted and she saw glimpses of an opulent ball room. A crowned man lay face-down in pool of blood. The weight of sword felt comforting in her hand. The blade came up at the ready as guards swarmed the room. The image of a shattering window filled her sight. Cold engulfed her as she fell into the icy ocean below the Hathak Palace. Then the experience faded.

Gasping, Myx was back in the Labor Camp, her knees stinging where they had smashed into the wet rock of the Washroom floor.

The masked assassin cocked his head in confusion. "Look, I don't need to kill you. So I'm leaving now." He raised his left arm in the air and he wiggled his fingers at Myx. "I apologize for the distress that I have caused you, but it was just a business deal. Good day."

Unable to control her emotions, Myx hurled herself at the man, tackling him to the ground.

The knife flung out of the assassin's grip, causing it to smash into the glass wall. Cracks formed, slowly inching their way outward from the impact. However, none of the river leaked through.

She climbed atop the masked man and pinned his arms to the ground. Myx paused and took a deep breath as she wondered how she knew a technique to subdue the well-trained assassin. But her curiosity eased as a wave of ferocity coursed through her, prompting Myx to send her fist at his armored face.

He bent his neck toward his shoulder to dodge. "You learned some new tricks, huh?" His hips buckled upward. The man counter grabbed her wrists and twisted under her. Rolling, he managed to switch their positions.

What was he talking about? "New?" Myx huffed, frustrated at her stupid attempt to avenge Alycee's death.

She shifted, uncomfortable of being so close to the corpse of her brutally murdered friend. All she succeeded in doing was getting more blood on her as she flailed in the overflowing tub water.

He shook his head. "I meant since the last attack. You were completely useless. After watching Alycee fend off my colleagues, I knew that I'd have to take her out stealthily on my own." The murderer's voice sounded rather amused despite the computerization. "I didn't plan on having to take care of you as well."

Myx groaned as more radiation passed through her bloodied skin. A warm sensation spread through her. She experienced flashes of when she had met Alycee—this time from Alycee's perspective.

Feeling invigorated from the wisps, Myx flung up one of her legs and curled it around his neck.

Clutching at her foot, he stumbled off her. The man pulled both of them to their feet. He kicked at her stomach and she swiftly jumped out of the way. Myx couldn't believe her speed. She reflexively knew when to dodge and when to attack as they fought in the next several moments. It was both thrilling and frightening.

And then the effects began to fade. She slowed and her punches grew sloppy. Myx dashed to Alycee's body and ran her fingers through the blood. Holding her hands to the drifting radiation, the alternating cool and warm numbness ran over her skin yet again.

She became more alert and ferocious. It didn't make any sense, but she wasn't going to question what was happening since it gave her the vigor to take on the assassin.

"I'm going to kill you," Myx growled, clawing at him. She nearly had her hands on the base of the red and gold mask, but he grasped her wrist.

"No one gets to see my face." The computer voice changed its tone, sounding upset. "It's part of being an assassin. I'm still planning on letting you live. However, if you get my mask off, I'll have no choice but to leave you dead with Alycee. That doesn't need to happen, though." He took a casual stance. "Go back to mourning your friend and let me leave."

Radiation wisps rushed through her again, almost as though they were attracted to her. Myx experienced visions of killing Alycee's assassination targets. She was stunned to learn just how many ways there were to murder people.

The masked man must have taken her silence as confirmation because he turned to leave yet again.

Myx began to panic as she felt her vitality drain. She looked frantically around the room as she tried to form a plan. And then she saw it. The fractures in the glass wall continued to grow along the barrier that held back the river. Retrieving the bloodied blade, Myx hacked at the center of the cracked pane.

Water spewed from a small hole. It wasn't sufficient for her plan, so Myx continued smashing at the wall with the assassin's knife. Slivers of glass shot out making shallow cuts along her arms. But she kept at it.

It wasn't happening fast enough. Myx switched the knife to one hand and used the other to heft a laundry barrel. With all her strength, she slammed all her weight against the barrel and hurtled herself towards the hole.

There was a deafening crack and the full power of the river burst forth. It threw Myx off her feet, but she retained her hold on the blade. Dazed grivin fish flopped around her as the waves rose and flooded the room. The soapy mass sent Myx hurtling through the Washroom towards the masked man.

Myx crashed into him as he reached the door. The water rushed past him, pouring into the hallway. Disoriented, Myx righted herself, still insanely insistent on completing her misguided attempt to have vengeance for Alycee.

Her prey sputtered and stumbled to all fours. The masked man crouched in the water and looked about in frantic motions. It took Myx a moment to realize that the killer was searching for his knife. He clearly hadn't seen her, since she bore the blade in her tightly clenched fingers.

But as she approached him, she stumbled on the soapy currents of the rising water.

The profound effects of the radiation/blood mixture began to wear off yet again; Myx felt groggy, like she hadn't slept or eaten in several days. Her legs threatened to buckle underneath her, but she kept moving forward.

Myx held the knife to the back of his neck. "Any last words?"

Rolling, the masked man moved out of the path of the blade. "What the hell happened to you?" He stumbled as his feet fell into an indentation of a stone tub. The assassin's face fell below the water before sputtering up to the surface. "You were this little, mousy woman and now you're—you're like Alycee!"

Myx brandished the knife. "It doesn't matter since you're about to join her in the afterlife."

He chucked a strange, computer laugh. "I highly doubt that."

"Let's find out." She sliced at him again and again.

The assassin turned and grabbed a loofah stick. It was a strange method for deflecting her strikes, but it proved to be a highly effective technique.

Something about the combination of blood and radiation gave Myx Alycee's memories and skills. She couldn't control it. As she fought, an occasional wisp would find her and she'd see a glimpse of Alycee's past. Thankfully, the assassin didn't attack her while she had a flash; he seemed to be sincere when he had said that he didn't want to kill her.

Still, she was filled with a new wave of vengeance after every memory flash and she fought with renewed vitality. And then Myx would feel the power start to slip; her vision grew blurry and her muscles began lagging.

"Someone looks tired," the assassin taunted, dropping his guard.

Enraged, she sliced more viciously. She knew it was sloppy, but it seemed to work on some level because the assassin had become accustomed to her well-placed strikes. Myx managed to cut a deep gash in the back of his shoulder.

He groaned and slapped the loofah stick hard onto her wrist. With a couple of quick jabs, he got past her defenses stepped behind her. He clasped his hands around her neck and squeezed.

The Washroom went black as she fell unconscious to the flooded floor.

Chapter 24

` Myx cringed as she beheld Alycee's body on the morgue table. Her friends gathered around, paying their final respects. The overseer gave them a wide berth, but still kept a close watch on them from the doorway.

"Do you think they'll let us burry her?" Voumatir asked, stroking what was left of her hair. Tears moistened his eyes. "I can't stand the thought of her being senselessly dumped in a mass grave."

"No," Myx replied, tying her pitch black hair into a thin braid over her shoulder. With Alycee's chopped off, she felt like wearing it like that would be a tribute to her deceased companion. "They don't burry people at the Camp." When they stared at her in confusion, she nodded at the incinerator across the room. "Corpses are cremated and their ashes are spread in the mines."

"Well then will they at least let us be the ones that cremate her?" Voumatir turned to the morgue overseer. "It would help me properly mourn my angel."

The elderly mortician brought them a bucket of water and sponges. "If you insist, you can clean and prepare her body." He took a step back and let them get to work, seemingly relieved to have a break from his tasks.

Myx kept quiet as she cleaned the blood stains from Alycee's throat. She wondered why her eyes were blindfolded. But when she tried to remove the cloth, the overseer scolded her.

"You leave that alone! It's Hathak custom to cremate with the eyes bound."

Rauno and Voumatir speculated in low voices on how Alycee had died, but Myx refused to reply to their inquiries. It was clear that it hadn't been an accident due to the gash below her jaw. However, the Camp hadn't given an official statement on the matter.

The overseer let out a blustery snore as he snoozed in the corner. Without the Hathak supervision, Bishing put a comforting hand on Myx's shoulder.

The touch loosened her tongue. Exhaling, she let all the details vent out of her. She summarized her final conversation with Alycee in one breath. "One of the assassins came back," Myx added, forcing back tears. "He said he watched us in the infiltration and knew that the only way to kill Alycee was in a surprise attack."

Rauno looked confused. "How come you're still alive?"

"He didn't want to kill me, for some reason." Myx bit her lip as she carefully pouring soapy water over Alycee's hair. She choked back the memories that threatened to surface. "I don't understand it either."

"He probably just wanted to get back home to collect his reward," Rauno offered, combing Alycee's damp hair.

Bishing pointed at a bruise on Myx's wrist and gave her a questioning glare.

"Something strange happened," she admitted, averting her eyes to the ground. "Alycee's blood was all over me. When the radiation passed through it, I suddenly knew everything about combat that Alycee had. I knew how to dodge and strike. I honestly thought I was going mad." Myx rubbed her arms where the blood and radiation had mingled. "It's like I was absorbing her life force. It didn't last long though; the blood was watered down and ran over my skin."

She couldn't bring herself to tell them that she also saw some of Alycee's memories. Although the skills seemed to have faded, she kept re-experiencing several flashes as random bits of radiation flowed through the morgue. But these moments weren't as strong as they had been before and they played too quickly to decipher any meaning from them.

"Are you saying that Alycee is living on in you?" Voumatir asked, looking both hopeful and worried.

"No. I don't have her abilities anymore." Myx shivered as a pastel blue wisp passed through the back of her bare neck. The radiation triggered the memory of the masked assassin's blade across Alycee's throat. She shook her head and continued explaining, "The skill transfer was only temporary."

Rauno had a creepy smile on his face.

"What's gotten into you?" Myx asked, feeling unsettled.

He didn't reply. Rauno simply pushed Alycee's body into the incinerator.

The room was larger than Myx would have thought. A stone table lay in the middle. A series of slits covered the rock, reminding Myx of an air vent or a water drain. She figured that's where Alycee's ashes would drop to then be collected before they could be scattered in the mines.

The men hefted Alycee onto the slotted rock while Myx needlessly supported the head.

With their task done, Rauno's smirk deepened. He moved to the furnace controls, but Voumatir blocked his path.

The alien held out his hands. His clear pink finger nails were beginning to turn light grey from radiation exposure at the Camp. "That's your 'escape plan' face. Are you thinking about bathing in the blood of the Handlers in order to get out? You're even crazier than I thought."

"It doesn't matter." Rauno became serious as he turned to Myx. "We'll step outside of the incinerator as you strip Alycee; the Camp has strict rules about not wasting materials."

Myx nodded as they left. She went about taking off the plain linen dress that Alycee had been placed in. When she was done, she joined the men outside the incinerator, putting the dress in the laundry.

Bishing pushed Rauno away from the incinerator controls and activated the blazing fire.

"Are you sure that you didn't just have an adrenaline high?" Voumatir asked, his voice low now that they were nearer to the sleeping overseer. "Bishing and I think that's what happened. It's not that we don't want to believe you, but the whole thing seems a bit far-fetched. I mean, you absorbed Alycee's life force?"

"I know her death has been hard on you," Myx said, trying to sooth him. "But that's what I felt. You can believe me or not. I just wish that I had been a bit stronger; then her murderer would have been brought to justice."

Bishing stepped away from the controls and patted Myx's shoulder as they waited for the incinerator to finish turning their friend to ash.

After several minutes, Rauno inspected the controls and determined that the process was complete. He pressed a lever and a jar of ashes slid out of the machine. "I know we are supposed to spread her around the mines—for whatever reason—but I need the calcium phosphate from Alycee's bone for my latest escape plan. Is it alright if I hold on to her?"

Myx yanked the jar from him. "You want to experiment of Alycee? I won't let you!"

Voumatir nodded, his sparkling blue eyes threatening violence on the researcher. "I agree with Myx; Alycee isn't a guinea pig."

"I know," Rauno sighed, pinching the bridge of his nose. "But I think she'd want to help us to get out of here. If her death can mean something, then it's the best way that we can honor her sacrifice."

Bishing signed something and Myx translated, "He wants to know what your plan is before he agrees to allow you to continue."

Rauno shook his head. "If I told you, you might let it slip to your Handlers. We've already seen what happens when they suspect that a prisoner is hiding something. I don't want Gotasun to have another reason to further harm you, Myx. You'll just have to trust me that I'll pay the upmost respect to Alycee's remains in our escape attempt."

Myx thought a moment. He was making perfect sense, and yet she was still reluctant. However, Alycee would have helped them how she could. Reluctantly, Myx handed Rauno the jar of ashes.

He took it and instantly began adding various compounds to it from vials he pulled from his clothing.

Voumatir stared at him. "Rauno, I thought that Parnuss warned you about hiding things in the seams of your clothes? One more mishap and they'll put you in that incinerator. But unlike Alycee, you'll be alive when the button is pressed."

"Parnuss did indeed threaten me," Rauno conceded, not deterred by Voumatir's comments. "Although I doubt he'd kill me. I'm too valuable in his scientist's research. But I think the risk is a small price to pay for getting out of the Camp." Rauno smiled as he stirred in various flakes. "Besides, if I get injured, it means I get to spend some time in the Infirmary with my nightingale."

"Wait!" Myx couldn't believe that Rauno glossed over a very important detail. "The Hathak are experimenting on us?"

Rauno nodded. "Not everyone. But Parnuss wanted to document the changes in an alien like Voumatir as the radiation alters his DNA. Some of the studies are run out of the Infirmary—if genetics affects the rate at which someone heals, or if it's simply how many wisps are absorbed, or a completely different factor."

Myx couldn't believe what she was hearing. She reflected on everything she knew about the Camp as Rauno prattled on about the various experiments being practiced.

"Oh, and Tieg!" Rauno continued, stirring his ash concoction. "He stumps all the researchers. I overheard one talking to Dolra about taking several prisoners to replicate the conditions of the transformation. But Parnuss says there's too much risk if the only reward is to have a bunch of walking flashlights."

When Rauno began making demeaning comments about the trial beauty treatments to make women more appealing, Bishing made a groaning sound and turned to leave.

Myx followed after him, determined not to learn anymore about the Camp's tests.

Also, she didn't want to risk hearing more about Rauno's escape plans. He had been right to be concerned about her being too informed. Although she was becoming more adept at it, Myx had yet to master the art of concealing information.

It had just been a fluke that she had kept Alycee's secret from Gotasun. But now she wondered if she shouldn't have been so tight-lipped. Perhaps her friend might still be alive if the Hathak had known that Alycee was the target of the attack on the Camp. Or she could have just as easily been killed sooner if Warden Parnuss knew that there was a bounty on Alycee's head.

She had learned too much information already. Rauno's revealing of the Camp's experiments plus Alycee's memory flashes combined in her mind to form a headache. Myx rubbed her temples as if she could force the facts out.

Being ignorant had never been more appealing. She longed to go back to the days when she knew nothing.

The next time Myx saw her Handler, she was sure to accidentally be suspicious. Hopefully she could use Alycee's life force to become as cold and emotionless as the deceased former assassin; she didn't want to give Gotasun any more reasons to torture her.

Chapter 25

Gotasun led Myx up and down the Main Street of the Camp. He would stop in front of one building and scratch his chin before shaking his head and moving to the next one.

"You have such poor motor skills, my pet," Gotasun said as he dismissed the idea of putting her at the Butcher's. "If I put you here and you cut your fingers off, you wouldn't be able to work for another week. You've already had too much recovery time."

As Myx followed, she inspected Gotasun. He didn't seem quite a trim as he had the last time she had seen him. His torso bulged as though he was bloated and his pace was noticeable slower as he shuffled along the stone paths of the Camp. It seemed like whatever diet he had been on ceased being effective.

The Handler strolled to the tunnel that led to the Farm. "Standing up and down all day planting seeds is too easy for even someone as simple-minded as you; and I'm still feeling inclined to punish you."

After visiting a dozen work stations, Gotasun eventually led her to an artist studio.

Myx was stunned to see that the Hathak allowed their prisoners to spend the day painting; she thought it'd be a nonessential use of the prisoners' time.

"We sell the artwork to various businesses and offices back home on Hathak," Gotasun explained, sitting her down at an easel. "So whatever you paint today had better be good enough that people would want to buy them." He brandished a paintbrush and placed it in her hand. "Make something pretty, my pet." The Handler's face was amused as he smirked and left the studio.

As Myx stared at the bare canvas, the room grew brighter.

Tieg stood over her shoulder, his white opal eyes wide and bright. Colored splotches decorated his face and bald scalp. "Don't know what to paint?"

She shook her head, spinning the brush between her fingers. "Bishing is an artist; this is where he should be. I hoped that countless hours of watching him create would help me know what to do. But my mind is completely blank."

"Good. Now that it's blank, you can fill it with whatever you want." Tieg handed her a booklet, his eyes beaming with encouragement "Here are samples of what they are looking for."

Myx flipped through the pages. Most of the pictures were basic nature scenes or floral patterns. Those seemed simple enough. She set the brush down, picked up a piece of charcoal, and turned to her canvass.

As she began, Myx experienced a flash of Alycee's throat being slit. She pressed her eyes shut and tried to imagine a better memory her deceased friend. She thought back to when the Camp was attacked by assassins. Alycee was so graceful and yet fierce as she took on half a dozen adversaries at once.

Her hand sketched the figure in her mind. The picture grew into an image of Alycee dancing amongst a pile of corpses. Myx quickly erased the bodies, but outlines of the charcoal remained. She hid the remnants by painting splashes of green along the bottom of the painting. As she brushed in Alycee's features, Myx realized that she had drawn in her own looks, with her dark black hair and pink tourmaline eyes fused to Alycee's towering form and long braid. It looked pretty decent so she kept it that way.

While selecting more colors to paint the background, she found her hand reaching towards the red. Her mind slipped into a vision of the bloody, flooded Washroom. Myx shook her head to erase the image, but the disturbing memory remained. Taking a deep breath, she put the red paint down and reached for the more shades of green.

"That's pretty," Tieg commented, looking over her shoulder. His glowing eyes illuminated the features of the painting. "Do you dance?"

"It's just wishful thinking," Myx lied, a little startled at how easy it was becoming. She evaded the topic, not sure if she'd soon revert back to her old, poor-lying self. "Should I add more people?"

"It's wonderful the way it is—or least it will be once you've finished the background."

Myx nodded and continued brushing green streaks onto the canvass.

As she worked, she wondered what Rauno's escape plan was. They had speculated earlier that morning. Voumatir mentioned an interesting notion about covering themselves in blood and running through radiation to absorb the life force of the blood's owner.

It seemed like a ridiculous plan. How were they going to get their hands on that much blood? Not to mention the fact that they would need it from people who could actually fight. Plus they would need to remain in an area of the Camp that contained a large concentration of radiation. There were too many holes in that theory for it to make sense. Besides, they didn't understand all the factors that had allowed Myx to battle like Alycee.

Rauno had said that he needed something called 'calcium phosphate.' It sounded like a complicated chemical. Perhaps he was planning on making a bomb? Shaking her head, she decided that she didn't want to know until he told her.

"So Tieg, I'm curious." It was probably a rude question to ask, but Myx couldn't help inquiring, "What really happened to your eyes?"

Tieg didn't seem upset at being asked such a personal question. He took a seat at the easel beside her and began painting a waterfall. "I told you that I was captured while doing a routine patrol. As I was checking the Tarasi perimeter, the Hathak attacked. Stun lasers sprayed all around me as they missed, blasting up bits of dirt and rock."

Myx divided her attention between listening to the elderly prisoner and continuing her picture.

"I stumbled behind a tree to get some cover," he continued, smudging blue across his canvass. "And that's when I noticed that the lasers had unearthed a thick crack in the ground that emitted radiation. Wisps spewed into the open air."

Myx gasped, her hand pausing over the water cup. "You discovered a Radiation Spring?"

"Yeah. I probably would have been handsomely rewarded by the Tarasi." He shook his head, the illumination dimming as he closed his eyes lids. "But the Hathak continued firing at me. An enemy soldier approached through the shots. The last thing I remember was him raising his stun rifle at me and then a stinging sensation in my eyes."

Tieg paused, his gaze focused on his painting. Myx followed his lead and resumed her work.

The older prisoner didn't remain silent for long. "I awoke in a radiation chamber two days later. Dolra figured that the combination of the radiation and the energy of the stun bolt to my eyes caused the luminosity. Of course, further exposure to the radiation while in the healing chamber probably added to the effect as well."

Myx was a thoughtful a moment. Rauno had mentioned at Alycee's cremation that researchers were curious about Tieg's ability. She decided to probe him for more information. "I wonder if the Hathak scientists are now somewhere shooting people in the eyes with stun riffles in a Radiation Spring. I'm surprised that they don't have you locked away in a research lab so they can study your transformation."

Tieg laughed, wiping a purple-smudged hand along his brow. "You sound like your friend, Rauno. He said something similar to that when I told him my tale."

"He certainly has some bizarre theories."

Myx turned back to her picture. With the background completed, it looked quite interesting. She quickly added little splashes of yellow, blue, and orange to represent radiation wisps. Satisfied with her work, she turned it into the overseer. He accepted it and told her to make him another.

Tieg's story had prompted Myx to create a series of paintings involving radiation. With the planet's obsession about it, she was sure to have her paintings sell well.

Chapter 26

Rauno raised a skeptical brow at Voumatir as Heikah dropped him off during breakfast. "I thought you were in mourning for your guardian angel?"

The alien set down his bowl of hot mash. "I've gotta find comfort where I can."

Myx narrowed her eyes at the pair of them, unsure of what they were discussing. Yes, Voumatir had been despondent the past several days as he missed Alycee. But he was surprisingly cheerful all of a sudden. And Heikah had appeared to be oddly chipper. Was it possible that the two of them had been passionately tangled the previous night? Being uneducated in love, Myx couldn't understand the intimate details of romantic pairings.

She turned to Bishing for an explanation about the other two, but his stare was transfixed on his meal.

Rauno lowered his voice and motioned at an empty place at their table. "Alycee has been gone less than a week. I can't believe that you'd finally give in to your Handler's advances after all this time."

"Heikah has been after me since the moment we arrived at the Camp," Voumatir sighed, running a hand through his ruffled, bright blonde hair. "It was only a matter of time until I succumbed to her whiles. Without my love here to keep me faithful, I decided to give in." He gave of a feint chuckle. "Besides, Heikah is a pretty decent lover."

The scientist was about to reply, but was interrupted by the appearance of Bishing's Handler.

Frezul's lips were twisted up in a menacing smile as she motioned at Myx's table. Bish began to collect his things, but the Handler stopped him. "No, mute. I'm not here for you." The elfin woman pointed at Myx. "I need Gotasun's pet. Let's go."

Bishing placed his thumb and index finger together, spreading his three remaining fingers in the air—his sign that everything was going to be okay.

Myx tossed her tray and followed, feeling very confused. Frezul hadn't waited for her, so she had to run to catch up. Despite knowing the rule about not asking question, Myx couldn't help the ones that sprang from her mouth. "Where is Gotasun? Are we meeting him somewhere? Or did Warden Parnuss decide to let you switch prisoners?"

Frezul frowned for a moment before smirking. "He's right; you are quite the curious girl." As they walked, the Handler wrapped her fists with a thick, white tape. She seemed pleased about something.

It didn't surprise Myx when she was led into the Reviewery. Another week had passed and she had been expecting to have her next Review that day. She had decided that she would remain strong for Alycee's sake; she would not to let her spirit weaken from the abuse she that suffered at the hands of the Hathak.

"Since Gotasun is busy today," Frezul said, circling the room, "I'm in charge of going over your weekly consequences."

Nodding, Myx closed her eyes and waited for the Handler to begin the review.

Frezul continued wrapping white tape over her knuckles as she spoke. "You get minus ten for each day of work you missed after your last punishment, which was three days. However, one of your paintings sold last night, so that's plus fifteen. In the Washroom, the deceased prisoner known as Alycee touched you a total of nine times as she cleaned you; minus one for each touch. The Warden was amused by some of the answers to your bio, so that's plus eight. However, we checked and some of your facts were incorrect. That's minus four."

The petite woman went over every little aspect of Myx's week. In the end, she was only at negative seven.

Frezul finished taping her hands and tossed the roll aside.

Myx was relieved that the punishment number was so low. She raised her hands above her head like she normally did for Gotasun and waited for the impact.

Grinning at Myx's lack of fear, Frezul adjusted Myx's arms so that they were out in front of her. Then the Handler sent both of her fists down onto the tops of Myx's elbows. "That's one."

"What the—" Myx cringed and clenched her mouth shut. She bit her lips, trying to bring the pain somewhere other than her burning joints. Gotasun never hit her like that. She looked at her forearms, expecting bruises and swelling to form. All there was were two pink marks where Frezul's fists had landed.

"I'm not like Gotasun," Frezul explained, rubbing the bottoms of her fists together. "He likes to show brute force to intimidate. However, I'm more precise as I attack the nerves. Now put your hands on your hips and brace your head against your shoulder."

Myx complied and braced herself for the next strike.

Frezul used the side of her hand to slice above Myx's collar bone. The base of the neck—just over the right shoulder—stunned and throbbed. Myx let out a sharp cry of pain and pressed a palm to where she had been hit. She crumbled to the ground, unable to stop the tears that flooded her eyes.

"Stand up and spread your legs." Frezul pulled at Myx's hair until she was on her feet. With her steel-toed boot, the woman nudged her thighs apart until the girl was in a wide stance. The Handler kicked the soft tissue at the back of Myx's knee.

The Handler paused after each strike, looking the young woman over as she planned her next move. The punishment continued for several minutes as the last four hits were doled out in small intervals. When the Review was complete, Frezul retrieved her roll of tape and left without another word.

Limping, Myx made her way to the Infirmary. She was suddenly grateful to have Gotasun as her Handler.

But then Myx was still curious why Frezul had performed her Review and doled out consequences that week. Perhaps it was because her last session wasn't effective? He had needed to use a staff to cause pain.

And why didn't Frezul ever punish Bishing? From what Myx could tell, the woman never laid a hand on Bish except for an occasional smack; it didn't make any sense.

As Myx arrived at the Infirmary, she plopped into the first bed by the door and waited to be treated. Dolra appeared a short time later and did a quick scan for damaged tissue. She deftly rubbed her stinging ointment into all the traumatized joints.

"Why can't you learn to follow the rules," Dolra scolded, her red jasper eyes looking even more vexed than normal. She returned the jar to the pocket of her stark-white apron and wiped away the extra salve from her gloved fingers. "I feel like I see you more than any other prisoner. Well, everyone besides that imbecile."

"Did you call for me, nightingale?" Rauno asked from across the room.

"No, but you can come finish up here." She waved him over with a sigh. "I've got someone in a chamber I've got to check on."

Rauno changed his apron. As he put the old one in the laundry hamper, he retrieved a wet wash cloth. He carefully wiped the ointment off Myx and discarded that as well. "I've got my own special blend for you. I've been watching her and I've got a salve that won't hurt when it mixes with radiation. You've been through enough without having to re-experience your punishments."

Myx watched him as he rubbed a gritty, grey paste into her sore joints. "What's in it?"

"A special recipe that I've been working on," he said dismissively. Rauno sounded defensive as he added, "I won't bore you with the details."

She nodded. "Yeah, I never know what you're talking about anyways." Myx lay there for several moments, trying to relax. She watched wisps float about the Infirmary as they escaped a radiation chamber. But eventually, her curiosity flared. "How's the escape attempt coming?"

He put the left over paste into one of his dozens of sewed-in pockets and lay a blanket over Myx to conceal the illegal paste. Rauno pushed her bed to the chambers as he explained, "I'm close. I just have a couple of things I need to test. I honestly don't know if it'll work or not. I've been doing research on my idea ever since we arrived at the Camp. It's based partially on some theories I came up with when I worked at the Institute."

Myx shifted on her cot as her joint pain began to flare up. "So there's no definite proof that you'll be successful?"

"Well, one of the stories I've heard recently made me believe that I'm on the right track." As Rauno got her settled in a chamber, he looked at the floating radiation wisps with an awed fascination.

She sat up and glared at him. "What story?"

"Why yours, of course." Rauno headed to the hatch and whispered, "The paste I gave you is made from Alycee's ashes. In the morning, we'll know for sure if we are correct in our hypothesis about absorbing another person's life force."

"Our?" Myx stumbled from the bed, limping toward him. "Rauno, I don't want to do this. Let me out!"

He shook his head. "This needs to be done, Myx. I'm sorry, but there's no other way."

The hatch closed with a hiss.

Chapter 27

Myx pounded the hatch until her knuckles bled. "Rauno! You open this door now!" She waved her bloody hand in the small, circular window. "Dolra? Are you there? Can you let me out? I changed my mind and I'd like to heal in my cell. Please?"

She wiped at the paste on her joints, but the radiation was already beginning to pass through it. There was a warm, tingling sensation. Rage welled up as Alycee's life force merged with hers. Myx performed a series of strikes that would have plowed through most humans. But the hatch remained intact.

"If I hear one more noise out of this chamber, I'll chain you down," Dolra said through the intercom. "Get some rest, missy."

Taking a breath, she slumped to the floor. Alycee's memories began transferring to her brain. The visions settled on showing her bits of Bishing. Myx folded her legs under her and focused on the images of her friend. The flashes slowed and she could perceive actual conversations.

Alycee approached Bishing the night in the hotel before they had signed up for the Tarasi military. Bish seemed rather calm, but there was the slightest hint of fear in his smoky quartz eyes.

"I'm not here to harm you," Alycee's voice said, sounding slightly gargled and broken.

Bishing pointed at his mouth and shook his head.

"Oh, yeah. Sorry. If you want, I'll leave. However, I'm growing quite fond of Myx. I don't understand what it is about that girl. She doesn't seem particularly special, but I feel drawn to protect her."

Bringing his finger to his throat, he made a slicing motion.

"No. I promise that I'm not here on a job." Alycee's field of vision shifted as though she were shaking her head. "After failing to kill the Hathak Emperor last year, there's now a bounty on my head."

He relaxed his shoulders and gave her a wide smile.

"I know. It's amusing." She let out a deep sigh. "It's all my fault and I want to do what I can to make up for my mistakes." Alycee tugged at her long braid, picking at the hairs that were out of place. "I did it on purpose, you know. I could have completed my assignment. Just understand that."

The vision faded and Myx was back in the radiation chamber. She stood awkwardly and went to lie in the bed. As she huddled into the blankets, she was back in a cell.

Only, it wasn't her cell.

She stood in the doorway of Alycee's prison bedchamber. Voumatir was in the corner, rummaging under the mattress.

"What are you doing?"

"Alycee! My gorgeous woman!" Voumatir pulled his hands away from the bed and grinned widely. "I was just trying to find the best way to leave you a note." He put a hand in his jacket, tucked something away, and then pulled out a piece of paper. "I hoped you'd think it was romantic to randomly find a love letter in your bed. But since you've caught me, I guess I'll just give it to you now."

Taking the note from Voumatir, she kept her eyes on him as she unfolded the paper. Her gaze shifted quickly back and forth between the alien and the note. "No. I'm not interested in you. And I don't like you going through my things. Leave."

Voumatir nodded, his plain blue eyes looking somber as they turned to the floor. "I know it seems creepy, toots, but I figured that since we are war prisoners that maybe it wouldn't be considered too disturbing." He met Alycee's gaze and took a step forward. "We should get all the comfort we can from each other. I won't give up until I figure out how to show you what I truly feel about you." He stepped away from the cot and moved even closer to her. "Can you forgive me for intruding?" Voumatir held out an expectant hand.

"What did you put away just now?" Alycee asked, ignoring his question. She tossed her brown braid over her shoulder so that it swung across her back. Her voice was firm as she added, "Show me what's in your pocket."

He shook his head, bright yellow hair falling onto his face. "It's embarrassing, my guardian angel."

"You don't embarrass easily. Show me or I'll get a guard to pat you down."

"It's just a picture that I drew of the two of us embracing." He fumbled with his tunic pocket as he searched for it. Voumatir frowned as he added, "I decided that it might upset you, so I wasn't going to leave it after all."

Alycee took a step closer. "Can you stop playing games? I know why you're really here."

"Because I'm pursing the most beautiful woman in the world." He removed his hand and held up the picture.

Before she could inspect the paper, a razor tore through it, coming at her face. Alycee backed away and put her hands up to defend herself.

Their skirmish went on and on. Myx's mind became disoriented as she tried to keep up with every strike and block. Alycee and Voumatir each exchanged a number of blows, but none gave any sign that they were going to give in. The razor was repeatedly switched between them as they took turns disarming each other in the small cell.

As Voumatir came at her again, Alycee managed to block a jab before twisting his arm around. "You're after the bounty, aren't you?" she asked him, tweaking his shoulder. "You lied about everything."

He dropped the blade to the floor and tried to squirm away. "Yes! You're right, toots." Voumatir's tone softened as he admitted. "I've been following you for months."

Alycee let go of Voumatir and pushed him away. Still in a defensive stance, she put a booted foot over the blade. "I won't die easily. If you're going to kill me, you'll have to do better than sneak into my cell."

Voumatir stared up at her, his breath coming out ragged. "How do you plan on stopping me?"

"I'm assuming that you're being protected by one of the Handlers—probably that vapid bimbo, Heikah." Alycee bent down and recovered the razor blade, her long brown braid swinging over her shoulder. "So I can't kill you yet. I could tell the other prisoners who you are. Maybe one of them will try to avenge the deaths of their friends from the day the Camp was attacked."

He was quiet a moment. "You could do that. But then everyone would find out the truth about you. And then who knows how many people's secrets will be revealed as well."

Alycee crossed her arms, one hand closing over the razor blade. She stepped aside so that the doorway was clear for him to exit through. "I guess we both agree to keep our mouths shut for the time being. But if you try to kill me again, I'll have no choice except tell everyone who you are."

"That's perfectly fair, toots. I love a good challenge, anyway." Voumatir blew her a kiss and gave her a malicious smile as he strolled out of her cell.

Myx awoke from the vision with a gasp, unnerved by what she had just seen.

Fresh wisps of radiation flowed into her, triggering a repeat of the interaction with Voumatir. She sobbed as the memories persisted through the night.

Chapter 28

The hatch popped open with a hiss. Myx launched herself off the bed and dashed towards the opening.

Dolra snatched her wrist and held tight. "What's the hurry, missy?"

"You're never here in the morning, Dolra," Myx sighed, frustrated at being detained.

The nurse pulled her closer and inspected her pupils. "I checked Rauno's pockets last night and found a strange paste in one of them. I was worried that he was experimenting again. It would explain why you were so upset last night."

"No, I'm fine. Really! I have to go find someone. Can I go now?" she pleaded, squirming under the stocky woman's firm grip.

"Just don't come crying to me when you grow extra toes or your hair falls out from the imbecile's nonsensical tests." Dolra released her and went about restocking the Infirmary drawers with her salve.

Myx stopped at the end of the row of beds. "Wait. Has that really happened?"

"Some bizarre events have occurred every time the Warden put Rauno on my work roster: ash-colored skin from combining flames with wisps, spontaneous blue hair growth on another, missing fingernails. I even caught the imbecile trying to grow gills on one of my patients." Dolra's red jasper eyes flashed a warning glance. "I wouldn't let him experiment on you any further."

With the nurse's caution repeating in her mind, Myx grabbed an energy bar for a quick meal and left the Infirmary. Munching on her meager breakfast, she took off down the Main Street in search of Voumatir. She asked the prisoners she passed, but none of them could help her. Next, she made her inquiries to the guards, telling them that she's his new accompanist in order to extort information from them.

Myx eventually learned that he was in the Handler's Ward.

As she approached, the Handlers eyed her, but didn't seem to care that she was there. They either didn't want to get involved because she wasn't their prisoner or due to the fact the she walked as though she was on a mission.

Myx was grateful that Gotasun wasn't around. Once she thought about it, she realized that she hadn't seen him since he dropped her off at the art studio two days previous. Frezul had said that he was busy the previous day, but gave no further answer.

What could he be up to that was more important than punishing her?

She shook her head and told herself to focus on the task at hand.

Voumatir sat a piano, tuning a guitar that the Warden had procured for him. He smiled as Myx approached. "Hey, you're looking pretty healthy this morning. I guess Frezul isn't as tough as she thinks she is."

Without warning, Myx pulled the collar of his shirt over his shoulder. Sure enough, there was a fresh, pink scar.

"What's going on?" He grasped her wrist and put his collar back to his neck. "Look, I'm still grieving over Alycee. If you want to get naked with me, you'll have to wait a couple of weeks—or at least until Heikah is done with me."

Myx pried his fingers off and took a step back. "I cut Alycee's killer in the shoulder—right where your scar is."

Voumatir shrugged. "That's really weird. What are the odds of that happening?"

She put her hands on her hips, hoping it made her look intimidating. "Where were you the afternoon she died?"

The alien laughed. "I was with Heikah, going through my Review. That's how I got that cut. Heikah was frustrated that I kept spurning her advances. She got tired of her little fists not doing anything, so she cut me instead. Dang, it hurt so bad. I remember wishing Alycee would be my nurse. If she had, then maybe she'd still be alive." He got serious all of a sudden. "Look, Myx, I know that her death hit you pretty hard. But do you honestly think that I would have ever hurt her?"

"I know you killed her."

"You're being paranoid." Voumatir put his guitar down. His dull blue eyes were beginning to transform into shimmering lapis irises. "The assassin snuck in and snuck out. You'll never know who murdered Alycee because he's probably moved on to a different planet by now. Just accept it and we can resume enduring the hell of this Camp."

Myx knew she was getting nowhere by outright accusing him. She switched her tactics. "Alycee told me that she failed to kill the Hathak Emperor. Apparently she was responsible for the War Declaration. Did you know about that?"

"What? Not our Alycee!" He shook his head. "She was such a skilled fighter, but I didn't have any idea that she would have gotten an assassination target like the Emperor."

"She seemed to think that you knew an awful lot of her secrets," Myx accused, walking around the piano. "Are you sure you didn't know anything about it? Or anything about Alycee's past?"

"No. I'm just a man whose true love was brutally murdered before we could get together." Voumatir sighed, tapping at random piano keys. "Why don't you believe me?'

Grabbing the metronome off the piano, Myx chucked it at him.

He snatched it midair and put it down on the bench. "Really? You're going to attack me now, hoping that it will unleash my assassin side?"

"Hah! So you admit that you're an assassin?"

Voumatir shook his head. "How did you know? Alycee promised to not to tell. Is it something to do with the weird life force transfer thing?" When she didn't reply, he sighed, "I really didn't want to kill you, Myx. I was hoping to reveal the truth about your past and watch the confusion that ensued. Oh, well. You wanted to confront me, so it's your entire fault that you're going to die ignorant about who you really are."

Myx rolled out of the way as he lunged at her. She adjusted her stance and kicked at his knees. He tumbled backwards, grabbing his guitar as he fell. Lying on his back, Voumatir held the instrument in front of him like a weapon, striking at her as she attempted to get close to him.

She grabbed the guitar fret board and snapped it off with her foot. The neck hung limp, only attached to the rest of the instrument by the strings. Myx spun the head stock around Voumatir's hand and pinned it across his chest as she sat on him. She deflected his other hand and arranged for the strings to lie across his throat.

Scooting forward, she put pressure downwards and choked off his air. He hit her in the ribs, but she barely felt the punches. After he fell unconscious, Myx snapped his neck for good measure.

Straightening, Myx adjusted her hair to make herself look somewhat presentable. She gasped as Gotasun entered the room.

"Oh, my pet, what did you do this time?"

Chapter 29

The shocked expression on Gotasun's face quickly eased into his normal condescending appearance. He circled the scene, inspecting Voumatir's corpse.

Myx clamped her mouth shut. She recognized that her Handler would soon resume interrogating her. After Alycee's death, he had questioned her relentlessly for days, but she had managed not to reveal her friend's identity. She wondered if she could do the same about the man she had just been witnessed killing.

The thought should have disturbed her—she was now a murderer.

Myx knew that morally she was no longer any better than the alien whose neck she had snapped. Even though Myx had been acting out of vengeance and Voumatir of greed, that didn't change the fact that she was responsible for taking a life.

And she had killed before. Myx shot that assassin during the attack on the Camp. But that had been in self-defense. Voumatir meant her no harm, and yet she had purposefully taken his life in her vendetta against Alycee's death. She had decent reasons for both kills; however, murdering the alien musician in cold blood wore more heavily on her conscious than when she gunned down that woman.

Another Handler appeared in the Ward. He greeted Gotasun before realizing that there was a dead body on the floor. After dashing out of the Ward, he returned with a squad of guards.

Chains were secured around Myx's wrists and she was escorted to her cell. Gotasun walked beside her, although he was surprisingly amused by something. She itched to ask him what was so funny, but she needed to focus on keeping her mouth shut.

Time passed.

Based on the number of meals brought to her, it had been about a week since her confinement. Handlers and the Warden had been in and out of her cell at all times of the day and night, asking her questions about what had happened and why she wanted to kill Voumatir.

With the strength of Alycee's life force, Myx was able to endure the examination without breaking.

Every time it was Gotasun's turn to be her interrogator, he looked oddly trimmer than he had before. Myx had noticed in the past that his weight tended to fluctuate over the weeks she had known him. But after seven days of spending hours at a time with him, she decided that there was something unnatural about his transformation. Remembering Rauno's explanation about the Camp's experiments led Myx to wonder if the staff was also a part of different radiation tests as well.

Throughout the long days, Myx experienced flashes of Alycee's life once again. She was getting better at not looking like she was having a seizure when they happened. Actually, having the memories helped her blot out much of the interrogations.

"I had cut Alycee's killer in the shoulder in the exact same place as the scar on Voumatir's shoulder." It was all she could say.

"How did you know to check his shoulder?" Warden Parnuss asked, looking her up and down. His salt-and-pepper hair seemed oddly darker than it used to be. "We have you on camera storming through the Handler's Ward to practically rip Voumatir's shirt off. After a few minutes of confrontation, we see you strangling him and then breaking his neck. How do you explain that behavior?"

She shrugged and looked away. Myx began retying her pitch black hair into a braid. "Voumatir was acting funny when we cremated Alycee. And then again the morning before that video footage. It made me suspicious. I didn't put everything together right away."

Keeping Rauno's ash experiment secret was of the upmost importance. It had occurred to Myx that she might have gotten a prestigious science job with Rauno in the Hathak government once the war was over. Being able to absorb the life force of the dead would truly give them an edge in the war. But she couldn't bring herself to hope that she'd be allowed to be involved in the research; it was likely she'd just end up as someone's lab rat for the rest of her life.

"When can I see my friends?" Myx glared at the Warden, raising an eye brow.

"Since you killed the last friend you saw, I'm reluctant to let Bishing or Rauno near you." Parnuss' turquoise eyes bore into hers. "It's rather suspicious that you've been involved in the deaths of two prisoners within a single week. Some of the Handlers are speculating that you killed Alycee as well as Voumatir."

The accusation made her explode. "I didn't kill Alycee! She was one of my closest friends. Yes, I did kill Voumatir, but only because he lied about who he was. He was the real murderer!"

She took a breath to calm herself. Myx sat back in her bed and shut her mouth tightly. Of course they knew that he was an imposter. Voumatir would have needed help from the Camp administration to keep his cover for as long as he did. But she was frustrated that she said so much at once. Myx needed to be more careful in the future about her emotions.

"I can't help you unless you give us more information." After waiting another ten minutes of her silence, the Warden seemed to grow bored. Parnuss eventually left the cell, shaking his head with a sigh.

During her confinement, Myx frequently wondered how Alycee and Bishing had known each other in the past. She replayed the memories—a skill she was getting better at. Alycee had said that she wasn't going to hurt Bishing, implying that she might have hurt him before. It was very jumbled and confusing. There were over thirty years of memories available to her from Alycee's past, all thanks to Rauno's ash experiment. After a week's worth of playing back recollections, she still had no idea what had happened between them.

Outside the cell, Parnuss spoke to someone. All the exposure to radiation had increased her sense of hearing. She closed her eyes and focused on the sounds.

"Traditional methods aren't working on her," the Warden said, his voice sharp.

"You know I how I feel about the alternative techniques," Gotasun groaned, followed by a pounding sound.

Parnuss' tone calmed as he replied, "She isn't intimidated anymore."

"Can't she be assigned a different Handler?"

"Switching Handlers won't make a difference," the Warden sighed. "We tried that by having Frezul doing Myx's last Review. It didn't seem to phase her much. The next day, she murdered Voumatir." He was quiet a moment before adding, "All that research was for nothing. I guess we'll need to find ourselves another alien to put through the trial."

Growing increasingly bored, Myx lost interest in their conversation. Sure, she was curious about what the "alternative techniques" were. But she didn't see the point in guessing. She was likely going to find out what Gotasun meant the time she saw him.

Myx leaned back on her hard cot and closed her pink tourmaline eyes to concentrate. She searched through more memories of Alycee and Bishing. Sorting through the past months in the Camp was tedious, but she had plenty of time to devote to her investigation. Bishing had always been quiet about his past, never revealing more than a couple details about his life before they met.

All the moments between Voumatir and Alycee were awkward. Knowing what she did now, she could see the schemes and manipulation in Voumatir's words. It disgusted Myx that she fell for his charm—that she had actually liked him. Of course it also Alycee's repulsion affecting her former fondness.

She wondered how their lives would have been different if Rauno hadn't been allowed to keep Alycee's ashes following her incineration. Voumatir would still be deceiving them. In all likelihood, he might have even left the Camp by then. Whoever had helped the crafty alien get his masked assassin friends in and out of the Camp would have found a way to give him an exit after he killed Alycee.

Myx wished that she had stolen some of Voumatir's blood when she killed him. She would have loved to experience a couple of his memories to figure out his darkest secrets. However, Myx was glad that she hadn't; she would have disliked being linked to the scum-bag's life force.

The cell door creaked open and Gotasun entered. He didn't seem to be at all happy as he said, "Hello, my pet. I shall now be keeping an eye on you at all times. That means that I'll be here when you sleep." Gotasun took a seat in the chair at the corner. He leaned back and laced his fingers behind his head. "Bedtime time starts now, my pet."

Chapter 30

Menacing, grey hematite eyes glowered at Myx as she attempted to sleep. Unsettled, she pulled her covers up to her chin.

If Gotasun was going to be there all night, she wondered if she should face him as she slept or turn toward the wall. On the one hand, she could react more quickly should he decide to attack her in the middle of the night. But that meant that he'd be able to see her facial expressions as she slept. However, if she were to sleep facing the wall, she'd at least get a little bit of privacy. She reviewed the endless list of pros and cons for both for several minutes, turning back and forth between her sides.

In the end, Myx decided to hide from his cold stare. Taking deep breaths, she calmed herself. After the ordeal of being interrogated all week, she was exhausted.

Myx was eager to be returning to work the next day. She never thought that she'd enjoying doing things for the Camp, but she found a sense of joy in painting. As she slept, her mind imagined different pictures sure could create with the radiation wisp theme.

There was a loud thud and she started awake. Gotasun just sat there with his thick, hairy arms across his chest, looking as though nothing had happened. He continued to regard her with his disgusted gaze. She settled back into her covers and closed her eyes, only to then hear a scraping sound.

She rolled back towards her Handler to see that he was now sitting several inches closer. Myx didn't bother facing the wall again; obviously the alternative method to unnerving her would be sleep deprivation. Propping up her pillow, she sat against the bed board. Determined to foil Gotasun's attempts to upset her, she decided to return his gaze and see if he would break before her.

But she lost. Being cooped up for a week had caused her to feel groggy and lethargic. Myx couldn't will her eye lids to stay open. She had no choice but to give in to slumber.

In her dreams, she thought of Alycee once again. Myx felt like she was becoming obsessed with the former assassin. Then again, Alycee was now a part of her life force, so it made sense that she'd think of her murdered friend.

They walked together through the Camp, often watching scenes of their memories in the various rooms and work stations. Her brain constructed an astral projection of the Alycee to facilitate the acquisition of her memories. The ghost-like figure walked her through the past events and added commentary as necessary. The pair relived their various conversations as they bonded in their captivity. Having Alycee with her was comforting and she drifted into a deeper sleep.

As they reached the dream-version of the mines, Myx tripped and fell into a deep radiation crevice. She awoke with her heart racing and sweat dripping down her face. Frantic, she looked about the cell.

Gotasun had a boot against her mattress. He bore a smug smile below his crooked nose. “What’s wrong, my pet? Can’t sleep?”

Sighing, she lay back down. Myx got a few more minutes of sleep before she experienced another falling sensation. “Do you realize that keeping me from sleeping is only going to make me more irritable and difficult to control?”

He shrugged. “Orders are orders. And it’s also quite entertaining. I love the exasperated expression on your face.”

Myx settled herself with a deep breath. “I’m not going to do an adequate job in the morning if I’m sleep-deprived. I do my best work after a good night of rest. I won’t be able to focus and the Camp won’t make a profit off my labors.”

Gotasun didn’t reply. He simply continued staring down at Myx, daring her to do something.

She was sure that he was waiting for her to go crazy and attack him. Myx decided not to give Gotasun the satisfaction. With Alycee’s skills, she could have easily taken him out, but she was already in enough trouble with the Warden. Besides, she was fairly certain that striking a Handler would earn her the death penalty. Myx would have to wait until after the war was done to get her revenge on him.

Turning over, she was determined not to react the next time Gotasun tried to rouse her. She got a bit of sleep before the lights came on. A moment later, Myx pulled her short blanket over her head to block some of the illumination. This left her toes exposed and chilly.

Still, she refused to give her Handler the satisfaction of knowing that she was uncomfortable. Even though sleep eluded her, she pretended to be off in dream-land.

Something cold and smooth pricked her large toe.

Myx kicked and felt Gotasun’s hairy forearm. He cursed and something glass clattered to the stone floor. She peeked her head over the side of her mattress to see a syringe.

Her heart began racing and she couldn't calm it. Myx focused on her breathing and found her happy place: the memories of her and Bishing walking along the streets of Capitaras before the war. She sat up and rubbed her chest in a desperate attempt to soothe it.

But nothing worked to lower her quickening pulse.

With her heart rate so high, she felt like she had when she killed Voumatir. Flashes of her murderous action came to her mind, mixed with images of Alycee's throat being slit and fighting the masked assassin. Myx blinked and she stood over Voumatir, snapping his neck over and over again.

The alien's dull blue eyes regarded her with amusement as his face spun all the way around. He grinned at her rage.

Tears stun her eyes as she stifled a sob.

Throughout the night, Myx had pockets of sleep, only a few minutes here and there. And then Gotasun would find ways to wake her. One time, she felt him putting her fingers in warm water; thankfully she awoke before it caused her to unconsciously wet her sheets.

In another instance, she became cold and rolled over without her blanket. The thin, cotton material sat crumpled in Gotasun's lap. As soon as she became accustomed to the draftiness of the cell, he put the wadded up blanket over her head and nearly suffocated her.

After hours of the sleep-deprivation, the bed sunk as Gotasun slid next to Myx. A finger stroked hey cheek until she opened her eyes.

Gotasun wore a cheery grin on his face. "Good morning, my pet." He slid his meaty hands below her back and knees and lifted her from the cot. The Handler chuckled as he dropped her to her feet. "It's time to go to work."

A chain jangled off the ring that had been secured about her neck. Even in her sleep-deprived state, the irony of the collar was not lost on her. Now she really was Gotasun's pet. Wiping at her tender, pink eyes, Myx trailed after her Handler through the stone streets of the Camp.

He handed her a protein bar and she chewed it as she trudged to an empty work station.

The Handler shackled Myx's neck chain to the table beside her easel. "I'll see you again in eight hours. Be sure to make something pretty for the over-seer." Gotasun turned to leave after stashing the key in his trousers.

Myx closed her eyes for a moment to rest them, but gasped awake as she slumped into a jar of violet paint.

"Don't be wasteful," the overseer scolded, smacking her in the back of the head.

Stifling a growl, Myx squeezed the paint from her oily braid and pawed the color onto the canvas. She arranged the color into a circle, hoping that it resembled the planet's sun, Lyrwen. It had been nearly a month since being outside the caves of the Camp; she wasn't sure that the star ever existed.

Her life in Tarasi was nothing but a hazy remembrance in her brain. The Camp was consuming her, altering her very soul under the massive physical and emotional abuse. And it didn't help that she had a second life force fused to hers. She felt like a lump of raw clay being formed into something new, except that her new form was pounded, crisped in a kiln, and then smashed against the stone floor—left in tiny little shards.

Myx longed for the days of ignorance back in Kaefh's shop, but she now understood that she could never go back to that life after all that had been done to her.

Chapter 31

Myx's chain clinked as she turned in her painting to the overseer. Scratching at the metal collar around her neck, she took an empty canvas with her free hand.

As she returned to her work station, she realized the lack of conversations from the other prisoners. Many glanced in fleetingly in her direction before awkwardly averting their eyes back to their art. Those closest to her noticeably inched their easels so that they could keep their gaze on her as they worked.

It appeared as though they had heard how she murdered Voumatir. However, some got up the courage to ask Myx clarifying questions about the event.

"Help me settle a bet," one man asked, poking his head into the studio. He looked down the Main Street before coming all the way in and sitting beside her easel. His pale blue topaz irises were wide in curiosity. "Is it true that you killed him because he wouldn't let you in his band?"

A female prisoner joined them from across the studio. "They say you killed Alycee out of jealously, wanting Voumatir for yourself. And then when he rejected you, you killed him too."

They continued alternating questions, not giving her a chance to respond.

"Are they starting a battle to the death? Does the last prisoner alive get to go home?"

"Were you responsible for the attack on the Camp?" the girl asked, hope welling in her red coral eyes. "Can your buddies help break us out? I can pay."

"I'd like to strangle the snoring guy in the cell next to mine." The man scooted closer and held up his finger. "Do you have tips on how to do it? Should I use my hands, or would a pillow work just as well?"

Of course, she simply ignored their inquiries. Myx continued drawing the colored wisps on her canvas without giving them a second look. She played back Alycee's childhood memories to distract herself, as well as get inspiration for her painting. The gawkers eventually gave up and walked away with a huff.

She swirled reds, blues, greens, and yellows to make the radiation "dance" like the wind. Adding white and grey streaks gave the colors dimension and depth instead of just looking like a disembodied rainbow.

Myx hadn't decided yet what kind of content she'd add to it. Perhaps she should bow to convention and draw flowers? Tieg had said that nature scenes were fairly popular. If she sold enough paintings, then maybe she'd earn enough points to not need another punishment. In the end, she sketched a field of bayrix buds changing from blue to yellow due to the radiation.

Rauno came by at lunch, delivering meals to the prisoners in the studio. He walked past her without a glance, moving to the back of the room first. Based on the smell, he seemed to be serving ceth noodles and lefen broth.

When he made it to her easel, Rauno set down the bowl and began to take off without even saying hello.

"I'm sure that you're upset with me, Rauno," Myx whispered, hoping he'd stay to hear her out. She set her pastels down and took a deep breath before continuing. "Yes, I killed Voumatir. But the alien assassinated Alycee."

He eyed her. "How do you know that?"

"Your experiment worked," Myx admitted, unable to conceal the blush of embarrassment. "From her ashes and the radiation, I have her memories and skills—permanently. Alycee found out that Voumatir was only following her in order to kill her and collect a bounty. All his flattery was to cover up his true intentions. I had no choice but to avenge her murder."

Rauno scratched at the thin, red beard on his chin. "I knew there had to be an explanation. But really? It worked?" He dug into his jacket and pulled out several vials of blood when none of the other prisoners were looking. "I took some samples yesterday when I was working at the Infirmary. Do you think that you could sneak into a radiation chamber tonight to use these on yourself?"

"You want me to bathe myself in strangers' blood to see if I can acquire their life forces?"

"No, not strangers." Rauno shook his head. "There's Tieg, Dolra, and myself in there."

Myx pocketed the vials. "How did you get Dolra's blood?"

"I drugged her tea," the scientist explained with a coy grin. "When my sweet nightingale grew dizzy, she let me take a blood sample to check her sugar levels to see if she was becoming hypoglycemic."

"Okay, fine. I'll try to get into a radiation chamber tonight. But I'm not sure if I can." She jangled her thick chain in front of her for emphasis. "I'm kind of under lock and key for the whole murder thing." Letting the links down softly, Myx let out a deep breath and changed the subject. "How's Bishing doing?"

Rauno picked up a bowl and sipped the lukewarm noodle broth. "Bish is a mess. He tried to see you; it took three guards to restrain him. I have no idea where he is now. But he doesn't seem to care if you killed Voumatir or not."

"That's a relief. I'm glad he doesn't hate me." Myx finished the rest of her noodles and put the bowl aside. "I hope I can get some sleep this evening. Gotasun kept me up all night."

"Oh?" Rauno raised an eyebrow at her with a smirk. "I didn't take you as the kind of girl that would pleasure her Handler for better treatment. Does this mean that he won't beat you anymore in exchange for some lovin'?"

"No! That's sick!" Myx gagged in disgust. "He's trying to keep me sleep-deprived. I got little ten minute snippets of sleep here and there. My energy is at an all-time low."

Rauno looked like he wanted to put a comforting hand on her; but the overseer kept a sharp eye on them. "Hang in there, Myx. You have Alycee to help you now." He looked conspicuously over his shoulder. "I've got to go. I'll try to talk to you again tomorrow."

Taking her bowl, he pushed his cart around the studio and collected the empty containers from the prisoners.

Hours later, she completed her fourth picture for the day. Many probably looked like they had been created by toddlers, but they were the best Myx could do in her sleep-deprived state. As she turned in the canvas, Gotasun appeared.

"That's pretty. See? You can still function when you're tired." The Handler unchained her from her work station and pulled her out to the Main Street.

She tugged at the collar and wondered how she was going to get away from Gotasun. And then she realized that he was taking her to the Reviewery. Perhaps he would let her be locked up in a chamber all night to heal? Dolra's salve kept up the injured prisoners half the night anyways.

Myx couldn't wait to see what kind of information and skills she would gain from the blood hidden in her coat. Tieg had been a valuable member of the Tarasi military most of his long life. And Rauno's keen mind would certainly help boost her intelligence. She was nervous about absorbing part of Dolra's life force, afraid that she'd turn into an unpleasant, shrieking harpy.

Of course, it would only be temporary since the blood and radiation combination didn't appear to be permanent; the best way to retain the life force seemed to be bathing in a paste of their ashes and letting the wisps complete the transfer.

Gotasun gestured for her to enter the Reviewery.

She walked past him and froze.

Chained to a post was Bishing. Frezul circled him, wrapping her knuckles with a roll of her white tape.

Chapter 32

"Have a seat, my pet." Gotasun walked to a bench at the far side of the room. He sat down and patted his lap.

Myx followed him, keeping her eyes on Bish. She stood beside her Handler.

Gotasun grabbed her wrist and pulled her onto one of his legs. He removed the key from his trousers and unlocked the metal collar. After tossing the restraints away, he skimmed his fingers up and down the tops of her thighs. "I thought you might like to see what a real punishment looks like. The mute hasn't had one yet and Frezul is eager to get started."

She wanted to resist, playing out several situations in her head where she struck him in retaliation for touching her so intimately. But it would only make her situation worse.

Frezul finished taping her hands and threw the roll across the room. The petite, elfin woman began spouting off offenses from memory. "Day 1—You tried to deny me as your Handler: minus ten. You worked diligently that day without questions: plus four. You didn't talk to your peers that day: plus two. You were late for curfew: minus five." She continued on and on, rubbing her taped knuckles all the while.

As they listened, Gotasun continued caressing Myx. She shied away from his touch, but he just moved his hands to a different location. He removed the tie on her braid in order to run his fingers through her dark hair.

"What do you think, my pet?" Gotasun asked, sticking his crooked nose into the curve of her neck. His calluses itched her skin as he stroked the length of her arms. He wrapped his arms around her torso and cupped her stomach as he added, "Aren't you happy that I gave you consequences after every week and not all at once?"

Myx gasped and turned toward him. "Frezul is doing a month of punishments at once?"

Gotasun put his hands on her shoulders and redirected her gaze at Bishing. "Don't worry. Frezul knows what she's doing. Sure, it'll hurt worse than anything the mute has ever experienced. But it won't cause any permanent harm; she knows how to traumatize the nerves without doing long-term damage to the body."

Myx remembered how much pain she was in after a session with Frezul. She could barely move afterwards and that was only after seven strikes.

She hoped that Bishing's lack of communication abilities would keep his final tally low. A lot of Myx's minuses had been because of something she had said. Bish was a good worker and he didn't seem to have difficulty following most of the Camp's rules.

"Alright," Frezul said, rubbing her taped knuckles. "That comes to minus sixty-four. Let's get started!"

Bishing moaned as his Handler sent her palm across his ribs.

"Got a good crack out of that." Frezul jabbed at his side twice more with the point of her forearm before circling him. She considered Bishing as though she were planning out all her attacks. "That's three. Sixty-one still to go."

As the consequences continued, Myx had a hard time watching. She averted her gaze and closed her eyes.

Gotasun put a hand on her chin and angled her face towards the on-going punishment. "Open your eyes, my pet. Watch every moment and be grateful that Frezul wasn't your Handler. Tell me that you appreciate how gentle I've been."

She obeyed, but kept her gaze to several inches away from the beating. Through clenched teeth, Myx said, "Thank you."

"What for?"

Heat rose in her cheeks as her anger flared. "For being gentle with me."

"That's my good pet." Gotasun patted her head as though she were a domesticated animal. "Now keep watching."

Myx wanted nothing more than to go to Bishing and hold him. She nearly leaped off Gotasun's lap, but his hands were too restrictive. Frezul continued thrashing Bish, occasionally looking over at Myx and smiling maliciously.

As Frezul did strike number seventeen—a roundhouse kick to Bishing's jaw—Gotasun let go of Myx and leaned back.

She stared at him, wondering what he was thinking.

He gave a taunting look, as though he wanted her to go to Bishing's aid. Lacing his fingers behind his head, Gotasun closed his grey hematite eyes.

Although on some level, Myx knew that it was a trap, she couldn't help but take the opportunity to get away from her Handler. She leapt off Gotasun's lap and ran toward her tortured friend.

She knocked over the distracted Frezul and pulled on the knots that held Bishing to the post. "I'm so sorry, Bish," Myx cried as tears began running down her cheeks. It was difficult to see what she was doing, but she somehow managed to loosen the loops enough to free him. "They are doing this to get back at me for my defiance. Can you ever forgive me?"

Bishing sat there, not moving. His smoky quartz irises narrowed as he took the rope from her. He twisted the cords back together as he re-tied his hands.

"Run, you idiot! Get out of here!"

Frezul laughed as she swept Myx's feet out from under her. "He has accepted that he needs to be punished. If you know what's good for you, you'd return to your Handler." She stood and checked the knots. "That's another minus ten for an escape attempt. Let's continue, mute."

Myx choked back a sob as she trudged back to Gotasun.

He seemed amused about something. "What was your plan? Were you going to take your silent friend and break out today? He can't even stand." Gotasun let out a bellowing chortle. "At least he knows that resisting will only lead to more trouble. I guess you haven't learned that lesson yet, my pet."

She didn't respond. Myx sat silently, determined to endure the rest of the session without another outburst.

Every once and awhile, Bishing would lose consciousness. Frezul called Myx over and told her to revive him. Splashing water on Bish's face, she got Bish to wake. She apologized and returned to Gotasun's lap.

The whole punishment lasted nearly an hour. When it was over, a pair of guards appeared with a rolling bed. Bishing was untied and hefted onto it.

"Since you're so close to him, you can go treat him at the Infirmary," Gotasun told her, releasing his grip on her elbows. "You'd better hurry. It looks like he desperately needs some time in a radiation chamber."

Bishing was barely conscious. Stepping to the back end of the bed, Myx pushed it down the Camp halls.

Myx whispered words of encouragement on their way to the Infirmary. "You were very brave. I'm proud of you for taking all that pain. But I'm going to care for you and get you back to health. You'll be up and about in no time."

Chapter 33

"I know it stings," Myx whispered, doing her best to sound soothing; somehow she had acquired Dolra's bedside manner and she was attempting to undo that persona. She continued rubbing the ointment into his traumatized joints despite his groans of protest. "It'll help you heal quicker. Dolra's salve is sadistic, but it's honestly the only reason that I'm still alive."

After so little sleep the past forty eight hours, Myx was starting to have a hard time doing basic movements. Her vision grew a bit blurry and she got ointment all over the sheets. It didn't help that she had a fussy patient, either.

Myx sighed and let the radiation to invigorate her before resuming her task. Trying to remain positive, she added, "It's nice to get a little alone time with you. Things have been so crazy the past couple weeks." Myx chose her next words carefully, unsure of hoe Bishing would react. "We haven't talked about the Alycee/Voumatir thing yet."

She waited to see if he gave her a questioning look.

He simply put a shaking hand on hers and pressed his lips together.

Myx wiped the ointment from her fingers and began re-tying her braid. "You don't want me to talk about it? Or did Rauno tell you what happened?"

Bishing held up two fingers to indicate that the scientist had indeed informed him.

"I'm glad that you don't think any less of me." Before she could say anything else, she re-experienced flashes from when Alycee and Bish had first interacted. Myx swallowed before saying, "That last day in the hotel when the police arrived—it seemed like you and Alycee had met before. I have her memories of the event and she clearly said that she wasn't going to hurt anyone. Why would she need to mention that, Bish?"

He rolled over and shut his eyes, clearly not interested in talking about it.

"Bishing, what aren't you telling me?" Frustrated, she pulled out a syringe from her apron and drew some of his blood.

Flinging his hands at her, Bishing tried to take the needle away.

She stepped toward the hatch and sprayed the blood over her arm. As the radiation passed through her, she received glimpses into Bishing's past.

Myx experienced a quick succession of flashes from their time in the Camp. Working with Alycee's memories had helped her become skilled at maneuvering through the information. Skipping through the unnecessary parts, Myx made her way to when Alycee and Bishing were alone in Capitaras.

The dialogue repeated, same as when she experienced it through Alycee's point of view. But this time she was seeing it as Bishing. As Alycee spoke, Bish's mind went even further back into a distant memory. Myx let her consciousness be swept to that moment.

She slowed down the remembered time, absorbing the details of her surroundings. It was familiar—the same Palace she had been in when she watched Alycee's botched attempt to assassinate the Hathak Emperor. Myx went forward in time and she rushed through the elaborately decorated halls to a large bedroom.

A woman lay on a bed, holding a small bundle of cloth. As she drew closer, Myx saw that it was a baby.

The woman smiled through the sweaty mess of black curls that obscured her face. She held up the bundle as Myx approached. There was something familiar about the dark-haired woman, but Myx couldn't place where she had seen her.

"Meet your daughter," the woman said, holding up the newborn.

The scene shifted and Myx was in a war room. She still seemed to be in the Hathak Palace, but there was nothing happy about this memory. Men and woman argued over a map of the Tarasi capital.

An armored man was chained to the far wall. Myx found herself moving to the prisoner. She, in Bishing's memory, brandished a knife and put it through the assassin's eye socket. The corpse was taken away and a masked woman was brought in next. She struggled against the restraints, not resolved to go to death without fighting.

Alycee's muffled voice spoke through the intricate mask. "Wait! I wasn't going to kill you!"

A guard pulled the mask off. Alycee looked perhaps fourteen or fifteen.

"I came to stop him," the young woman explained, her purple tanzanite eyes wild. "I didn't become an assassin to murder little babies in their cribs. Check your security footage. I saw the alarm and purposefully tripped it. Please believe me!"

An uncomfortable amount of time passed as a decision was reached. All the while, the teenage assassin sobbed and pleaded with her captors.

Since Myx was only temporarily experiencing Bishing's memories, she found it difficult to stay attached to one specific scene. The flashes threatened to pull her back once again, deeper into Bish's consciousness. But she resisted, wishing to stay where she was and see what had happened to her deceased friend.

Alycee was unchained and given back her weapon. A group of guards escorted her out of the war room.

Myx was sent spinning as the scene changed again. She looked down on a younger version of Kaefh. She held the hand of a little girl with long, dark hair. The child—who looked about five years old—had brown, inquisitive eyes.

"I don't want to leave, Daddy," the girl said, her voice oddly devoid of feeling.

"Daddy will come see you shortly, Princess," Kaefh explained in her curt way. "So will Mommy."

"Where is Mommy?"

"You'll see her tomorrow." Kaefh picked up a bag and pulled the girl along with her.

The memory shifted, showing an elaborate funeral procession. Dozens of black-clad guards escorted a tiny casket. A hologram of the little girl was projected over the marching mourners.

"Now that the whole planet thinks that she's dead, she'll be safe." Myx could feel her mouth making the sounds, but they were in a man's deep voice.

Myx was then back in Capitaras, across the way from Kaefh's shop. A younger version of Myx—perhaps ten years old—dusted shelves inside. She spoke with a little blonde-haired girl and chased the younger child about the shelves.

She sped along through the memories. Myx could feel pressure on her physical self as Bishing wiped the blood splatter from her arm. But the imprint had already set into her the moment the radiation passed through it. However, she still felt a sense of urgency to see more of Bishing's memories since the blood transfer was not a permanent, strong connection.

Night surrounded her, but the decorations told her that she was back in the Hathak Emperor's Palace. Satin sheets fell over her frame as she lay in a wide, plush bed. A figure lurked in the doorway.

She stumbled to her feet and searched for something in the shadows. The lights came on and she was face to face with another masked assassin.

"I know you," Myx said in the Hathak Emperor's voice.

"I have a new mission, Your Majesty," Alycee said, now not much younger than when Myx had known her.

There wasn't much of a battle. The Emperor managed to dodge a few blows, but the assassin quickly subdued her target. A knife sliced through Myx's mouth, severing her tongue. She fell to her knees, choking on red, hot blood.

Chapter 34

Myx gagged as she returned to her own mind. "Why didn't you tell me that I'm your daughter?" She stared at Bishing across the radiation chamber, feeling hurt, betrayed, and yet also relieved. "Not only that, you're also the Hathak Emperor!"

Bishing sat up, wincing. He made signs with his hands.

"I don't care that you were going to enlighten me someday. I care that the moment never occurred!" Myx took a breath, but it wasn't enough to calm her. She slumped to the floor, tears stinging her pink tourmaline eyes. "I'm a princess. Not just that—I'm a princess of a society that has enslaved me for the past month. I don't understand how this happened."

She had been led to believe that her parents were dead; that's what Kaefh had always told her. On some level, Myx understood that they didn't say anything to protect her. But all the lies exposed at once made her feel like they didn't respect her enough to tell her about her own life.

If Bishing had planned on joining her shortly after Kaefh left the Hathak Palace, what had kept him from joining them in Capitaras? From the memories, Myx could tell that Bishing looked in on her occasionally. But why hadn't he come to her? Was he still in charge of the Hathak Empire? Did he think he'd be a bad father? Or maybe the assassination attempt on her life had made him fear for her safety? She wanted to shout all the questions at him.

"Why get involved in my life now?" Myx huffed, pacing in the small chamber. "You were the one who wanted to sign up for the Tarasi military. But we could have lived in obscurity away from the effects of the war."

He shook his head, refusing to answer.

"Tell me," Myx demanded, standing over him.

When he rolled back towards the wall, she decided that she needed to calm herself down. Bish also needed to heal properly before they could have a productive conversation.

Remembering the blood samples from Rauno, Myx almost hopped into a different chamber for the night. But she didn't want to be anywhere near the radiation; it increased the strength and frequency of the absorbed memories. On her way out of the Infirmary, she wiped the remainder of Bishing's blood off her arm and tossed the rag away.

Myx wondered if Gotasun would be in her cell. Probably not since he assumed that she'd stay with Bishing as he recovered. But her Handler wouldn't have predicted what had just happened.

In her cell, Gotasun sat in the chair, his eyes closed. Suppressing a sigh, Myx made her way to her bed as quietly as she could manage. Ahw covered herself with her blanket and waited for the sweet release of sleep. But her mind still raced, unable to rest from the thoughts and questions about her past.

As she drifted off, her mattress sank. An arm curved around her stomach. "Good evening, my pet."

Unable to deal with her Handler getting handsy, Myx said, "I don't like that. Please stop." She sat up and gently pushed at his arms. He didn't budge, so she pressed harder. "Gotasun, I won't sleep with you."

"I'm your Handler. It's your job to do what I want."

"You're ugly, unpleasant, and pathetic." Myx knew she should have held her tongue, but she couldn't control herself anymore. "If you need to get your jollies but raping prisoners, then you're the sickest man I've ever met!"

Gotasun put a hand in her hair and yanked her head back. "I will have you." The other set of fingers caressed her abdomen. His lips found her neck and trailed down to her shoulder. "It all depends on you how that happens. If you're complacent and do as I say, I promise not to hurt you too much."

Tired of being a victim, Myx rammed her elbow into his chest.

He fell off the bed, gasping.

Myx stood on the hard mattress and jumped. Gotasun grabbed one of her legs mid-air and she slammed into the stone floor.

As he climbed on top of her, Myx calmed herself to remember Alycee's fighting skills. Adrenaline rushed through her and she knew what to do. She rolled, managing to turn her upper body towards the ceiling. Myx struck Gotasun in the face with her fingers spread out like a claw. Her ragged nails scratched against his enraged, hematite eyes.

She got to her feet and made her way to the door. But the Handler—still blinded—rammed his whole body against her.

Pinned against the cell wall, Myx could feel the vials of blood dig into her ribs. Gotasun felt for her arms; he was so muscular and she wasn't strong enough to push him off. Her chest felt like it was being crushed as he pressed his massive weight against her.

"You're going to pay for that, my pet," Gotasun growled in her ears. He ran his bare teeth over her shoulder. His tongue ran along her upper back. "I'll make you beg me to take you—over and over again."

"I'm tired of your threats." Myx grunted and sent her heel upwards into his groin.

Gotasun stumbled to the ground, clutching at his genitals.

Taking advantage of his defenseless state, Myx did a downward kick to his abdomen, adjusted her stance, and stomped on his head for good measure. He fell unconscious as blood spurted from his once-again broken nose.

Chapter 35

The few belongings Myx still had were in a small sack under her cot. She collected it, took Gotasun's keys from his belt, and left her cell. Locking the door behind her, she turned to see that the halls were surprisingly clear of guards. Myx flung the sack over her shoulder and took off down to the Main Street of the Camp.

She needed a plan. The least-watched place in the Camp at that time of night was probably the mines. Pick axes were locked up in a guard station. But now that she had keys, she could easily get into one. Maybe she could find her way through the mines and discover a path to the wilderness? It was a crazy idea, but it was better than the alternative: stay in the Camp and be tortured before being executed.

Myx tucked into an alley as a pair of guards passed by. The vials of blood jabbed into her side and she winced; the keys she had stolen from Gotasun jangled loudly in her pocket.

After waiting a moment, she stepped back out onto the Main Street and continued on down to the mines. There were few other prisoners or guards out so late at night. Myx tried to look like she was running an errand when she passed anyone.

One of the guards seemed rather suspicious. He approached Myx and asked, "Do you need an escort back to your cell?"

She had never been good at lying. But she was finding herself spew falsities with relative ease lately. Myx composed herself as she replied, "No, thank you. I'm just fetching something for my Handler. Gotasun is having one of his cravings and sent me to make him an ohbic and frewsha sandwich."

The guard made a disgusted face at the combination but let her continue on her way.

More questions came to mind, distracting Myx from her rage as she strolled quickly past the Washroom.

If Bishing was the Hathak Emperor, why didn't he tell the Warden who he was? Was there a usurper on the throne? Was he only a disposable figure-head and not really allowed to have any real power? There were so many possibilities and nothing made sense. Of course, logic wasn't her strongest skill. What little she had was thanks to Alycee's life force merged with hers. Still, it wasn't enough to answer her queries.

But she knew how she could gain some new insight.

Myx dashed into the empty mines. Radiation-infused rocks glinted in the moon light shining through narrow crevices in the ceiling. Wisps flitted out the giant chasm, adding multi-colored illumination, but it still wasn't enough to see well.

Using Gotasun's keys, Myx removed a flash light and pick axe from one of the locked cabinets. She ventured deeper into the caves, following the dense wisps of radiation.

After traveling down a series of tunnel, she set her axe down aside and pulled out the three vials of blood. Myx didn't know whose were whose. She took the tops off all three and reminded herself that the transfer effects would be temporary. Swallowing her anxiety about covering herself with other people's blood, she poured each vial over her left arm.

Radiation flowed through Myx and memories soared in her brain. They ran so fast that they became jumbled. She had a difficult time focusing as her mind was over-stimulated with a dozen decades of experiences. Myx didn't need the memories, just the logic skills from Rauno, Tieg, and Dolra.

Being infused with three life forces at once was dizzying as the memories began to set in. Due to Tieg's advanced years, his flashes seemed to drone on and on as he paroled the Tarasi-Hathak border along the equator of the planet.

What was most revolting was simultaneously watching and feeling Dolra's and Rauno's love making in the radiation chambers. She pushed away those intimate thoughts, but the vast number of their trysts still meant that Myx was forced to feel things that she really didn't need to experience.

However, she was able to side-step those memories by focusing on the thousands of chemical compounds that swarmed Rauno's mind; Myx became fascinated by the sheer number of elements that could be combined to create fiery explosions.

It took nearly half an hour to calm the flashes. Perhaps if she had actually gotten sleep the past two days, she might have gotten a handle on her mind a little easier. She could feel the life force losing its vitality, fading more and more with every minute. Myx began thinking again of her predicament. Pouring a couple more blood drops onto her arm, she prepared for another wave of memories, hoping for a logic booster to set in.

She focused on what she knew about Bishing. He was the Hathak Emperor. There were a number of assassination attempts on his life—as well as Myx's when she was a small child. Bish had sent his daughter away and promised to meet up with her a couple days.

That turned out to be untrue because she didn't meet him for another twelve years. Bishing occasionally came by to check up on her—well, more like spy on her. He lost his tongue when Alycee tried to assassinate him. A few weeks later, Bish became involved in Myx's life. Six months after that, war broke out because of the assassination attempt. But how were they connected? That was an awful long time for the Hathak to prepare for a war that had already been brewing for decades.

And then Bishing wanted to join the Tarasi army. Myx had made the decision to go with. Now they were in a Hathak Labor Camp, captured their first day in their military training.

There were a couple reasons why Bishing would have left the Hathak Palace behind. Either he was tired of being the Emperor or he found out how cruel the Hathak were. Both made sense to his current situation. Myx realized that she really couldn't blame him. And yet, she couldn't understand why he wouldn't tell her what was going on.

Perhaps Bishing was ashamed of his decisions as Emperor and thought the Camp was a worthy punishment? But then why involve Myx? She hadn't done anything wrong. He could have just signed up by himself as penitence.

And where was her mother? Did she die in an assassination attempt? Is she still at the Palace? Maybe someone was keeping the Empress prisoner to make the Emperor more compliant. Or did she take control of the government, forcing Bishing to flee the Hathak? It would explain why he never said anything; he could have thought he was protecting Myx from discovering that her mother was evil. It could be why Bishing took up arms against his former people. Myx still didn't like that idea, but it was the most probable one she could think of.

There was a soft white glow ahead before Tieg appeared. "Just as I thought."

Myx hid the glass vials in her jacket pocket. "What are you talking about?"

Tieg sat down beside her. He saw the blood and gasped. "Are you alright? Let me take you to the Infirmary!"

"I'm fine," Myx replied, wiping away the blood. She experienced a flash of when Tieg was captured—his eyes being simultaneously blasted with lasers and being healed by the newly exposed Radiation Spring. "Why did you think I was here?"

"I saw you rushing through the streets. You seemed upset." There was something tight in his voice as he inspected her arm with his luminescent white opal eyes. "I've known a couple prisoners who had that look—like they had just hurt someone and didn't know what to do. Sure enough, I overheard a couple guards talk about how the Warden was looking for you. So I followed, but got lost in the maze of mine tunnels."

Myx tugged at her unraveling braid. "I have to escape tonight. Otherwise, they're going to kill me."

His unnerving, glowing eyes betrayed no emotions. It was difficult to understand the motive behind his next words. "As someone who has lived a bit longer than you, I'm going to have to recommend that you turn yourself in."

"Don't tell me that you're a spy for the Hathak."

"Not at all," Tieg assured her. "The punishment is usually less severe when you admit your mistake than if you run away and they catch you. Besides, even if you make it through the mines to the lake at the end, it's the first place they'll check. And it's a five day hike back to Capitaras."

"How do you know that?"

"I was a patrolman," he replied, his voice sounding a little off once again. He ran a hand across his sweaty, hairless scalp. "I know these parts pretty well. Actually, it was near here where I had my, uh, accident." Tieg paused, averting his gaze to a vein of colored rocks along the mine wall. The elderly prisoner rubbed his eyelids before adding, "Myx, there's something that I need to talk to you about."

His next words were indistinguishable as Myx was pulled to Tieg's memories. They were faint and distorted. She figured it must have been due to his accident. Her vision wasn't normal. Instead of seeing people trudge through Camp, she saw people-shaped auras roaming through the halls and work stations.

At first, they all looked the same. But as she sifted through the events, she realized that she could detect certain people based on their color. It took her a few moments to realize that the color matched their radiation-enhanced irises. Myx saw her pink tourmaline aura often; however, since she was only experiencing the memories from blood transfer, she didn't have enough control to really decide where the memories occurred to her.

"Myx? Are you okay?" Tieg stood over her collapsed form, his white shining eyes opened wide in concern.

"What are you?" she whispered, trying to understand what was happening.

Tieg helped her to her feet. "I see that Rauno's experiment is beginning to take effect. I'm glad that I was able to tell you about me without using words. It's really quite difficult to describe what is happening, Myx."

"Well—" She didn't know the polite way to ask her next question, so she blurted out, "But what is the point of seeing people's aura? It seems rather pointless."

He smiled at her comment. "Yes, Warden Parnuss has been wondering that same thing. That's why I'm not in isolation; they are experimenting on me here at the Camp to see how they can actually use my ability. Except, they don't know the extent of my new skill."

Myx thought back to the flashes of Tieg's memories and came upon a startling revelation. "You can find people. Is that how you knew where I was?"

"Yes. And how I know that the guards are searching for you." His serious disposition broke as he said, "I've got to say that it was quite entertaining to see you take on Gotasun. Sure, I couldn't see much of what was happening; I actually thought that you were being intimate for a moment before I realized that you were fighting."

"Oh, I nearly forgot about all that." Myx felt her anxiety begin to take over; she ran her fingers through the tip of her lengthening black braid as she paced the width of the mine tunnel. "Can your special sight help me get out of this Camp?"

Tieg closed his eyes and shook his head. "Myx, I think you need to accept that we might be here for quite awhile." Brilliant white light illuminated the tunnel yet again as he resumed his warning. "The guards say that we could get ransomed if we behave, but no one has been released yet. I heard talk of them getting ready to release that man, Voumatir, before he was, uh, killed."

With a sigh, she realized that he was right. "Except that I just assaulted my Handler. I'll likely be sentenced to death instead of being ransomed."

"It's a difficult choice. But turning yourself in will likely help you. You've become a real problem to our captors, Myx." Tieg put a comforting hand on her shoulder. "However, this is your decision; I won't turn you in if you decide to escape."

Myx considered what Alycee would have done. As competent as the former assassin was, she would have accepted whatever consequence was fitting for her act of rebellion.

With a shaking hand, Myx took Tieg's arm and let him escort her to her likely doom.

Chapter 36

Myx's curiosity was piqued as she placed papers in the shredder.

Parnuss had warned her about reading the files as she worked; she was already in enough trouble as it was. Until the Warden could figure out what to do with her, Myx was going to be chained up in his office, doing whatever menial tasks he told her to do.

Shackles clanked as Myx looked over the to-do list written in the looping Hathak script: make copies, dust the furniture, proof-read a speech, and taste-test Parnuss's lunch, etc... Every couple of minutes, the turquoise-eyed man would push himself out of his plush office chair and add something new to it. With a contented sigh, the Warden chalked the words "rub feet" to the bottom of the list.

Myx did her best to be grateful that she was allowed to work instead of being locked up in her a cell all day. But she hadn't heard yet if there was going to be a trial or anything. She was at least appreciative that there hadn't been any talk of execution yet.

Still, her punishment didn't seem to be appropriate for her crime. Myx had attacked her Handler and she should have a much worse consequence than becoming Warden's glorified lackey. Perhaps Parnuss was keeping her away from the other Camp prisoners to minimize the rumors; it wouldn't go well for the Hathak staff to have the Tarasi thinking it was acceptable to assault their captors.

Myx also wondered if maybe the Hathak were placating her since they had obviously pushed her further than she could manage.

She decided that she didn't have enough information to come to a conclusion. And her attempt to learn logic through blood-transfer had failed miserably, so she couldn't think through her predicament.

So Myx put her attention back on her tasks.

"How has your experience at Camp Hathak been?" Parnuss asked, looking up from the screen in his hands. His turquoise eyes looked oddly serene as he waited for an answer.

Putting another stack of papers into the shredder, she simply shrugged. Myx didn't understand why he wanted to know, so she didn't want to give him a proper answer yet. When the Warden repeated his question, she busied herself with arranging the papers that were yet to be destroyed.

"This is for posterity." The Warden set aside his screen and removed a pen and notebook from his desk drawer. "Don't you want future prisoners to have a better time than you did?"

"I'd rather you not ever have more prisoners," Myx mumbled under the hum of the shredder. She had been determined not to answer his inquiries, but she felt rage well up inside her. Unable to control herself anymore, she exploded. "This place makes no sense! I understand the purpose of enslaving us. But the whole Handler situation is preposterous. Some get one while others don't. Why is that?"

Myx sent a fist into the side of the paper shredder. She wanted to stop and breathe, but the words continued to shoot out of her mouth.

"A few get beat to within an inch of their life and are then healed over night—only to endure more humiliation and hardships the next day. And then others simply do menial tasks without any kind of harm. Can't you see how wrong this Camp is? Don't you have a soul?" Myx tossed a stack of papers into the air for dramatic effect. "I mean, I was only defending myself when I attacked Gotasun. He was putting his hands all over—" She paused, biting her lip to choke down the memory. "You can't kill me for that!"

The Warden smiled. "Technically, I can do as I wish. But I've decided not to kill you." He motioned for her to sit across his desk. "Last week, when we were detaining you for killing inmate Voumatir, an envoy arrived. They've been negotiating the release of some prisoners. Well, we can't just let anyone leave. But I'm prepared to return a couple of my biggest nuisances."

The sleep deprivation had slowed Myx's brain function; it sounded like Parnuss was going to set her free. "Can you repeat that?"

"You've been a pain ever since you got here," he said, his voice flat and unemotional. "Gotasun is one of my finest Handlers, and you've been constantly fighting him on everything. With you gone, perhaps we can restore some semblance of tranquility to this Camp."

Myx blinked at him, finally processing what he said. "You're really going to let me go?"

"I don't have much choice, young lady. The President has offered quite a bit of money has been exchanged for two of my prisoners." Warden Parnuss pressed a button on his desk and the door opened.

Sievly came running in, tears running down her rosy cheeks as she ran fingers through Myx's dark hair.

Kaefh looked like she wanted to embrace Myx as well. But she first set about unlocking the chain that linked her foster daughter to the shredder. She then grabbed her foster daughter roughly by the shoulders and pulled her into a tight embrace. "I knew you'd get into trouble if you left with that man. And now you get to come back home with us where it's safe."

"Just get her out of my Camp," Parnuss ordered, waving them away.

They left the Warden's office and made their way down the Main Street to the hangar.

Rauno was there, looking uncharacteristically sad. He ran a hand though his thickening red hair, his mouth pressed shut in a moping grimace.

"You're being released, too?" Myx asked, patting him on the back.

Rauno shifted uncomfortably, scratching at his scraggly beard. "Yeah, I guess. They think I've been too disruptive to daily life at the Camp. The women are all taking it hard that I'm leaving." He let out a discontented sigh. "But my future bride must be elsewhere."

Myx had a series of residual flashes, experiencing Rauno's and Dolra's romantic dalliances. She shook her head to clear the traumatizing images from her over-taxed brain.

"Whose ship is this?" Rauno inquired, as he led Myx up the ramp.

Sievly turned around from the cockpit. "It's President Naichom's. She put up the money to ransom you two. She would have loved to help more people, but the Hathak were asking for an awful lot per prisoner. Still, having you two back will give us great insight into the mindset of our enemy. We will win this war soon!"

"They told us that the Hathak were close to being victorious," Myx explained, shifting in her chair.

"It's been pretty even so far," her foster sister replied, regaining some of her composure. The young woman's face had changed much; being a press Intern for the Tarasi President must have taught her to have a better command of her emotions. "There is much to tell you, but there will be time for that later. For now, you should rest. It'll be about an hour before we get back to Capitaras."

Myx settled in her chair. Although she had little energy, she couldn't bring herself to sleep. Being free made her too emotional. Plus the revelations about Bishing and Tieg added mysteries for her to contemplate.

And then there was Rauno's lack of enthusiasm about going home.

She put a hand on his shoulder. "What's wrong?"

"I don't know if I should tell you or not," he admitted, not looking at her.

"Rauno, please." She tried to keep her voice soft and without too much power. "I hate it when people keep secrets. You're one of the few friends I have left."

The scientist put his hands within his tunic and clutched at one of his hidden glass vials. He turned to her, his emerald eyes welling up in tears. Rauno let out a shaky breath as he explained, "Well, you have one less friend; Bishing passed away last night."

Chapter 37

Myx itched to ask Kaefh about her past. She wondered how an old Hathak spinster ended up the caregiver of the Emperor's daughter in a small Tarasi store. It was bound to be quite a story. But Sievly calmly urged Myx to get some sleep for the rest of the journey.

Rauno closed his eyes, but his sleep seemed to upset him even further. His breath became ragged and his facial features were tight with worry.

Hearing that Bishing was dead hadn't hit her right away. A part of Myx wanted to believe that it was all a trick and that he was really alive, on his way back to the Hathak Royal Palace. But she knew that it was too much to wish for. They would probably be cremating him about now. And then their little group would be down to only two.

She couldn't question Bishing anymore. Myx regretted taking off on him when she learned the truth; she should have stayed and demanded answers.

The lack of sleep caught up with her yet again. The energetic effects of the colored radiation wisps had begun to wear off as they jetted away from the Camp. Myx drifted off to a deep void of sleep.

When she awoke, she was back in her old room above Kaefh's shop. Myx was confused; surely the Tarasi government would have wanted her to be kept in a secure facility. She turned to see Sievly reading some official-looking documents. Her foster sister put the papers down and moved closer.

The sky outside her window was dark purple at the setting of Star Lyrwen. Smears of soft orange and pink on the horizon changed hues as wisps altered the color of the clouds.

"Hmm. What time is it?" Myx asked, painfully easing herself to a sitting position.

"Dinner is almost ready." Sievly moved behind her and began combing through Myx's black, tangled hair. "You slept all yesterday, that evening, and the whole of today. You must have been so exhausted, sis."

Myx assessed her faculties. "I'm fine now—just a bit sore and lethargic. But that's probably from sleeping so long." She caught a whiff of Kaefh's cooking. "Can you help me downstairs?"

Kaefh scrambled about dining area, her short frame barely peaking over the tall counters. "Good! You're awake. Come sit."

"Thank you," Myx said as she her cup was filled with mint tea "Where's Rauno?"

"He's been with President Naichom all day," Sievly replied before blowing on her drink. "I heard a rumor that he proposed to her. One of her service guards threatened to lock him up for eternity if he ever asked the esteemed President such an impertinent question ever again. I think one of the valets got a video of it. I'll show it to you later."

Myx shook her head. "I've seen too many of Rauno's failed proposal." She took a sip of the soup Kaefh served her. It felt good to actually eat something steaming hot; all her meals at the Camp had been lukewarm. "So how did President Naichom know about the Camp?"

Sievly pulled her yellow curls over her shoulder and sat back in her chair. "She received an anonymous letter a couple weeks ago. It mentioned you, Bishing, Rauno, a woman named Alycee, and a man named Voumatir. Since I was your foster sister, President Naichom sent me to negotiate terms of release. I thought someone more experienced should go; I'm only fifteen after all. But Naichom insisted." She stared into her tea, a finger absently twisting in her hair. "I was saddened to hear about the deaths of Alycee and Voumatir. I didn't believe the report that you might have killed both of them."

A twinge in Sievly's green malachite eyes suggested to Myx that her foster sister really did consider it but wouldn't admit that someone dear to her was capable of murder.

"You have an appointment with President Naichom in the morning," Sievly continued, picking up a spoon. "I know that you slept all day, but I think you should get some more rest after we get some food in you."

Throughout the meal, Kaefh remained mostly silent. She only spoke up about food or making general comments on their life while Myx was gone. Kaefh appeared to not have forgiven Myx for running away from home. Near the end of dinner, Myx asked her foster mother if they could speak alone.

"What is it, my dear?" Kaefh asked, clearing the dishes. Her yellow-brown sinhalite eyes seemed to be avoiding Myx's pink tourmalines.

"I know who Bishing was." Myx waited to see how she would reply.

Kaefh turned her attention to wrapping the leftovers. "I don't want to hear about the snake that took my girl away from me."

"But I heard that you were actually the one who took his baby away." She raised an eyebrow, but Kaefh remained silent. "Do you have anything to add to that?"

"He was worried for your safety," Kaefh said, her words bitter and harsh. "Assassins kept coming for you. No matter how much security was established in the Palace, the villains always made it through. The Emperor had no choice but to send you away."

"Why didn't he come with us? Surely someone else could have ruled in his place." Clearly her throat, Myx asked, "And what about my mother?"

Shaking her head, Kaefh said, "I couldn't tell you. She came by occasionally, but just stopped visiting one year." Kaefh set out a slice of xifan cake and slid it across the table. And then she returned to her rant about Myx's father. "When Bishing eventually came back for good, I'll admit that I was a bit jealous. I raised you by myself most of your life! He thought he could swing by and take you away from me forever? I didn't like it. I tried to tell him to leave, but he never listened—that stubborn man!"

Myx ignored the cake and put her arms around Kaefh. Although she sensed that her foster mother was still hiding something, she decided that it didn't matter at the moment. All she desired was to be held by the aggressive little woman who raised her. "I'm sorry that I ran away. I shouldn't have. Then I wouldn't have been put in that dreadful Camp."

The tears began to flow from all the pent up emotions. They clung to each, sobbing into each other's shoulders.

They were interrupted by the sudden appearance of a dozen armed soldiers who came storming into their home. Their shoulder patches bore the sigil of a grey figure absorbing half a dozen multi-colored wisps of radiation.

Sievly glided down the stairs. "I guess the President is ready to see you now."

Chapter 38

Myx eyed the service guards with a new level of anxiety. She couldn't quite figure out what upset her. It wasn't that she was going to see the President of Tarasi, nor that she was surrounded by dozens of well-armed muscular men.

As their transport glided through the crowded streets of Capitaras, Myx realized what was bothering her. She craved their blood. The guards' vein pulsed with their irradiated life force. Myx was curious about what kind of abilities she could acquire from them. Disturbed by her desire, she moved to the back of the transport to find Rauno surprisingly alone.

"You're looking better," the researcher commented, seeming much more like his cheery old self. "Did you get to catch up with your family?"

"Yes, I did." She nodded and secured herself to the seat next to him. "I got a couple of answers, but I still have more questions to ask. There will be time later, though." Myx pushed down all the uncomfortable feelings and redirected the conversation towards him. "What about you? Did you get a chance to see your loved ones?"

Rauno shook his head, his emerald eyes staring out the window and the violet sunset of Star Lyrwen. "I don't have any loved ones."

"I'm sorry to hear that." Myx reasoned that was why Rauno was at the President's Estate the previous day, allowing him the opportunity to propose to Naichom. "I'm sure you'll find your special lady to cherish someday. In the meantime, I'll keep you company."

"Yes, I've enjoyed all the 'conversations' that we've had," Rauno replied, sounding stiff and cryptic. He winked at her and continued, "I had some lovely 'conversations' in a morgue last night with a couple of very helpful citizens. When we have some free time, I'd like to tell you what we 'conversed' about. Would you like to have a 'conversation' with me like that?"

Myx glared at him, not sure what he talking about. What was he hinting at? And then it hit her. "Like the ones we had with Alycee?"

"Yes, just like those." Rauno lowered his voice. "The morgue is so fascinating. I've been learning what happens with people's remains—not just cremation. I know you had a fascination with it when you worked in the Infirmary with Dolra. Maybe the Tarasi will let you train to work in the medical field?"

From what he was saying, Myx determined that he was actually talking about acquiring the remains of corpses to continue their experiments.

"That'd be great," Myx replied, hoping that she and Rauno didn't sound suspicious.

They sat in silence the rest of the trip to the President's Estate. Myx had never been to that part of Capitaras. Everything was clean, bright, and sparkling despite the late hour. She wished she had known that she'd be going to see the President; then she could have made herself look a little more presentable when she awoke.

Sievly joined them at the back of the transport as it touched down at the Estate. "Sadly, President Naichom is tending to an emergency this evening. But some of her most trusted advisors are waiting to debrief what happened to you at the Camp. Please follow me."

She polished her green Intern Charm as she led them through the pristine halls of the President's Estate. Thick currents of radiation wisps floated about the wide rooms and vaulted ceilings. Despite the broad bans of colored energy, the view wasn't obscured. Myx took in the luxurious decorations that rivaled the grandeur of the Hathak Emperor's Palace.

Occasionally, Sievly would inform Myx and Rauno of some obscure history fact or anecdote about when the planet was colonized, but the pair had little enjoyment in the explanations.

Eventually, the group was escorted below ground level to the basement. An attendant handed Myx and Rauno goblets with a blue, sweet-smelling liquid.

Hesitantly, Myx and Rauno drank their glasses.

"It will relax you," Sievly explained with her earnest smile. "Then you'll be alert and be able to more easily access memories that might be repressed due to trauma."

Men and women in lab coats rushed about, typing information into various screens and consoles. The attendant took back the goblets and motioned for them to sit in the plush lounge chairs at the middle of the room.

"What's going on?" Myx asked, feeling even more anxious than she had in the ride over.

"They have a way of mapping visual and auditory memories," Sievly explained, putting a comforting hand on her shoulder. "I don't understand the science of it, but they are going to take you back through all your experiences at the Camp. It will give our analysts a more complete picture of what happened to you. We are very sorry to put you through this; take comfort in knowing that it'll help us better know our enemy. Please remain as calm as you can."

"You want me to relive all the horrors I suffered? That's just—"

Rauno interrupted Myx. "If it will help get back at the Hathak, I'll gladly undergo this trial."

Sievly smiled at him. "Thank you for your cooperation. The operators will speed through most of it, sending sections of the recording to psychologists for analysis. The military would simply like to focus on the main events. So there will be a bit of fast-forwarding involved. We believe we can get through a whole week in one night—a total of two or three days to get through your whole month." She paused and smiled at them before adding, "Then you'll be free to pursue your own passions."

Myx nodded, although she was still reluctant to have the government poke around her head. She didn't like the idea of the Tarasi using Rauno's discoveries to make super soldiers from the corpses of those that have already passed.

Scientists placed thin rings around Myx's and Rauno's heads. The translucent crowns glowed a soft green.

Everyone turned their attentions to the two screens at the front of the basement. Someone behind Myx said that they were going to the date of recruitment. On the screens were projected the recruitment center—one from Myx's perspective and one from Rauno's.

The scenes zoomed forward and they were in the training center. Apparently that wasn't interesting enough for the military because they jumped forward yet again, only stopping briefly to save the section of the Hathak spacecraft firing on them' the Tarasi chattered about studying the enemy's movements for tactical purposes.

She wanted to ask if she could just sleep through it, but she knew they'd say no. Otherwise, they wouldn't have given her the liquid that was going to make them more alert. Myx tried not to pay too close attention to her own screen. Instead, she watched Rauno's. He hit on the Camp Handlers that approached him. None seemed to think he was humorous, so they moved on to other prisoners.

There was sick feeling in her stomach every time she saw Voumatir talk to Alycee. She had originally thought that it was cute how much he seemed to care for her.

But it had all been an act to get close to her to kill Alycee. The alien had been lying with every breath as he waited for an opportunity to earn his bounty. Seeing his fake devotion only strengthened Myx's resolve to take on the Hathak and get justice for her friend's death.

Chapter 39

After hours of reviewing Myx's and Rauno's raw memories, the scientist let them leave the President's Estate. Myx was relieved that they hadn't yet seen Rauno's experiments. It left time for the two of them to test a few more theories before the Tarasi took them away to be studied like lab animals.

Rauno had hinted earlier that he prepared a few more samples. If they could get some alone time, Myx could treat herself with the compounds.

At the Estate hangar, Sievly said, "The transport will take you wherever you would like. As an Intern of President Naichom's Inner Circle, I'm recommending more rest. But you slept so long and you probably aren't tired." She handed Myx a small pouch of coins. "As your sister, I'm telling you to go relax in a Radiation Spring for a couple hours; you could use a bit of pampering." Sievly embraced her and she left.

"That's perfect," Rauno said, getting into the transport. When settled in his seat, he pulled out several different vials of varying grey colors from the lining of his jacket. "While we're at the Spring, rub these in. Of course, the effects might be more potent if you ingest them."

Myx was horrified. "I'm not going to eat dead people!" she hissed, reluctantly taking the vials. "Are you trying to turn me into a cannibal?"

He shrugged, smoothing his ginger hair. "When you think about it, you kind of already are. You've ingested and absorbed the life force of another person, as well as partially digesting the memories of several others."

She didn't want to admit it, but he was right. There was no other word to describe what she had done other than cannibalism. Myx shook her head to displace the awful images.

At the nearest Radiation Spring, they parted ways to the different gender parts of the spa. Myx found a secluded area and rubbed one of the pastes into her legs. She had become quite experienced in dealing with the sudden memory flashes. From what she could tell, the ashes' owner was excellent at puzzles. The events ended quickly, however; most likely the life of a little boy who had lived only a few short years.

The next paste that she massaged into her arms had many memories attached as it; she skipped through the lovely life of a woman who worked part time as a clerk from a small business while also raising a family of six children. She died peacefully in her sleep at an old age.

There was one vial left. She rubbed this into her chest and abdomen, hoping that this corpse had some useful skills for taking on the Hathak. Radiation flowed through her and she saw flashes of Alycee.

It didn't make sense. Was Rauno trying to strengthen her connection to their deceased friend? No, that wasn't it. If it was Alycee's memories, then she'd see through her eyes. This person saw a lot of her. But many of the memories were not of actual interaction with Alycee; they were from far away, as though they were watching from a distance.

Myx blinked and she was on a street, tucked at the edge of an alley. A transport flew down the road and she walked directly in front it. There wasn't any pain as her legs were hit. Her eyes closed, but she was still conscious as she heard the voices of her friends.

She fast forwarded through the memories and she was in front of a hospital, looking at a scowling Alycee. Another jump ahead and Myx was in a taxi, following Alycee's transport. Again, she pushed ahead through the flashes and she was in the recruitment center, signing up for the military as Voumatir. Myx tried to break through the images, but she couldn't get back to her own mind and body.

At the training center in orbit around the planet, Voumatir placed a call. "Yeah, she's here. Come get us." He hung up and headed over to bother Alycee.

There were a couple weeks of quick memories at the Camp. She scrolled through them, not wanting to see Voumatir pretend to like Alycee. Mixed in were romantic liaisons with his Handler, Heikah. Watching the alien she murdered make love to the superficial Hathak woman made Myx sick to her stomach. Myx skipped through those, still feeling traumatized from viewing Rauno's and Dolra's intimate moments.

Voumatir spent a bit of time working in the Warden's office during that time as well, even though he had said that he was assignment to the farm. Parnuss let Voumatir do simple tasks and didn't seem to mind if he slacked off a bit.

On the day of the attack on the Labor Camp, the staff, guards, and Handlers barricaded themselves in the Warden's office and Voumatir took off to the battle, dressed head to toe in his masked assassin gear. He didn't engage in battle; he simply watched Alycee and took notes on how she fought.

Myx flashed through his killing of Alycee and being killed by Myx since she had been there on that occasion. Bits and pieces caught her attention and she was amazed at how quickly and gracefully she moved as the wisps transferred some of Alycee's life force to her.

As Voumatir's neck was snapped, the memories ended.

Dipping into the Spring's water, Myx washed off the residual paste. She splashed her face to clear the tears. Leaving the bathing area, she patted herself dry and dressed.

Myx carefully planned her next words to say to Rauno; she didn't appreciate being given Voumatir's remains that way. When she saw him, all the diligently chosen sentences left her brain and all that was left was her rage.

"How could you do that to me? What possessed you to give me the life force of Alycee's murder? It's like he's always going to be inside my head—a part of me until I die."

"I thought it would help give you closure about Alycee's death," Rauno said calmly, rubbing an herbal lotion into his skin. "Besides, now you have the abilities of two assassins. We have a much better chance of exacting justice on the Hathak mongrels that enslaved us. Doesn't that make you at least somewhat happy, Myx?"

He was right. As good of a fighter as Alycee was, it wouldn't be enough to help her do what needed to be done. Now she could use Voumatir's knowledge, too.

"Fine. I guess that was a good move on your part." Even though she wasn't happy about her situation, she accepted it. She tied her long black hair into a braid as she moved to the Spring exit. Through the glass walls, she spied their chauffer transport on the street outside. "But what about the little boy and the old lady? How are they going to help?"

Rauno continued messing with the vials sewn into his jacket lining. "I honestly didn't know about the others, Myx. I just nabbed a handful of ashes from a couple of newly cremated corpses."

Myx suddenly had an idea. It was creepy—not to mention illegal. However, she was sure that Rauno wouldn't mind. "What do you think about a late-night stroll through a graveyard?"

Chapter 40

Mud trailed everywhere in Myx's room, running from the window to the closet to the bed. Cursing softly, Myx rushed about, mopping up the wet dirt with clean sheets from her linen cupboard before her family came up to get her for breakfast. She barely finished her task as she heard soft creaks in the wooden landing outside her door. After wrapping her filthy shoes in the soiled sheets, Myx tossed the bundle onto the balcony just as Sievly came bursting in.

"You were out fairly late," her foster sister commented, pulling Myx onto the bed. She picked up a brush and began pulling Myx's black hair into a pair of tails. "Were you with Rauno all night?"

"We were resting at a Radiation Spring," Myx replied, blinking her sparkling pink irises. She ignored the fact that she now hated hair tails and added, "Thank you for the coins."

Downstairs, Rauno was being berated by Kaefh. "What a disgusting video! I couldn't believe someone could be so crude to someone as enchanting as President Naichom. May you spend eternity alone and without love!" Her mood shifted to a more pleasant tone as she welcomed her daughters and served them breakfast.

After their hot meal, Myx and Rauno were picked up promptly by the President's security force. Sievly joined them once again, although Myx couldn't understand why her foster sister was there; she was simply a Media Intern.

Back at the basement of the President's Estate, scientists connected them with their green head-rings and sat back to watch the "show."

From what Myx could tell, Rauno didn't seem to have it as bad at the Camp as she did. Sure, he almost died during several of his escape attempts and in the mass assassination attack, but that was the extent of his woes. He never sustained the kind of beatings that Myx did at Gotasun's and Frezul's hands. Rauno even had cushy jobs like delivering packages to various parts of the Camp or preparing meals. It wasn't fair that she was basically tortured while others skated by with hardly any humiliation or pain.

Rauno's face turned red as they came across memories of him and the red-eyed nurse wrapped in a passionate embrace. The scientists skipped forward, but Myx saw them make copies of the footage out of the corner of her eye.

Every time Bishing appeared on the screens, Myx took calming breaths to soothe herself. She sipped from a goblet of the attention-inducing liquid to clear her mind. The pain of losing another dear friend was beginning to set in. But she hated that she was mourning the death of the man who was secretly her father.

There were too many questions she desired to ask. Confusion and hurt muddled her thoughts on top of the pain from re-experiencing the trauma of the Camp. Myx bit her lip to bring herself out of her anxiety and instead focused on Alycee's life force stirring inside her.

It was a long morning of re-experiencing the second week of memories. The scientists paused at midday and they were brought a late lunch. Myx and Rauno ate while still connected to the machines. They sipped more of the blue beverage that kept them alert; it also opened and relaxed their minds to allow any repressed memories flow fluidly.

"Are we continuing on?" Myx asked, still shaken from re-experiencing week two at the Camp. "I don't know if I can handle any more today."

An attendant adjusted the ring around her head. "There's plenty of time today to go through another week. We'll be moving on shortly." He awkwardly patted her shoulder as though to comfort her before he cleared her lunch dishes.

Rauno fidgeted in his seat, looking uncomfortable. "I'd like to end for today, too."

The Tarasi scientists weren't going to let them stop yet. Myx understood why Rauno was nervous; they were coming upon Alycee's death and their experimentation with her ashes. It appeared that he was also worried about their government learning their secret—just as he had been about the Hathak discovering it.

Frustrated, Myx ripped the glowing band off her head and stormed out of the room. The guards didn't stop her, but she heard someone's heeled shoes following after her. Myx ascended the staircase and made it to the ground floor before someone grabbed her arm.

"I know this is difficult," Sievly said, turning Myx towards her. "But we really need to see what is in your head. Don't you want to get back at the Hathak?"

Myx looked away, not wanting to meet the pleading, malachite gaze of her foster sister. "I do, but it's—" She groaned as she attempted to come up with a good excuse. "It's painful and I thought I had put it all behind me when you and Kaefh brought me home. Can't I just get on with my life, Sievly?"

She shook her head. "Myx, this is really important. We can't help your friends back at the Camp without you."

Sievly always knew the right words to say to someone. If Rauno's discoveries could help the Tarasi win the war. There was still the morality of their research to consider, but Myx was less inclined to worry about that if it could help rescue Tieg and the other prisoners. Perhaps she could get a bit of justice for herself by demanding to get to deal about Gotasun in exchange for her cooperation.

"I have a condition," Myx said, her voice soft. "I want freedom to do what I want with my tormentor."

"I believe that's something I can arrange," Sievly assured her.

When they descended into the basement, documents were drawn up.

Rauno's interest was pique. "Do I get to make a demand?" He whispered something to Sievly that Myx couldn't quite hear.

With their demands recorded and settled, the former captives returned to their plush seats, sipped from the goblets of blue energy juice, and let the scientists reattach the glowing green bands.

"This way, I get to see how the radiation interacts with the pastes," Rauno said, leaning back on his couch. "Don't worry; the Tarasi military will use our research wisely."

Myx wasn't a hundred percent sure about that, but it was now out of her hands. She mimicked his peaceful slump and tried to relax as she watched Alycee's throat be slit by the masked assassin she now knew was Voumatir.

The scientists, of course, became more interested in the screen as Myx fought off the intruder. They mumbled together in little clumps during the battle. Men and women stared at her, looking confused, scared, and awed. When the skirmish was over, they made a copy of the memory and sent it away for military researchers to review it.

"I didn't know that you could fight like that," Sievly gasped, leaning over her shoulder. "What happened?"

Myx nodded at the screen. "Keep watching."

Alycee's funeral was skipped over and sent away for analysis as well. Myx was grateful for that. After the conversation about the interaction of the blood and radiation, Sievly excused herself and left the basement. The scientists continued re-experiencing the memories of Myx's and Rauno's third week at the Camp.

Some scientists commented on how beautiful her painting was when she was finally released from her solitary confinement.

None seemed to care about the abuse Myx had gone through at Gotasun's interrogation the following days. However, there were whispered sympathies as they watched Frezul's form of punishment and the painful recovery that Myx went through the following day.

Explaining Voumatir's death was going to be tricky. At least the scientists were going to wait until the following day to go over the final week. Myx and Rauno had time to prepare what they were going to say. And surely the analysts would have gone over the memories of Alycee's funeral by then; they have eager questions for her. The next day was going to be even more emotionally daunting than this one.

The scientists took off the head-bands and began packing up for the night. Several left right away, but some stayed late to continue their work.

Myx and Rauno waited patiently for Sievly to return. She came down the stairs shortly, followed by a familiar-looking lady with long dark hair and flowing black dress.

The women were accompanied by a dozen armed guards. Baring the uniform patches of the Estate's emblem, the towering sentries circled the basement in synchronized steps and stood at attention.

Sievly gestured to the beautiful woman. "Myx, Rauno, may I present President Naichom?"

Chapter 41

When Rauno stepped forward, a pair of guards did as well, raising their weapons in warning.

"Madame President, you're looking radiant as always." Rauno didn't seem at all bothered by the presence of the armed soldiers. He continued closing the space between him and Naichom. "I must be in a museum, for you truly are a piece of art."

The dark haired woman cocked a smile at his persistence. "You already used that line on me yesterday, dear Mr. Rauno. Perhaps your charm is starting to slip?"

"I am deeply humbled by your sharp memory. May I say that—" Rauno pressed his lips together tight as Naichom raised a hand at him. He bowed deeply in respect for several moments before stepping behind Myx.

"This war takes up so much of my time. I apologize for not seeing you sooner." President Naichom gave the impression of being the kindest woman on the planet while also exuding a presence of strength and dignity. She smiled, her warm yellow garnet eyes beaming as she extended her hand. "It's a pleasure to finally meet you."

Myx accepted Naichom's gesture. "Don't worry about it, Madam President. I understand that your time is often not your own."

Naichom turned to the other rescued prisoner. "Mr. Rauno, my researchers have discovered some interesting information from your memories. I'd like to discuss them further with you. Would you and your protégé be so kind as to join me for dinner?" She smiled warmly at Myx. "I hope you haven't you made other plans."

"I'm sure my foster mother will understand why I won't be home right away." Myx dipped her head in respect.

One of the guards raised a fist and the others changed formation.

Naichom waved for her guests to follow. She turned and headed up the wide, shallow steps.

At the ground floor, Sievly hugged Myx and whispered, "Good luck, sister."

A squad of guards stepped onto the end of a moving stair well, venturing further up the President's Estate. Naichom glided up the mechanism, her gaze fixed forward. Myx took Rauno's hand and tugged him along; she remembered he had a slight fear of mechanical transports, even though he often hid it well. Together, they trudged up the steps to close the gap between them and the ruler.

Naichom nodded her head at an approaching landing, she stepped off without hesitation.

Myx supported Rauno as they awkwardly leapt off the ascending steps. Some of the guards were unable to jump off with them since the girl and scientist blocked the way. So they raised themselves over the banister and landed on the carpeted floor with a series of thick-booted thumps.

The President waved them down a grand hallway, which eventually led to a luxurious dining room. The table was already prepared for three. Covered trays of food sat around the place settings. Thick ribbons of radiation flitted about the furnishings and dishes, infusing their mysterious powers into the meal.

"My scientists have figured out how to hone the wisps to make food taste better," Naichom explained, taking a seat at the head of the table. She removed the tray covers, letting the smells further invigorate the room. "That and the fact that I have the best chef on the planet will make this the greatest meal you've ever eaten. Please, help yourself to anything that you desire."

Rauno and Myx sat at either side of her and began scooping the various dishes onto their collection of plates.

As they dined, Rauno monopolized Naichom's attention. The Tarasi President asked him questions about his research and the practical applications of it; she didn't seem at all upset that he had proposed the other day.

Myx regularly attempted to discuss possible ethical dilemmas in using the abilities of the deceased to strengthen the living. When she was ignored, she let herself be distracted by the wide wisps. Many seemed to almost be sucked down into their food as they ate. She rubbed her tired, pink tourmaline eyes as though she was sure that she was seeing things. Her curiosity was interrupted when the President addressed her.

"My dear, we can't worry about the sentiments of reality when millions of lives are in danger," Naichom explained in a hard but gentle voice. "I have a duty to protect my people and I'll do what I need to in order to keep them safe."

"With that mentality, we can validate doing anything," Myx scoffed, playing with her qiva beans.

Naichom turned to Rauno. "I've very much enjoyed our conversation, but I have something I need to discuss with Myx. Alone." She pointed at a door in the corner. "Would you please go down that hall and tell my chef that we'll be ready for dessert in ten minutes? Please do me the favor of staying in the kitchen during that time. Thank you."

"As my President commands." Rauno put down his utensils and left the banquet hall.

"Why aren't you happy?" Naichom asked, raising an eyebrow at Myx. "You're free now."

Myx pondered the question for several moments before answering. "Well, three of my friends are dead. One was killed by another. I snapped his neck in retribution. And the third turned out to be my father, who died when I because I decided to stop treating his wounds." She took a breath in an attempt to calm herself, but it had the opposite effect. "On top of that, I have the life force of two of them inside me and I've experienced select memories of the other. And I think that Rauno's experiments are too dangerous. We don't know what will happen if we continue exploring the fusion of ashes and radiation."

"Like I said earlier," the President said after a moment of hesitation, "I can't help but use everything in my power to keep my people safe. However, I'm sorry for the loss of your friends. If you aide me, we can prevent the deaths of many more."

Wisps floated through Myx and she had an idea. "Give me some of your blood."

Naichom shook her head and calmly replied, "I can't allow you access to my secrets. It would put you in danger."

"I can handle myself," she assured the Tarasi President. "I've got the memories and experiences of two highly trained assassins within me. Don't underestimate what I can and can't do. Now give me some of your blood or I'll refuse to be a part of your research."

"Even if it means that you won't get your revenge on that man? What was his name? Gotasun?" The President put a hand on Myx's—a seemingly gentle gesture.

Myx gasped, clutching at Naichom's wrist as more radiation passed through her. Since her feelings about her father were resurfacing, she saw flashes of Bish's memory of her own birth. A dark haired woman held the baby. The woman's face became clearer: a younger version of President Naichom.

"Did you have a vision? What did you see?"

She stared at the President, her grip loosening. "You're my mother?"

"I knew I wouldn't be able to hide that from you forever," Naichom sighed, pushing away from the table. Her yellow garnet eyes became distant as she continued, "Only a few people know. You'd have been killed years ago if more people had known who you were—not to mention the fact that you are the child of both the planet's leaders."

Thick ribbons of radiation shot through Myx, as though they knew that she needed the extra strength that the energy provided. But the wisps also brought on more flashes from Bishing's life.

Naichom resumed her account. "When some of the prominent men and women in the Tarasi government found out that the Hathak Emperor had a daughter, they sent countless assassins to kill you. I wasn't President yet, but I was being groomed to run for the position in couple years; the former President was preparing to retire, but not before making one last move on his enemy."

History had never been one of Myx's best subjects in school, but she had faint memories of the propaganda broadcasts for Naichom when she was a little girl.

The President took a drink of maroon wine from her goblet. "Bishing and I planned on hiding you in plain sight in Capitaras. Faking your death seemed to work as well; the assassins came less frequently, until they finally stopped altogether. I was still living in the Hathak Palace, and traveling to Tarasi frequently wasn't safe. Kaefh proved to be an excellent caregiver in our stead. So we ceased our expeditions one year, believing it was the best decision for all of us."

The radiation stimulated memories from Bish's blood transfer, images helping narrate the President's tale. Myx felt tears run down her cheeks, but she was too engrossed in the tale to bother wiping them away.

"But now my dearest love is dead," Naichom sighed, looking weak for the first time since Myx had met her. "I should have run away with him when I had the chance. The three of us could have traveled the galaxies as a whole—albeit broken—family." She put a hand on Myx's. "You're all I have left. Could you ever forgive me for abandoning you?"

Myx didn't know how to answer. That seemed like an awful lot for Naichom to ask of her. "Why didn't you raise me yourself, here in Capitaras?"

Naichom set her cutlery down with a clink against her dinner plate. She closed her eyes and took a deep breath. "As much as my dear Bishing and I loved each other, we didn't see eye-to-eye on how to raise you. So he paid Kaefh to hide you from me. To a certain extent, I can't help but agree with his decision."

All her life, Myx had wished to know her parents. She convinced herself that she would love her natural mother and father no matter what they had done—just so long as she had a chance to finally meet them. Well, she hadn't been true to her promise when she learned who Bishing really was. But Myx was determined to be forgiving of Naichom in order for the opportunity to get to know her biological mother.

"I want to start over," Myx whispered, twirling pieces of shredded vegetables with her fork. "However, a mutual trust needs to be built."

Naichom nodded. "Yes, I agree. There is much to tell you. Would you be acceptable if you came to stay at my Estate? Maybe we can take a vacation when the war is over? What do you think about that?"

"I'd like that. But first I need to spend a couple days with Kaefh and Sievly. My priority is to rebuild my relationship with them."

The President was about to answer when the windows shattered.

Armored figures came crashing through the splintering glass, aiming firearms at the women.

Myx tightened her grasp on her fork, spun, and stabbed one of the attackers in the back of the knee joint. She blocked another soldier's movement and used their firearm to shoot another in the shoulder. Several were injured in those first few moments, but there were plenty to take the place of the wounded.

All the while, Naichom urgently fingered the broadcast display over the dining table. The President raised the alarm, signaling for her troops to deploy to the banquet hall. With that task done, she spun and fought off the nearby assailants.

Despite the number of arriving Tarasi guards, they were still out-numbered 3-to-1 by the Hathak. They swarmed the space, separating Myx from Naichom.

Still, the President was able to hold her own in battle. Being unarmed didn't seem to unnerve her. She engaged in hand-to-weapon combat without even the slightest hint of fear in her yellow garnet eyes. With each skirmish, she successfully disarmed her opponent before shooting them with their own rifle.

Myx kept close to the dining table, where she had access to the polished cutlery. After much trial and error, she figured out the weak spots in the Hathak soldiers' armor to plunge whatever forks and spoons she could get her hands on.

Although it would have been more effective to keep taking guns from the attackers, Myx still wasn't confident in the use of ranged weapons. She experienced flashes of the assassin attack on the Camp and how she had nearly shot Alycee; so she only took firearms from the Hathak as a last resort when she couldn't get into a good angle to stab with a dinner knife.

More enemies burst through the shattered windows. Tarasi soldiers fell unconscious in larger quantities than their ranks could refill. Soon, everywhere Myx looked was nothing but the Hathak. But she fought on.

And then she realized that none were approaching her any longer. The Hathak stood several feet away, making an empty ring around Myx. She hefted herself onto the dining room table to get a better view of the hall. Through the crowd of soldiers, she could see Naichom surrounded similarly. Four of the Hathak approached her, a sizzling stun baton in each of their hands. The President slumped to tiled floor as she was shot with the paralyzing energy.

Myx flung herself off the table, desperate to save her sole-surviving parent. But a pair of armored soldiers pinned her arms behind her back. Tears stun her face as she called out her mother's name. There was a searing red heat on her shoulder before her vision went black.

Chapter 42

"I've already told you what happened!" Myx snarled, pushing away from the table. She stomped about the room, rubbing her shoulder where she had been stunned. "We should be figuring out how to get President Naichom back. Why are we wasting time?" Heat rose in her cheeks as her pulse raced. "Stop interrogating me!"

Service guards raised their weapons. The man who was questioning her raised a hand and they relaxed.

"We will, miss," the stern-faced man assured her, his voice monotone. He added a note to those he had already scribbled during her interrogation. "I just need to be sure that I have all the information before I proceed."

The man repeated everything he had written, making marks in a different colored ink as Myx confirmed the details of the attack yet again.

After the debriefing, Myx stormed out of the President's Estate with Rauno. They had the transport drop them off at the nearest bazaar, promising to return in a couple hours. Instead of shopping like they had made it seem, they made their way to where they had stashed Alycee's vehicle before signing up for the war.

Being in this transport brought a flood of memories to her consciousness. Myx used Alycee's life force to learn how to operate the vehicle. She casually drove through the streets of Capitaras, growing accustomed to controls.

Once they were confident that they hadn't been followed by the service guard, Rauno used the onboard map to locate the nearest morgue.

"If the Tarasi want to waste time asking questions, we will have to act." Myx approached a young woman at the morgue reception desk. She held up an ID she had pocketed from an Estate officer—a little trick she picked up from Voumatir's life force. "I'm here on behalf of President Naichom. I need access to your lab. Please show me and my assistant to the bodies. Your presence will not be necessary."

The woman batted her long lashes as she examined the badge. She smiled and motioned at a pair of wide, swinging doors.

Hours blurred past as Myx and Rauno searched through the ashes of those that had recently been cremated.

Myx looked up each person's bio to determine who had skills that she currently lacked.

All the while, Rauno cremated small bits of flesh they had acquired during their night in the graveyard. He wasn't entirely sure how much DNA was needed, so this experiment would help him better understand the amount of flesh necessary to transfer the life forces. When he finished burning the stolen corpse tissues, Rauno placed various lab equipment in the incinerator to make fake ashes to refill the urns they had emptied.

On several occasions, Myx spied the scientist refilling the various vials stitched into his jacket lining. Myx had been reflecting on Rauno's behavior the past two days, trying to determine the reason why he felt the need to keep dozens of chemicals on his person at all times. It was easy just to dismiss him as crazy, but she sensed there was a deeper meaning.

As she watched him, she noticed the man ease slightly with each new acquisition. He wouldn't have admitted it, but Myx knew that Rauno became noticeably anxious when the Tarasi researchers made him re-experience his love-making with Dolra. He would shake it off before then hitting on one of the female attendants. And yet he still hadn't returned to his normal, unrelenting self. However, it seemed that having his vials full of various concoctions was his coping mechanism for dealing with stress.

When she was done making her selections, Myx handed the ashes over to Rauno, letting him make pastes from the remains. He stirred them together with the bits of puréed flesh he had taken while grave-robbing the previous night. Rauno seemed a little too eager to be desecrating the dead. But Myx knew it was his scientific curiosity taking over and not a morbid fascination with death.

As he worked, Myx put the ashes of cremated office supplies into the urns to cover up that some of it was missing. By midnight, they had an entire liter-sized jar of paste prepared.

"Do you think that it's a good idea to blend everything together?" Myx asked, realizing that it was a little late to be questioning the mad scientist. "It might adversely interfere with the radiation's effects."

Rauno shook his head as he bleached his work table. "Think of it like a smoothie—several parts blended together, but still keeping its essence."

"I thought I told you that I hated the cannibal analogy," Myx grimaced.

With their tasks completed, they left the morgue and strolled down the street to a Spring. Rauno flirted with the attendants while Myx sneaked the jar of ash paste into the women's bath.

In a secluded corner of the Spring, Myx applied the salves. She covered herself from head to toe in the white-grey mush, trying not to think about how she was rubbing her skin with dead people. Every time radiation passed through her, it tingled hot and cold.

Some of the deceased had random skills like juggling, pet grooming, and sewing. She also picked up a couple abilities that might come in handy someday: mechanical engineering, carpentry, map-making, and investigative skills. Myx didn't know how all that would fit into her plan, but she felt more confident in having new abilities.

Myx cleaned herself up and returned to Rauno. Still damp from their dip, they slid into Alycee's transport and headed to Kaefh's shop. It was time to make her farewells to her goodbyes to her family.

"I know you don't approve of this, but I have to go," Myx said to her foster mother.

Kaefh held her tight, the short woman's chin digging into Myx's collar bone. "The last time you left me, you were held prisoner for a month." Tears fell down the elderly woman's cheeks, moistening Myx's shirt. "How do I know that you'll come back to me and your sister? You could end up dead for all we know! What kind of parent would I be if I let my daughter face danger again?"

Myx pulled away from the embrace. "I'm not the same girl I was back then. I have no choice but to go after Naichom. Please understand that." She wasn't sure if Kaefh knew that Naichom was her biological mother, but she hopped that the foster parent could at least realize that Myx had gone through a drastic transformation.

Kaefh stared, seeming to know what Myx meant. She nodded and moved across the store. Pulling down an old box from a low shelf, Kaefh opened it and removed a scrap of paper. "If you must go, then I can at least do something to help you." She handed Myx the sheet. "It's coordinates to the Hathak Emperor's Palace. Whoever took over after Bishing left would be ruling from there."

Sievly came down the steps, a heavy bundle of bags balancing precariously in the fifteen-year-old's arms. "I've packed some things for you—provisions, clothes, tools, and a few other necessities." She dropped them unceremoniously before pulling Myx into an embrace. "Stay safe."

Rauno hefted the luggage over his shoulders. He gave the family a few moments of privacy as he loaded the transport.

"Go through the servant's quarters," Kaefh explained, pointing at the paper. "These are the instructions that I got from Bishing before taking you away from the Palace. Just back-track my steps and you'll make it to the Emperor's traditional quarters."

Myx nodded and tucked the scrap into her pack. She gave the women one last hug before leaving the store.

After settling into Alycee's vehicle, she and Rauno began their journey out of Capitaras.

"Are you sure this is the best plan?" the scientist asked, tentatively adjusting the controls. There was something else in his voice that suggested that he was manipulating her for something. "You and me against the entire Hathak Imperial Guard? Although I'm completely behind you, I can't help but wonder if we should get reinforcements."

"What do you mean?" Myx replied, already knowing what he was going to say; she had already been contemplating the same thing, except she was unsure if it was the best plan.

Rauno shook his head. "I keep thinking about everyone back at the Camp. We are free and clear now, but all our friends are still suffering. I'd like to do something about it. Besides, it might be a nice practice run for your new abilities. I know it's a crazy idea; I thought I'd suggest it anyways since you're use to my insanity."

She thought quietly for several moments as she input the coordinates into the map. Myx wanted to help as well, but it was an unnecessary stop. Every moment Naichom was in the Hathak's hands was a moment that her mother was in terrible danger.

However, Rauno had a point about needing more man-power. They could certainly use help. And all the prisoners would be sufficiently motivated to take down the Hathak. On top of that, she could finally get retribution on Gotasun for everything he did to her. It was a tempting suggestion.

In the end, she replied, "What kind of rescue plan did you have in mind?"

Chapter 43

Rauno reached over Myx's shoulder, setting the transport's autopilot mode. "I told Sievly what we've been planning." He rummaged through their pile of luggage and tossed Myx a bulky sack. "She seemed to think it was a good idea since she packed us our Camp clothes."

"Then shoo so I can change." Myx removed her old rags. She had hoped to never wear them again. But since it was for a good cause, she didn't mind.

They parked the transport in the river outside the Camp mines. Myx had found a remote amongst the drawers that could control the vehicle from a limited distance; she used it to send the transport below the water's churning surface.

Taking a deep breath, Myx led Rauno through the twisting tunnels of the mines.

Wisps twirled through her, unleashing a barrage of memories. Myx thought of her deceased companions and all the lies they told her. Barely comprehending what she was doing, she turned on Rauno and pulled him into a hammerlock. The two of them struggled in the brightly-colored, radiation-infused dust. It didn't take long to get the spindly man pinned on the ground.

"What are you doing, Myx?" Rauno groaned as Myx put more pressure on his shoulder joint. "Get off me, please. We need to save our friends!"

"I've been lied to by every friend I've met this year. Bish stole me from my mother. Alycee was sent to kill me when I was a child. And Voumatir—well, his list of imperfections just keeps expanding." Myx maneuvered Rauno so that she could sit on his chest and look into his quivering emerald green eyes. "I want to know what your secret is."

"You know me. I'm an open book; I don't have the capacity to lie."

Myx experienced a residual flash of a closing radiation chamber door. Rauno pulled Dolra onto his lap and kissed her. The blood transfer from those two wasn't complete, but she saw bits and pieces of their amorous activities. In the past, she resisted watching it. But now Myx let herself feel their affection and tenderness for each other. And then she understood that the nurse and scientist were truly in love. She needed to hear Rauno admit it.

"Why did you really want to come back here?" Myx asked him, standing to her feet.

Rauno massaged his upper arm, still lying in a pile of rainbow dust. "You never told me if you were able to try the blood of Tieg, Dolra, and myself. I didn't want to bring it up until you were ready to discuss what you may or may not have seen. Yes, I have selfish reasons for coming back." He sat up and met her gaze. "I need to save my love; Dolra is just as much a prisoner here as we were."

"What? No, Rauno. You're confused." Myx ran a hand through her loose, pitch black hair as she paced the width of the tunnel. "Dolra has brainwashed you! I wouldn't be surprised if she was secretly your Handler all along. What other lies has she filled your head with?"

"Myx, not all the Camp staff are Hathak." Rauno got to his feet and moved in front of her. "Think about how miserable Dolra was. If she was here of her own free will, you'd think she'd be a bit cheerier. Yes, she was afforded more freedoms than the rest of the Tarasi prisoners. However, Dolra and the other Tarasi staff were secretly part of a psychological experiment. I don't understand all the ins and outs of it, but essentially the Hathak were trying to figure out how to break the bonds of patriotism."

Every time Myx thought she understood something about the world, she was reminded of just how ignorant she really was. She closed her pink tourmaline eyes and tried to shut out the rage that began welling up inside her.

"No, don't calm yourself, Myx." Rauno took her hands in his. "Use that anger as fuel. We have a long battle ahead of us and I need you to be prepared."

"Just to be clear, you're assuring me that this isn't a trap set to lure me back to imprisonment?" Myx looked the scientists up and down to see if he displayed any signs of deceit—yet another ability she had gained from Voumatir. But the man appeared to be in earnest. "Alright, then. I'm ready to begin. Let's go rescue your nightingale."

The mine tunnels twisted and turned in a maze. It took a bit of effort to navigate without venturing in circles. But eventually, Myx saw a soft white glow ahead. Tieg's opal eyes illuminated the cave as he and other prisoners gathered radiation-infused geodes.

"What are you doing here?" Tieg asked, not looking up from his work. "I thought they released you two."

Myx snuck behind a barrel of digging tools and whispered, "They did. But we decided that we needed to free everyone else, too. Having liberty isn't as fun when your friends are still slaves. Rauno and I have a plan, but we need a distraction."

The scientist removed a jar of matches from his jacket and tossed it at Tieg. "Do you think you can cause some trouble with those?"

Tieg discreetly picked the jar up with the minerals. "Yeah, I can put on a bit of a show for you."

Myx snuck forward, crouching behind wheel barrels as the prisoners hefted the altered rocks. When the guards weren't watching, she and Rauno moved to the next one over. And then they reached a point where it wouldn't make sense to push the carts since the rocks were meant to be dumped down a massive hole in the ground. The prisoners looked to Myx for an idea, but she needed a moment to think.

"The barrel isn't going to deposit itself," the overseer scolded. His voice grew louder as he approached. "What are you waiting for?" The man was nearly to them when there was an echoing boom through the mines.

Rauno peaked around his barrel. "Good ol' Tieg. That's exactly what I would have done."

A case of tools billowed with smoke as flames ate up the wood handles of the axes and shovels. Radiation passed through the explosion's remains, giving off glittering flares of color. Guards rushed toward the fire, leaving the mine entrance unattended. Myx and Rauno slipped out unnoticed in the commotion.

"We should go to the Infirmary first," Rauno said, keeping to the shadows of the Main Street. "Dolra has some sedatives that we can use on the Handlers."

Myx nodded. She still didn't care for the nurse, despite Rauno's comment that she was a also held against her will. But taking Dolra with them meant that Myx would eventually get a chance to interrogate the woman and finally know the truth.

The Infirmary was mostly empty. Apparently things had quieted down a bit since Myx and Rauno left the Camp.

Dolra was busy mixing chemicals together. A stark white apron covered the front of her stocky frame. Her red jasper eyes concentrated on adding the precise ingredients to make her healing ointment. She didn't notice them enter.

Rauno crept up to her, raising his arms as though he was going to tackle Dolra. As he reached the nurse, he grabbed her shoulders, spun her around, and planted a kiss on her lips.

"You stupid, arrogant man! You think you can leave me and just come back here as though nothing happened?" Dolra smacked him across the chest before pulling him in for another kiss.

"I'm sorry, nightingale," Rauno whispered, caressing her face. "I tried to stay, but the Warden said that the Tarasi specifically wanted me to be released."

Myx averted her eyes. "Can you leave your reunion for later? We're sort of in a hurry."

"Sorry." Rauno wrapped his arms around the nurse's wide waist. "I can't help but love this adorable creature. I found my woman in the most unlikely place."

Dolra tugged on his shirt. "I can't believe you made me love you, imbecile."

"We don't have time for this," Myx scoffed. She headed to the medicine cabinet and found the sedatives. "Help her gather what she needs."

Rauno moved his hands to Dolra's wrists. "My love, will you escape with us? We're planning on breaking out as many prisoners as we can. I want you to come with me so we can start a new life in Tarasi."

Dolra huffed, her red jasper eyes softening. "And what will I do in Tarasi? The other prisoners will insist that I'm Hathak and I'll be put in jail for the rest of my miserable life."

"I promise I won't let that happen. We will find evidence that proves you were a captive here." Rauno kissed her again. "Meet us at the mines in one hour. Bring as many prisoners as you can. Get them to help you bring the wounded. Do you think that you can do that for me?"

The nurse nodded and began gathering medical supplies to take with her.

Myx and Rauno left the Infirmary and headed to the Kitchen. Based on the time, the Handlers should be eating soon. They didn't have much time to spike the lunch.

But since it was nearly meal time, the Main Street was full of guards. So they made a pit stop and darted into the Laundry. They were met with stunned glances from half a dozen prisoners.

"Who's ready to be free?" Myx said with a nervous smile.

She hadn't really thought about how she was going to break the news to the Tarasi captives. But that seemed to get their attention. They listened intently as Myx explained what was happening. One of the older prisoners instructed them to hide in laundry baskets.

It was a quick ride to the Kitchens as they were pushed down the Main Street. Any guards who stopped them were told that they were simply collecting dirty towels.

The Kitchens were empty save for a couple prisoners.

Myx repeated their plan, getting tired of saying the same thing over and over. She gave the cooks some of the sedatives and said, "Spike the soup and drinks with these. It'll take some time for them to kick in. But when everyone is unconscious, make your way to the mine tunnels."

Their task was done shortly. The prisoners took the food away to be served. Left alone in the kitchen, Myx and Rauno weren't sure what their next plan was.

Myx wracked her full brain for ideas. "We'll need to get some keys for the weapon lockers in order to defend ourselves from any Hathak staff that doesn't eat lunch quite yet. That way we'll also be armed when we infiltrate the Emperor's Palace."

Rauno agreed. He stuffed a couple knives from the kitchen into a pillow case as well. "We should take every weapon we can get our hands on."

She nodded and began assisting him.

As they finished filling the sack, the door opened.

"I thought that we released you two," Heikah scowled, rage welling in her orange amber eyes.

It took Myx a moment to realize why that Handler would hate her so much. She had very little interaction with the flighty, incompetent woman. Myx then remembered about Heikah's relationship with Voumatir when the Handler shouted, "You killed my alien!"

Chapter 44

The female Handler let out a growl as she launched herself over the counter between them.

Myx side-stepped to the left, but her back jammed into an open drawer.

Heikah seized her throat and squeezed.

Gasping, Myx reached behind her for something to use as a weapon. But Rauno had already cleared that drawer of knives and forks. So she grabbed a handful and spatulas and hurled them at her attacker.

The maneuver distracted Heikah enough for Myx to slip out of her grasp. After taking a deep breath, she charged her entire weight at the slim woman's legs. They tumbled to the ground, each reaching through strands of loose blonde and black hair as they attempted to subdue each other.

Rauno made no move to intervene. He gave them space as he continued ransacking the kitchen for dangerous implements that could be used as weapons.

As they fought, Voumatir's memories flooded Myx. She had become competent enough in working with them to also keep moving while they filled her mind. Due to the nature of her surroundings, the flashes seemed to focus mainly on interactions with Heikah. Voumatir smooth-talked the Hathak woman in a similar fashion in which he had attempted to woo Alycee. From what Myx could tell, he wasn't sincere in his love for either of the women.

In fact, Voumatir seemed rather frustrated with both Alycee and Heikah. Myx saw flashes of hundreds of easier romantic conquests over the span of his adult life. This revelation fueled Myx's hate for the alien, and her strikes became increasingly intense as she fought her opponent.

Heikah's head fell back to the floor with a thump, blood dripping from a rip in her lip. She clutched at her face, screaming, "Don't make me ugly!" over and over.

Myx ignored her pleas as she performed some well-placed strikes to the woman's abdomen. She kept herself in the right mindset to allow Alycee's and Voumatir's memories of martial art training to guide her. Clearing Heikah's arms with one hand, Myx used her other one to bash the side of the Handler's jaw.

She was about to knock the amateur Handler unconscious when Rauno stepped in between them. He stopped Myx's fist in his out-stretched hand. "That's enough. Let's just tie her up and leave."

Heikah began sobbing, rocking back and forth in the fetal position. "Please," she gasped, looking up at Myx. "Please. Take me with you. The Warden has been punishing me ever since you killed Voumatir. Parnuss says that I failed him. If I fall short once again, he's going to make me a prisoner too. I wouldn't survive here! I can assist you in escaping the Camp if you help me. Can we make that deal? Please, please, please."

Myx considered the offer. They had just talked about needing a key for the weapon lockers. However, there was something off about the Handler. "Fine. But one step out of line and I'll snap your neck just like I did with Voumatir. Now take us to the nearest weapons stash."

Nodding, Heikah stood and pulled her keys off her belt. "There's one at the guard station across the way. I know that he's going on his lunch break in a minute. When he's gone, I can put the weapons in the laundry hamper." She grabbed the basket and motioned for Myx to get in. "If I betray you, you can always jump out and stab me with a knife."

Taking a blade from Rauno, Myx got into her hamper and arranged the sheets over her head.

A couple minutes later, they were in front of the guard station.

"I hear there's cake in the break room," Heikah said in a sweet, flirty voice. "It's got chocolate frosting, dotted with fresh bilq berries. Go ahead and get a piece. I'll keep an eye on the monitors as long as you promise to bring me back some."

"What happened to your face?" the guard asked, sounding suspicious.

Heikah sniffed. "One of the psychiatric patients attacked me. I guess the test trial on her had an adverse affect, fueling her jealousy; it's not my fault everyone envies me beauty."

"So why are you telling me about the cake?"

Heikah's voice broke as she replied, "I'm still on probation and I'm not technically allowed to have any treats. So I'm forced to bribe people to get me my chocolate fix."

Someone brushed past the laundry hampers. A couple moments later, Heikah put a pair of riffles in the basket. After awhile, Myx had a quite a collection of variously designed guns in her hiding place. When Rauno's hamper was full as well, Heikah pushed them along down the Main Street.

"Where are you taking us?" Myx whispered as quietly as she could manage.

“Somewhere we can talk in person without worrying about being walked in on.” Heikah continued pushing them along. Eventually, she opened the top of the basket. “Let me help you out.”

Myx accepted her hand, stepped out, and stretched her legs. And then she realized where she was. “The Reviewery?”

“No one is signed up to use it today,” Heikah explained, locking the door behind her. “I know you don’t care for this room. However, it’s the only place we won’t be disturbed. Now, I know that I’m just along for the ride, but I think you should consider taking the Warden hostage.”

“And why should we do that?” Myx asked, not following the logic.

“He has the defense codes. I can only open the hangar; without those codes, you won’t make it more than a couple hundred yards away from the Camp before the guns blow you out of the sky.”

Rauno pursed his lips before saying, “She has a point, Myx. And we can’t get all the prisoners out on Alycee’s transport. We’ll need the Camp’s vehicles to evacuate everyone.”

“I’m still not comfortable working with a Handler,” Myx mused, looking Heikah up and down for any signs that she was lying. Thankfully, one of the life forces she had absorbed had been a detective in the Tarasi police. The woman appeared to be telling the truth.

“I already told you: I want out of here. It’s not like I can just transfer to another Camp.”

Myx sighed, throwing her hands in the air. “Alright. How do you propose we get into the Warden’s office?”

“Parnuss doesn’t mind Handlers coming in and out of his office. He likes to socialize,” Heikah explained, growing oddly chipped about something. “It won’t be suspicious that I swing by. If I bring a man and woman prisoner with me, he’ll think I’m there to ‘party.’ He’s got some drugs he likes to play with to get the prisoners do what he wants. Parnuss usually dismisses the guards before that. It’ll be a good time to turn on him and inject him with his own narcotics.”

Myx and Rauno agreed to the plan. They covered their heads to conceal their faces and took off to the Warden’s office, leaving the hamper of guns in the punishment room for the time being. However, Myx kept blades concealed under her prison clothes in case she needed to slice Heikah open for betraying them.

Heikah didn't have any trouble getting past the guards as she pushed Myx and Rauno into the office. "Hi, Warden! I brought you a couple presents." She rubbed her hands up and down Myx's and Rauno's bare arms. "Why don't we dismiss the guards and have a bit of fun?"

Parnuss nodded his head. "That'd be great. I'll be right with you."

Stepping out of the office a moment, Heikah told the guards to leave for an hour. When she returned, she pulled a gun on Myx. "You are so gullible, little one. I can't believe you fell for that." All signs of the flighty, incompetent Handler melted away in an instant, replaced by a glare of cold hatred. "No matter. I can finally avenge my lover's death. You took my Voumatir from me, so I'm going to end your life."

"This is why you never trust a Handler. As Myx raised her hands, she knocked off her head cover. "I guess you were aware that Voumatir was an assassin and was going to leave the Camp shortly after carrying out his mission? You probably wouldn't have ever seen him again."

"You don't know what you're talking about," Heikah scoffed, her haughty amber eyes looking crazed as she became riled up. "He's the one who made the deal to have all of you brought here—in order to collect the bounty on Alycee. He even promised to split the money with us. But now that he's dead and can't collect it, we don't get anything."

Parnuss raised a hand and Heikah ceased speaking. "You never knew when to stop talking, dearest sister. I'd rather you not reveal anything sensitive to these two." He turned to Myx. "It's so lovely to see you again. There is much we need to discuss. Have a seat."

Chapter 45

Myx cursed herself for not having a more well-thought-out plan. In hindsight, it was ridiculously obvious that she and Rauno never should have listened to Heikah. And yet, with the combination of nearly a dozen life forces fused with hers, the Handler had still managed to lie without showing any of the signs; there was more to the woman than Myx had originally thought.

Parnuss pulled a pile of paper documents from his desk and tossed them to Myx. "This is my proof that Alycee has been eliminated. It also includes my contract with Voumatir, explaining the Camp's involvement in the assassin's death."

A thick package fell from the folder. Myx fingered it, surprised to find it was soft. She let out an unconscious gasp as she realized it was Alycee's cut-off braid.

Ignoring the bundle, she perused the papers. It was a fairly easy task as she accessed the speed-reading skill from the elderly clerk whose life force she acquired the same day as Voumatir's. The files confirmed everything she had seen in the alien's memories and filled in all the little details she had been missing; although Myx had complete access to Voumatir's life, it was hard to find something unless she had some slight idea of what to search for.

"I went to the trouble of writing up a report about why you killed Voumatir," the Warden added as he smoothed his salt-and-pepper hair. "All I need is for you to sign it. Then you and Rauno can walk free out of here once again. Do we have a deal?"

"Any chance I can get in on the bounty deal instead?" Myx asked, meeting his gaze.

The Warden laughed, his turquoise eyes beaming in amusement. "I don't know what happened to you, but you're not the same mousy girl you had been when you arrived."

"Heikah over there has just threatened me and my friend," Myx replied, poising a pen over the signature lines. "Why would I validate the events in these documents when she has promised to kill us?"

"She's just upset," Parnuss explained with a shrug. "It makes Heikah feel better to threaten people. My sister-in-law is getting tired of hiding her true nature."

The Handler growled, "Don't talk about me as though I'm not here. For over a month I've pretended to be this simpering, incompetent little lady when I just wanted to make someone bleed. Please, Parnuss! Let me cut open my lover's killer."

"Settle down, Heikah," the Warden ordered, his voice dropping to indicate how serious he was. "I'll soon send you back to the battlefront to appease your blood lust."

Rauno was awfully quiet during the whole conversation. He seemed to be waiting for something to happen. His emerald eyes continually darted at the clock on the wall. He gave Myx a comforting smile, looking as though he knew something that she didn't.

"I deserve the chance to avenge Voumatir!" Heikah shrieked, grabbing a letter opener off the desk. "The money doesn't matter. All I want to do is put holes in her!"

She came at Myx, but faltered a moment before falling to the floor.

Rauno jumped out of his seat and held a knife to Parnuss's throat. "What are the defense codes?"

"They're in the top drawer of my desk," the Warden replied calmly.

Myx didn't understand what had happened, but she moved to back up Rauno. She opened the drawer and found the codes. When she pocketed them, Rauno put a large clear square on Parnuss's arm.

"Sedative patches," Rauno explained as the Warden slumped unconscious in his chair. "I put a small one on Heikah when she helped me out of the hamper. That one had a delayed affect since it was only a partial piece." He moved to the Handler and put a larger patch on her. "That should keep them asleep for awhile."

They quickly ransacked the Warden's office, looking for things that could be helpful to their cause. Myx found a number of firearms stuffed under Parnuss's desk and Rauno came across some knives in fake books on a shelf. Rauno took the Warden's jacket off him and held it open as Myx filled it with their new weapons. If anyone stopped them, they could just say that they were taking Parnuss's coat to be cleaned.

Myx was about to leave when Rauno stopped her.

He pulled up the broadcast screen and accessed Parnuss's private account. "Before we go, how about we take the Warden's digital files for leverage?"

"You really are a genius, huh?" Curiosity rose in Myx as she wondered what her record said. Would it explain why she was singled out amongst the prisoners for extra doses of trauma? Would it describe the reasoning behind Gotasun's verbal and physical abuse?

She itched to read it, but their tasks weren't completed yet.

As they made their way back to the Reviewery, Myx and Rauno discreetly told all the prisoners they encountered about their plan and had them make their way to the common room when they could. They ceased telling them to go to the mines since they needed more make-shift warriors to arm as they stormed the Camp hangar.

But before that could be accomplished, they needed to retrieve their laundry hampers full of weapons; it didn't take long to do so since most of the guards were unconscious from the sedation in their lunches.

Back at the common room, they distributed the guns and knives to the prisoners.

"Here's what we're going to do to," Myx said, grabbing a gun for herself; no one was going to take this one from her. "We're going to storm the hangar and take the ships. We'll load up into them and then head to the mines to collect the other prisoners."

The group of now-armed prisoners made their way to the hangar. There were occasional guards that popped up, but they were quickly dealt with.

Myx led the attack on the hangar, using her assassin skills from Alycee and Voumatir to take on a number of guards without much help from her peers. She transferred smoothly between hand to hand combat and ranged fighting as she swung the stolen stun pistols at those too far away to grapple with. Myx found it easiest to wound the guards just enough for them to back away from the fight, only to be finished off by the prisoners.

The sight of blood no longer made Myx woozy. Several of the survivors gagged at the scent of blood as is spilled and covered the hangar floor. Bile soon mixed with the red pools as prisoners lost the remains of their latest meal.

"Hurry into the ships," Myx urged as they dispatched the last of the guards. "Rauno, can you input the defense codes? We're not going to get far with the automated guns online."

He nodded, taking the paper from her.

Moving to each ship, Myx made sure that there was at least one flight-capable person that could handle flying the craft back to Capitaras. She gave instructions to the pilots for picking up the remaining prisoners at the river by the mines. Before they took off, she also explained that they were to wait for her and Rauno and not leave Camp until they gave the all-clear.

Rauno returned, looking more like his cheery self than he had in days. "We should check for other prisoners who haven't heard about the escape plan."

Myx had already planned to that, but she only nodded as she reloaded the charges of her stun pistols. She assessed the minor cuts on her arms and legs to see if they needed to be treated. Thankfully, her blood had already clotted and sealed the sliced skin.

"You're quite a pain, little mouse," a woman coughed from across the hangar.

They turned to see Frezul's petite form rise from a pile of bodies. Blood dripped down her well-pressed Handler uniform, but none of it appeared to be hers.

"I'll take that as a compliment," Myx replied, aiming a pistol at Frezul.

She didn't seem nervous. "You get one free shot."

Something felt off about the situation, but Myx pulled the trigger.

Frezul barely moved as the lasers zapped her chest. She cracked her taped knuckles and moved closer. "My pain nerves are all dead, so I can't feel anything. Now say your goodbyes to the mad scientist; these are your last moments together."

Myx tossed the stun pistols at Rauno and removed a knife from her back holster. Before she could move in to attack, another figure appeared in the doorway.

"Hello, my pet," Gotasun smirked, lowering a rifle from his shoulder. "I never thought I'd see you again."

Rauno moved closer to Myx and whispered, "We can't win this battle; we should run."

Her Handler smiled. "He's right. Frezul only has one weakness and you'll never get close enough to exploit it." Gotasun turned towards his fellow Handler and let off a shot.

A spray of bullets shattered Frezul's right hand. Blood spurt down the tatters of the white tape around her knuckles. Gotasun's rifle aimed towards the left, but the woman rolled out of the way. The piles of corpses exploded as they were needlessly filled with more holes.

The rifle clicked as the last bullets sprayed out of the muzzle.

Frezul used that moment to begin her assault. "Looks like someone has developed feelings for his plaything," she said in between jabs. Her right arm stump curled in the cloth of her uniform. Despite what she said about her pain nerves, the petite woman appeared to be in complete agony as blood spurt out of her forearm. Her words came out loud and crazed as she assaulted Gotasun's joints. "Gone soft, have you?"

He didn't appear to be as skilled a fighter as Frezul. Gotasun tried blocking, but was repeatedly too slow. It wasn't long before he slumped to the floor, no longer able to stand on his swelling knee.

Pity clawed at Myx's stomach. She sighed in frustration before going to her Handler's rescue. Despite everything that Gotasun had put her through, she felt a sense of duty to protect him. Sure, he beat her senseless once a week and emotionally abused her. But he had turned on Frezul and showed her the woman's weakness. So Myx snuck up on Frezul and sliced off her remaining hand when she pulled her arm back for a punch.

"I only saved you so I could get my revenge," Myx explained, sounding defensive as she partially lied to him.

Gotasun coughed up blood and clutched a darkening bruise on his abdomen. "I have some information that you need to know. But before I tell you, you have to promise me that you'll take me with you. With Dolra leaving, the Camp doesn't have the staff to care for all the injuries. I like my survival odds of coming with you."

Myx contemplated putting a bullet in his head right there. But she was intrigued by what he thought that she didn't already know. Plus, it would give her the opportunity to deal with Gotasun in a manner more pleasing to her desire for revenge.

"I'm going to enjoy having you as my prisoner."

Chapter 46

Grabbing a pair of restraints from an unconscious guard, Myx chained up Gotasun. “Start walking,” she ordered, jabbing a pair of fingers in a tender part of his shoulder.

“Just remember what I nice Handler I was,” Gotasun groaned through clenched teeth. “I could have been much worse, like the psychopathic Frezul that I just helped you fight off. I spoiled you in the best ways I knew how, my pet, because I’m not as vicious as some of the others.”

As they made their way through the Camp, the trio came across pockets of confused prisoners who didn’t know what was happening. Myx and Rauno armed them, which came in handy when they came across stray guards.

Back at the mining river, the ships of prisoners awaited their arrival. Tensions seemed high as Myx surveyed the scene. A select few of prisoners remained outside the vehicles, their weapons raised at the ready in case of more guards and Handlers appeared. Many seemed rather uncomfortable at taking directions from an eighteen-year-old, but they were just going to have to deal with that if they wanted to be rescued.

Dolra sat on the riverbank, her hands twisted up in rope. “You have to untie me! I’m the only one who can treat the wounded.” Red jasper eyes blazed, almost as though her rage lit them. She pointed a bound finger at the injured prisoners. “Do you want them to die of sepsis?”

“I’m sorry, but we can’t trust a Hathak,” Tieg said in a gentle voice, his white opal eyes glowing through half-closed lids.

Rauno sprinted to Dolra’s side. “My nightingale has saved dozens of you from death over the past weeks and she doesn’t deserve to be treated this way. She’s also Tarasi—the same as us. Now cut her loose, you animals!” He clutched at the restrained nurse and planted a deep kiss on her lips. “If they harmed you, I’ll repay them tenfold!”

“Can you believe these idiots?” Dolra scoffed, giving Tieg a vicious glare with her red jasper eyes. “They thought I was going to poison everyone.”

Myx nodded at Tieg and the elderly prisoner untied the knots.

“It’s alright, my love,” Rauno cooed, stroking her ruddy cheek. “You’re free now.”

“We’ll have plenty of time later for that, my imbecile.” Dolra stood and moved to the injured prisoners. “Help me get my supplies onboard.”

Those that weren’t wounded loaded the invalids into the biggest ship. As the afternoon wore on, the Hathak attempted to reclaim the hangar. But they were easily overwhelmed and taken care of. However, some of the staff held up white flags and asked to be brought with them. Myx reluctantly agreed to take them as their prisoner—at least until they could sort out who was really from their side of the planet.

Tieg scanned the walls, as though searching for something. The action confused Myx until she remembered that the elderly gentleman could sense people’s auras.

“Way to stay vigilant.” Myx waved over a dozen more Tarasi. “I want all of you to keep an eye out for any more arrivers. If they are Tarasi, catch them up on our plan. If they are Hathak defectors, put them with Gotasun.” She passed her former Handler over to the others so that she could oversee preparations for their departure.

“Aren’t you ready for our private conversation?” Gotasun called out. His grey hematite eyes bulged at Tieg, clearly uncomfortable at the being left with him. “What I have to say will affect your plans, my pet.”

Myx ignored Gotasun and went to check on Dolra and Rauno with the injured Tarasi. The scientist seemed to have regained his cheery, optimistic disposition now that he had been reunited with his love; he danced about the cargo hold, checking vitals and dispensing the appropriate medicine.

Dolra roughly grabbed Rauno’s wrist and inspected the ointment in his hand. “You didn’t add anything, did you?”

“Oh, my Nightingale,” Rauno cooed, smiling at Dolra’s rough touch. “I promised that I’d stop experimenting while we’re fleeing the Camp. I will have plenty of time to test my theories once I’ve returned to Capitaras; President Naichom has promised to reinstate me at the Institute. I’ll be able to provide for you when we’re married.”

When the couple began arguing about whether or not they were ready to wed, Myx checked in on the other ships. She oversaw the distribution of the surrendered Camp staff amongst the cargo holds of the different vehicles.

Tieg began leading Gotasun towards one of them, but Myx stopped him.

"I want you and Gotasun with me." Myx motioned for Tieg and her former Handler to follow. Using the remote, Myx had Alycee's transport float back to the top of the water.

The Hathak man smirked beneath his crooked nose. "Aw, my pet. I think you're starting to like me. I knew that you would eventually—if we gave our relationship a little more time. Can I just tell you how excited that I am to be a part of your elite team?"

Meeting his amused gaze, Myx replied, "Don't flatter yourself. I just don't trust the other prisoners enough to deliver you safely to the rendezvous. I'm looking forward to dealing with you personally when my next task is complete." She summoned Rauno, who soon popped his head out of the ambulance ship. "I know what I'm asking is difficult, but I need you with me as well. Say your goodbyes to Dolra; she'll be fine for now."

Not giving him a chance to argue, Myx strode away. She visited each transport to pass out coordinates. After getting the go-ahead from Tieg, the caravan of ships shot away from the Camp and towards their destination.

Myx allowed Rauno to pilot Alycee's transport. Tieg and Gotasun were silent about the constant jerking movements they had to endure, but they seemed fairly uncomfortable as they slid under their loose restraints; they stifled groans each time their shoulders slammed into the vehicle's walls.

The collectively let out a deep sigh as the Camp disappeared in the distant horizon. Thankfully, the defense codes they had taken from Parnuss had been genuine; they hadn't blasted out of the sky as they escaped.

The constant rocking and shaking did little to upset Myx anymore. She sat back and looked through the profiles Rauno had stolen from the Warden's office. Most of it was dull, but some was wildly entertaining. However, she had failed to learn the names of most of her fellow prisoners, so she wasn't sure who a lot of the info was about.

And yet, her readings served the purpose of distracting herself from the fear of seeing what was in her own file. She had originally been excited to learn everything. But anxiety set in when her fingers approached the icon labeled with her name.

The next distraction from the truth soon came into view on the front screen. The shimmering, crystalline Hathak Palace rose against a desolate, rocky valley.

The small fleet touched down in a field hidden below a series of mountains. A dozen stolen transports landed in a crude circle around Myx's transport and the prisoners descended their ramps, looking rather uneasy.

Myx motioned at the gathered Tarasi and addressed them all. "I know that we've had a rough month. Living in the Camp was brutal and humiliating. We didn't know if we were going to survive. But we did. And now we're free to pursue our own interests once again. However, we are still at war with the Hathak. They have shown themselves to be ruthless and relentless in their mission to make us all their slaves."

Several of the Tarasi gave grunts of consternation at the mention of being slaves.

A man at the back of the crowd bellowed, "They'll never take us again!"

The woman beside him added, "Let's make them our slaves instead!"

"Bring out our captives so we can brand them as—"

Waving her arms to silence her people, Myx continued, "Please, let me finish. Last night, a force of elite Hathak warriors stormed President Naichom's Estate and kidnapped her." She accessed her life forces, searching for persuasive rhetoric skills. "I've come here intending to free her as well. Now I can't make you fight with me, but I need a few volunteers to help me infiltrate that Emperor's Palace to find Naichom."

"Why should we risk our lives for the President?" the man asked. "She could have ransomed for all of us to be freed, but she didn't."

"The Hathak wanted too much money," Myx explained, her patience being taxed. "But since she freed me and Rauno, we were able to use our knowledge of the Camp to get everyone else out without bankrupting the Tarasi government."

Many of the former prisoners didn't seem assured by her words. They grumbled amongst themselves.

Myx had a difficult time quieting them all down again. "If you don't want to come, you may stay here and help Dolra tend to the wounded. Anyone who would like to be a part of the team that rescues President Naichom can come speak to me. I'm leaving at sundown."

She turned from the crowd and returned to her transport. Myx sought out Gotasun, who had been tied to a latch on the exterior of the transport. Untying his bonds, she released him.

"Time for your revenge?" Gotasun asked, shaking out his joints.

"You said you had information that I need to know." Myx kept her face blank, not letting herself show any emotion. She pushed the feelings down like Alycee always did. "I'd like to hear it now. If I like what you have to say, I won't keep you tied up anymore. Agreed?"

Gotasun shook his head. "That's a good offer, but your timing is bad. You see, I overheard what you're planning and I'd like to come with you."

"Why would I agree to that? You'd probably just run away and warn the Emperor."

"Naw, I wouldn't do that." Gotasun pulled out flat, wooden box from his jacket. He tapped the surface in different places and it opened. "Here's my identification card. It'll help you understand who I am."

Myx took it from him. "A Tarasi service guard? How were— Who did you— What were you doing as a Handler at the Hathak Camp?"

"I was undercover," Gotasun explained, his harsh expression softening. I'm aware of your parentage, my pet. President Naichom saw that you and Bishing had signed up for the military and she was worried for your safety. She sent out several of us to various Hathak facilities in order to keep an eye out."

She tried to interrupt him with her question, but Gotasun continued.

"I told you that I was spoiling you—which was technically true. I would have been nicer if I could, but the Warden watched us Handlers carefully. Besides, it seems that those beatings toughened you up quite a bit."

Myx couldn't believe what she was hearing. Was anyone around her who they really said they were? She didn't like being in the dark.

"You can come with, but you're to never leave my sight."

As she shook Gotasun's hand, Rauno came clamoring around the side of the transport, his emerald eyes frantic. "The Hathak are here! Strap in. We're about to go for a bumpy ride."

Chapter 47

Gotasun slung Myx over his shoulder and dashed to the other side of the transport.

"Put me down!" Myx order, trying to sound authoritative while her face bounced against his hefty backside.

"The mad scientist said to strap in, so I'm going to strap you in." Gotasun flung her into her chair and lashed down her seat restraints. "If the Hathak are coming, my priority is to keep you safe." He plopped beside Myx and barely managed to belt himself in as the transport took off with a lurch. "I know you probably don't understand how far my loyalty to President Naichom goes, but that doesn't change the fact that I will fulfill my duty to her."

Tieg sat in the front seat, at the co-pilot's position. His hands flew over the controls, which were lit by his glowing, white opal eyes. He spoke through a communicator and gave bearings to the over vehicles in their make-shift fleet.

Myx undid her straps and lunged forward. She grabbed the communicator from the protesting Tieg and announced through the speaker, "Forget the mission. I want you to head back to Capitaras. Tell the Tarasi what is happening. The enemy ships are only trying to get us to leave their air space. They might let you go if they see that you don't intend to fight." She ended the transmission and let Gotasun pull her back to her seat.

The supposed Tarasi service guard hadn't had time to strap himself back in when the transport veered suddenly to the left. Gotasun's face made a sickening squish as it made contact with the vehicle's wall. He stumbled into his seat, blood dripping from his broken nose.

"What are we going to do, Myx?" Rauno asked, his hands flying over the consul. "We came out here for a reason: Naichom needs us!"

The communicator boomed with half a dozen different voices.

She turned it off, not wanting to hear anything else the freed prisoners had to say. Myx tied her pitch black hair into a braid over her shoulder as she told the men, "Head in the direction of Capitaras. We'll come back later on tonight and try infiltrating again."

Rauno was having a difficult time with the controls. "I haven't flown anything this fancy since I was a teenager."

Gotasun undid his belt once again and shakily moved to the flight panel. "I have."

"Why is he even here?" Tieg pushed at the beefy man's hands. "He should be locked in a crate, tumbling freely around a cargo hold."

"No time to explain," Myx replied, getting out of her seat. "Rauno, move. I'll fly."

Tieg looked confused as he asked, "Are you even old enough to operate this vehicle?"

She ignored him. Since she had Alycee's life force in her, she knew how to fly her transport. Myx's hands glided over the controls and the vehicle leveled out. She thought about tactical maneuvering and she was able to access Alycee's training memories. Myx expertly steered the transport around the Hathak ships.

As she flew, Myx reflected on her plan. It probably hadn't been the smartest idea to come to the most secure place on the planet with a bunch of untrained men and women who had just broken out of a Labor Camp.

Myx flew south of the mountains. The Hathak ships pursued, but kept their distance.

A natural Radiation Spring spouted out of thick cracks in the rocks. Thick colored wisps floated lazily away from the ground and rose in the violet light of Star Lerwyn. Despite the lack of expression in Tieg's eyes, Myx could tell that the man was anxious around the energy from how his body stiffened as each ribbon passed through him.

The Hathak ceased pursuing the caravan of vehicles. Myx had begun to relax—that was until she passed a mountain peak.

A storm of swirling colors raged to the east, shooting out of the ridges of the rocks.

This radiation was unlike any she had ever experienced. These shimmering bits of energy seemed like they could explode at any moment. Radiation shot through the transport as quick as a blink.

When they passed through Myx, she had a series of memories from the dozen life forces she had absorbed. She couldn't control them the flashes. While her brain fixated on all the memories, it couldn't also access the knowledge of how to fly Alycee's transport. Myx froze, her hands not sure what they needed to do to control the vehicle.

"What's wrong?" Rauno asked, leaning across the aisle to inspect the console. "That mountain is awfully close. Why don't you move us a little to the left?"

"I can't," Myx groaned, trying to will her fingers to move.

Gotasun stepped forward. "The Radiation Storm looks bad, too. We should get out of here." He tried to access the flying controls, but Myx's arms were in the way. "I'd rather not die here, my pet."

The three men tried to move her from the seat, but all of her muscles stiffened at once. Memories continued flashing through her consciousness like jolts of lightning.

"Hey, mad scientist!" Gotasun shouted suddenly. "Don't you have anything to help her?"

Rauno searched through his pockets and pulled out an ointment. He quickly spread it over Myx's arms. "This is a topical muscle relaxant. It should help everything to loosen up—hopefully before we crash into one of those peaks."

All at once, Myx was experiencing her life forces' moments. She tried to focus on a single one to regain control, but it didn't work. Her head ached and her muscles felt strained.

Secretly, she wished for death. Myx was tempted to veer the transport into the mountain side. But she banished that thought since her concern for Rauno and Tieg—as well as her desire to get more answers out of Gotasun—stopped her.

Outside, the Radiation Storm continued to rage. Several rays seemed to dart directly towards them at the last second instead of shooting out into the atmosphere. Every jolt gave her an overwhelming sense of power, while also making her heart feel like it was about to implode; it was both terrifying and thrilling.

Another ray hit her and she began to spasm. Her hands flailed and hit several controls that she didn't mean to touch.

The transport hung in mid air a moment before plummeting toward the ground.

Myx was too frightened to scream. She shut her pink eyes and waited for the impact. As they hit, the ship bounced and rolled. Thanks to the invigoration of the thick wisps, her whole body felt numb during the impact.

"Everyone alive?" Myx asked, trying to turn around.

Each of the men grunted in affirmation. The cockpit had gone dark save the soft glow coming from Tieg's illuminating opal eyes. Gotasun crawled across the cockpit and helped Myx out of her seat.

Rauno checked the controls to see if anything still worked. "It's no good; half a dozen systems are non-functional."

Lethargic, they carefully gathered what supplies they could and crawled out of the ship.

During the supply search, Myx felt helpless as they men scavenged the ship without her. The relaxant topical cream Rauno had spread over her forearms prevented her from contracting her muscles, so her arms hung limply at her side.

Tieg's white opal eyes scanned the mountains.

"What do you see?" Myx asked, joining him a distance away from Rauno and Gotasun.

"I can just make out faint glimmers of auras." Tieg rested a hand on the cliff's rock face. "It's just sparkling dots, but I'm confident that's the way back to the Emperor's Palace. My best guess is that it will take about a day to walk there."

"Is everyone still alright with our infiltration plan?" Myx asked, not sure herself if she wanted to still do it.

"The nearest town is a week's trek away," Gotasun explained, blood still dripping from his crooked nose. He hefted a large pack of weapons onto his back and grimaced, likely from the injury he sustained from Frezul's attack. The undercover Tarasi officer continued to wince at every step, but he led the way towards down the winding mountain path. "We don't have a choice anymore."

Chapter 48

"It's been two days. Why won't anyone tell me what's going on?" Gotasun trudged in front of the group since no one was comfortable yet having him behind them. He massaged an ointment into thick purple bruise on his bare, hairy chest. "You can trust me. I'm a member of the Tarasi service guard. Now explain to me what happened with the transport crash!"

"Yeah, yeah. We heard you the first hundred times you asked." Rauno readjusted the pack on his back. "There's nothing else you can say that will make me tell you anymore. For all we know, you could be a triple agent. So you will never learn about Myx's medical history."

"Medical history?" Gotasun scoffed, kicking at a rock. "So she's got this mysterious illness, and yet she's also somehow going to rescue President Naichom? I should have just stayed at the Camp and taken the chance of Warden Parnuss discovering who I really am." He was quiet a moment before saying, "What is our plan, anyway? Or are you keeping that from me, too?"

Rauno gestured for Tieg to stay with Myx before motioning for Gotasun to scout ahead with him.

Myx stopped at a stream and removed her shoes. She plunged her sore, aching feet into the icy water. Her health hadn't improved much from the Radiation Storm. Although she was growing more accustomed to controlling the flashes, Myx still had a difficult time moving while her brain experienced the random memories. It made their progress slow as they journeyed to the Emperor's Palace.

Only Rauno knew about the ash trial. However, Tieg at least understood that Myx had been experimenting with the radiation and that it was affecting her body.

But she didn't trust Gotasun enough to trust him with her secret; no one she met seemed to be who they said they were. Myx had looked up her former Handler's file in the records they stole from the Warden's office, but there was nothing to suggest that Parnuss suspected Gotasun of being Tarasi.

With her jumbled head, Myx was starting lose track of her preparations. And then in a moment of lucidity, she remembered something. "Tieg, can I talk to you for a minute?"

The elderly man joined her at the river's edge and passed her a canteen. "Feeling better?"

"Yes, thank you." Myx was indeed in better spirits—except that two days of walking had exhausted what invigoration the Radiation Storm had bestowed on her. She tied her lengthening black hair into a neater braid as she said, "So, you know certain details of my, uh, condition, and I know certain details about those glowing eyes of yours."

"You're wanting me to finish the tale we never seem to have time for?"

Myx pulled her shoes back on did up the laces. "If you don't mind. You see people's auras, right? Does that mean that you might be able to detect President Naichom's in the Emperor's Palace?"

Tieg pursed his lips. "I'm not sure, Myx. It's possible. I met the President on several occasions during my military days. But it's been a few years. I'll need to remember her exact eye color so that I know which aura to search for. They are beige feldspar? Maybe pale golden agate?" He rubbed his forehead. "You've seen her recently. What do you think?"

She shook her head. "No, her irises are more like yellow garnets."

"Then, yes, I should be able to find her."

Rauno and Gotasun returned, still grumbling about the plan.

"It's not going to work," the Gotasun hissed, plopping down along the riverbank. His shirt was ripped open, revealing a mass of purple contusions and faded scars across his broad, barrel chest. "There are too many holes. No offense, my pet."

"Stop calling her that!" Rauno snapped, kneeling between Gotasun and Myx.

Putting a hand on his shoulder, Myx said, "It's alright, Rauno. There's no need to get upset about that."

Gotasun had a point; they needed a better idea than simply depending on her extra life forces to solve the problems that arose during the rescue attempt—not that Gotasun even understood that aspect of their plan anyways. His frustration was justifiable.

Despite not having a clue as to how they should begin, Myx at least understood that a good leader depended on the wisdom of her advisors. "What do you think we should do?"

Rauno kicked off his shoes. The scientist waded into the river and paced back and forth among the knee-high water. "I don't think we can take on all the Palace sentries with just us four. Perhaps we should turn ourselves in and explain our situation?" He bent over to refill the empty canteens as he continued. "The new

Emperor might be sympathetic when we say that Myx is the former Emperor's daughter."

Myx shook her head gently. "No, that won't work. We don't know why Bishing gave up the throne. It's possible that he was forced out."

Gotasun winced as he rubbed a wet scrap of clothe along his broken nose. "Let's tell them that you're Naichom's daughter and that you've come to negotiate the terms of her release. Maybe they'll let her go if you promise to marry the Emperor's son, or something?" He tugged at her lengthening dark braid—almost in a playful fashion. "That's how a lot of political problems use to be solved back on Earth."

"I'm not marrying some guy I've never met before," Myx groaned, swatting his hand away. "Would it work to knock out a couple guards and take their armor? Then we could walk about the Palace as we please without being stopped."

Tieg shook his head. "That's the oldest trick in the book. There are bound to be measures against that."

Gotasun removed his shirt completely and dunked it into the cold water. There was an attractive ruggedness to his girth that Myx had never noticed before. She sucked in a shallow breath and averted her gaze from his muscular form, her cheeks growing warm.

"I thought you had all this planned out," the former Handler snapped, water dripping off his towering form onto Myx as he confronted her. "Why would you come all the way out here without knowing what you're doing? It's the stupidest thing I've ever seen. I can't believe I'm a part of it."

"If you hate it so much," Rauno scoffed, "then just leave us alone. I'm sure they'll find your body in a couple weeks."

"This isn't helping," Myx said as loud as she could manage. She stood, glaring into Gotasun's grey hematite eyes. "Look, we'll be at the Palace by nightfall. We need to figure out what we're going to do before we get there. Now stop bickering and start thinking!"

After their brief rest by the river, they continued their journey in silence, led by Tieg's aura-seeking eyes. When the Palace came into view a couple hours later, the group had yet to come up with any decent ideas.

"We could get captured," Tieg offered without enthusiasm. His eyes darted around the perimeter of the group. He looked increasingly nervous as he spoke at a quicker tempo. "Then we could break out of the jail cell with some chemicals that Rauno has hidden in his shirt. That at least gets us into the Palace."

They thought a moment, but were interrupted by a blinding light that shone against the purple evening sky.

With a threat present, Myx became alert as adrenaline pumped through her body. Rauno put a hand on her arm and she felt something sticky beneath it. When he took it away, she saw a patch like the ones Rauno had used on Parnuss and Heikah. Only this patch gave her an energy boost instead of knocking her out. Myx raised her newly-acquired pistol, her grip strength returning in the anticipation of battle.

"Identify yourself," a woman said behind the lights.

"We've come to negotiate the terms of President Naichom's release," Myx replied, putting as much authority into her words as she could manage. "Take us to her immediately."

The female's voice sounded oddly metallic as she said, "The Tarasi have already sent an envoy. We told them to leave and never return. Now I'll give you one more chance to tell me the truth. Who are you and why have you come to the Emperor's Palace?"

"Fine, you got me. We're not diplomats." Myx wondered if she could lie more convincingly. "We're part of an elite force that is currently infiltrating the Palace as we speak. We're just a bit late to the party. But nonetheless, we're just as lethal as the marines posing as guards."

The woman laughed loudly before making a hand gesture at her soldiers. "We'll get to the bottom of this at the Palace."

Stun rays erupted simultaneously from every gun trained on them. Tieg fell forward, followed by Rauno. Gotasun managed to evade and block several bolts before collapsing onto Rauno with a grunt.

Myx searched through her arsenal of life forces as she dodged blasts. But none of her fighting personas could help her. Alycee's knowledge of being knocked out told her to relax her muscles to make the impact of hitting the ground less damaging. She did so as something hot hit her arm.

Unable to fight any longer, her vision went dark.

Chapter 49

Myx gasped awake. The rail-less cart she was slumped in hit another bump in the road and she nearly fell over the side. She clenched her toes against the uneven wood as her bound arms dangled down towards the dry ground. Gotasun pressed his forearms against her thighs to steady her as she painfully rolled back inside.

Rauno lay crumpled beside Myx's feet, with Tieg sprawled atop him. Both still seemed to be unconscious.

Shoving away from Gotasun with a groan, Myx surveyed her surroundings. The Emperor's Palace rose in front of them. It appeared just as it had in Alycee's memories, its height rivaling the distant mountains as it rose from the bare valley.

There were easily fifty guards around the entrance and at least a dozen more surrounding the cart—all well armed with rifles strapped to their backs and stun guns on their hands.

Frustrated yet again, Myx determined that no amount of life forces would have been enough to allow her to get all of them out of their situation. However, the stun bolt had somehow cleared her head and she was able to think again, masking the painful attack she had suffered before the transport crash. Feeling invigorated, she racked her brain to figure out how they could escape and find President Naichom.

"Wake up, guys." Myx nudged the men with a kick of her boot.

"At least they took us alive," Rauno commented, wriggling under Tieg's weight. "I'd like to marry Dolra before I die."

"You and the shrew?" Gotasun asked, sounding amused. "Good luck with that."

Tieg had a difficult time getting up with his wrists bound. As he looked around, his illuminating irises gave everything a soft glow. He theatrically darted his gaze at each guard and bulged his eyes. Several looked at him like he was a monster and took a step away from the cart.

"Now that I've scared them into keeping their distance," Tieg whispered, "maybe now we can continue making our master plan."

Gotasun seemed oddly calm as he glued his gaze on the Palace. "My pet, we never had a chance to finish our conversation. But I suppose it won't matter fairly soon, anyways. I'd just like to caution you to be ready for a startling revelation."

Myx looked over the beefy man. Although he still had considerable girth, he was much leaner than he had been when they first met over a month ago. He had claimed to be a Tarasi service guard, and Rauno had given her proof that many of the Camp staff were not Hathak. She still had a hard time wrapping her head around all the true identities of those who had lied about who they really were. But what else could Gotasun possibly want to tell her at such a time?

The former Handler met her gaze, his grey hematite eyes oddly serene as he said, "I know I have a lot to make up for, but I hope somehow you can understand that everything I have ever done has been in your best interest. My pe—Sorry, Myx." He took a deep breath before adding, "I hope what I did was enough to prepare you for what will happen next. I—"

There was a loud cracking sound. Myx looked over her shoulder to see a fully-covered armored woman raping her staff on the cart. Her voice was muffled and thickly accented as she said, "Quiet down. I don't want to see you being so disrespectful in front of the Emperor."

"We're going to see the Emperor?" Myx asked, feeling anxious at the prospect of finally getting some answers.

"I told him of the situation and he's curious about how you plan on making him release Naichom," the guard replied, once again sounding like she was from a different planet. "Perhaps if you continue to amuse the Emperor, he'll let you live."

Further inspection proved that she was indeed the lady who had earlier led the Hathak soldiers in capturing the four of them.

At the front of the Palace, guards hefted them out of the rail-less cart. The trio was then led through a luxurious annex, the wall studded with gemmed rings in ornate patterns. There was something strangely familiar about them.

"What are those?" Myx tried unsuccessfully to shake the uneasy feeling that the gem rings gave her.

"Those are irises from Hathak's enemies, acquired over the past centuries of feuds." The armored woman's voice seemed to change in tone once again. She chuckled and pushed Myx along with her staff. "If you're lucky, your pink tourmalines won't end up with them. Now keep moving."

The Hathak were even more brutal than Myx had thought. The Emperor's Palace was decorated with the eye parts of the dead? Still, she supposed it wasn't nearly as creepy as covering herself with human ashes in order to absorb the corpses' knowledge and abilities.

Seeing the irises sparked one of her own memories. Myx thought back to preparing Alycee's corpse before cremating the ex-assassin. There had been a thick fold of fabric tied across her face and Myx thought it a strange ritual. But hearing about the Hathak's brutal decorating custom finally answered her question on the purpose of binding corpses' eyes.

The squads of guards ushered them through the annex to a wide staircase that spiraled up the sides of a lavish ballroom. Occasional wisps of radiation flitted around them before passing through the walls to the next room. The gemmed irises glowed faintly at the touch of energy.

As they ventured down the endless halls, Tieg continued gazing about him. Myx assumed that he was searching for Naichom's aura.

"Anything?" Myx asked Tieg in her softest voice.

Tieg shook his head. "I can see small glimpses of auras here and there. But I think the armor blocks my sight."

In front of Myx, Rauno fiddled with something. She hoped he was secretly preparing some kind of explosive that would get them out of their situation. However, as they turned along the corner of steps, Myx caught sight of a ring on his left hand.

At first, she didn't understand what it meant. But then Myx remembered a past conversation where Rauno had explained that rings use to be a symbol of love and marriage. Her heart was saddened that her friend had finally found his wife just moments before his life might very well end.

At the top of the staircase, the armored woman directed them to the large door, also adorned with the irises of the dead. They stepped through, greeted by even more radiation. But these were more like waves or thick ribbons than little wisps of energy.

Myx seized as the bands shot through her. Her companions linked their arms together to make a chair for her.

The armored woman made a hand gesture at her soldiers and they all departed. The doors shut with an echoing thud. Alone and without any escort, the woman led her Tarasi prisoners across the high-vaulted room, her staff resting over one shoulder.

As they approached a dais, Myx noticed that it was a throne room with a pair of large gold chairs seated high above the floor.

The men pressed their faces close, making animated facial expressions at each other. From what Myx could tell in her overwhelmed state, Rauno seemed to be suggesting that they attack the armored woman. Gotasun appeared to be skeptical and wanted them to wait. She could see Tieg very well since he was positioned behind her. But the elderly man must have sided with Gotasun since Rauno's normally calm demeanor was scrunched up in frustration.

Armor clanked as the woman bowed before the empty thrones. "My Lord Emperor, I've brought the intruders. What is your will?"

Gotasun faced Myx. "I'm not the only one who doesn't see anything, right? It's not like the Hathak Emperor is a ghost or is somehow able to be invisible? But then again, Tieg has glowing eyeballs, so I guess anything is possible."

A robotic voice echoed from all corners of the throne room. "Welcome honored guests! I hope you have been treated with respect."

Rauno shrugged. "Well, all I can say is I'm grateful we haven't been tortured."

"I've heard tell of your excellent mind, radiation researcher. But I'm not ready to address you yet. Take a step back. Gotasun, come forward."

The trio of men eased Myx to the floor. The air was dense with thick wisps, the colorful ribbons moving swiftly about the vast hall as though creating a small Radiation Storm in the heart of the Hathak Palace. Tieg and Rauno stayed by Myx's side as Gotasun obeyed the Emperor's voice and moved towards the thrones.

"You have done a great service to my people," the voice said in an affectionate tone. "I shall like to reward you for your service to the Hathak—despite being a member of the Tarasi service guard. One of my attendants will present you with a commendation worthy of your works." A door at the side of the throne room opened. "Leave us. I'll send for you again shortly when the rest of this business is concluded."

Gotasun nodded and left after giving Myx a mischievous wink. The door shut behind him with a reverberating thud.

"Step forward, Tieg." After the older man walked to the dais, the emotionless voice continued, "While incarcerated at the Camp, you showed excellent valor and leadership skills. I would like to appoint you as Hathak's new ambassador to the Tarasi."

Tieg was quiet, likely weighing all the pros and cons of the situation. He scanned the walls with his glowing white eyes as though he were trying to determine the location of the Emperor's aura. “It would be my pleasure to take on that role. When do I start?”

“Immediately.” The same door reopened that Gotasun had just gone through. “My advisors have several terms they’d like you to take to the Tarasi leadership. Please join them and add your input.”

After Tieg was gone, the Emperor’s robotic voice addressed Rauno. “There is an opening at the Hathak University. I’d like to offer you a tenured position there. Would you be interested in continuing your research?” After several moments of silence, the voice added, “Before you answer, I’d like to tell you that you’ll have unlimited resources and freedom to choose your own areas of study.”

Rauno turned back to Myx. “I’m sorry, but I’ve got to accept. I know we came here to rescue Naichom. However, I never anticipated that the Emperor would be so generous with us.” He addressed the throne. “Sign me up. But I want to bring my love, Dolra, back here so that we can wed.”

“That shouldn’t be a problem. Come make the arrangements with my staff.”

Myx was soon alone in the room with just the armored guard.

“We saved the best for last,” the voice said, sounding warm and oddly affectionate. A panel behind the throne opened and a finely dressed figure walked through.

She gasped as the Emperor came into view. “Why aren’t you dead?”

Chapter 50

Bishing strode past the golden thrones, his opulent, embroidered clothing glinting in the reflection of the thick wisps. A metallic collar hung from his neck, resting over his vocal chords.

A swarm of Hathak and Tarasi broadcast drones flew out of vents along the top of the throne room. They positioned themselves in a dome-like formation, a series of arches stretching up from the floor and reaching towards the ceiling before creating the other half of the frame.

Stopping in front of Myx, Bishing smiled down at her. "I'm sorry for the deception," the robotic voice said, the sound coming from the collar. "I thought this was the best way."

"The best way to do what?" Myx asked, not sure if she wanted to hug him or rip his smoky quartz eyes out. She glanced at the surrounding camera drones, feeling self-conscious at having such a personal event televised to the entire planet.

There was a clank as the woman guard removed her helmet. Her accent disappeared as she said, "To prepare you."

Myx turned to see Naichom discarding pieces of armor. "Mom?"

Naichom and Bishing met at the middle of the room, kissing as their hands ran up and down each others' arms and back. They whispered tenderly to each other between pecks, oblivious to the fact that their abandoned daughter stared at them in shock.

Bishing winced as Naichom's hands raked over his abdomen.

"Still tender, huh?" the President cooed in a soft, caring voice. But her words became cold as she added, "If you hadn't taken my daughter away from me, I wouldn't have needed to have Frezul beat you to within an inch of death." Naichom gently pushed Bishing away from her lips, but stayed in his arms. She turned her attention to their guest. "Welcome home, Myx. You must have many questions for us. We can answer just a few now, so choose only the most important."

Myx began pacing the room to calm herself, but it only riled her up more. "Why were you dressed as a guard? I thought you were being held prisoner."

Hunger gnawed at her stomach, reminding her of the arduous journey she had just endured in order to save her mother. Even though the wide wisps would only trigger more memory flashes, she still yearned to sink her hands into them to invigorate her weak body.

"And Bishing was supposed to be dead. Why is he not dead?" She swallowed down her hunger and focused her rage on her mother and father. "Until a week ago, I thought that my parents had abandoned me, never caring about my life or who I was. Now you're telling me that I'm the heir of both civilizations? I just—" Myx choked down a sob as her voice cracked. She remembered the drones and took a breath. "I just don't know how to handle all this."

Naichom stepped out of Bishing's embrace and approached her daughter. "You were weak. Your father and I worried that you wouldn't be a good leader. I simply can't believe that Kaefh let you grow up to have no skills; we should have chosen a better guardian for you."

"At least Kaefh was there for me! You were absent from my life for twelve years." Myx paused as she processed her next thought. "Did you let me get captured and sent to the Labor Camp in order to toughen me up?" She waited for them to respond, but all her parents did was give each other exasperated looks. "What made you think that was an acceptable thing to do to your own child?"

Bishing reached to put his hands on Myx's shoulders. However, he hesitated when she pulled away. "It's more complicated than all that. The Camp wasn't controlled by the Hathak; it was under the jurisdiction of your mother."

Myx felt like she had been punched in the stomach. A wave of nausea passed over her. If she had eaten anything in the past day, she likely would have emptied her stomach right there on the throne room floor. She turned on the Tarasi President. "You captured us because you were mad at Bish for hiding me under your nose in Capitaras?"

Naichom's face brightened. "The Camp has prepared you even better than we thought!" Her yellow garnet eyes beamed as Bishing wrapped his arms around her once again.

"As much as I hated that plan," Bish whispered in his metallic voice to Naichom's ear, "I'll admit that you were right about that. I never should have doubted your wisdom in how to strengthen Myx. Her transformation is astounding."

The President turned back to Myx. "And yes, dear one. My beloved and I had already decided that Kaefh would accompany us as your nanny when we left the trials of this planet behind. We were prepared to abdicate before journeying through the galaxy together." Naichom put her head on Bish's shoulder. "In a moment of weakness, I decided to stay and continue ruling. Bishing became upset that I wouldn't leave, so he arranged for Kaefh to care for you away from my meddlesome schemes."

Bishing ran his fingers through Naichom's sleek, dark hair. That tender touch seemed to ignite a passion in the woman since she jumped into his arms and twined her legs around his hips.

Myx turned away, rubbing her temples. All her life, she wondered what her parents were really like. She ran every scenario through her brain until she determined that she no longer cared why they didn't raise her themselves. But hearing about all the manipulation involved and seeing just how twisted her mother and father were made Myx want to run away from it all.

Still shaky on her feet, Myx began creeping back the way she had come in. She repeated to herself that this wasn't what she wanted; Kaefh and Sievly were her real family and she would never leave them again.

A staff zoomed into view. Naichom's hair was stuck up in the back from her embrace with Bishing. Her yellow garnet eyes bore into Myx's pink tourmalines. "We're not done here."

Myx side-stepped out of the staff's reach and took off running at the doorway. Wind swept towards her knees and Myx instinctively knew to roll out of the way. As she righted herself, she crouched down into a deep stance with her hands up, guarding her face and torso.

Naichom swung at her again and again, not giving Myx a chance to recover or strike back in between the swooping arches of the club.

Bishing stood to the side of the throne room, appearing as though he didn't really care about the outcome of the fight. But on occasion, he would remind Naichom to, "Be careful," or to, "Be gentle," as he rubbed and injury at his abdomen.

Sweat poured down Myx's brow and gathered at her chin. She watched for an opening in Naichom' strikes, but the movements were so quick that they blurred together. All Myx had time to do was dodge as they wooden staff swung at her. One hit nearly took; however, the club hesitated for half a second before Myx was able to jump out of the way.

Clearly, Naichom was going easy on her. And that infuriated Myx further than anything that had already happened that day.

Chapter 51

"You will let us continue our tale." Naichom hooked one of Myx's knees with her staff, knocking her to the ground. The President then raised the weapon so that it rest on her own shoulder. "Like I said, we will answer some of your questions. But your father and I won't let you leave here without knowing as much of the truth as we're able to tell you."

Radiation swirled about Naichom. Several ribbons seemed to zoom straight at the President's chest, around her silver broach.

And yet, Myx hadn't been touched by a single wisp during their entire confrontation. Her entire body ached as she tried to will herself to move. Other than that last move when Naichom tripped her with the club, she had not been struck. Why did she feel as though all the strength had been zapped from her body?

There seemed to be something else going on that she wasn't being told about her situation.

Bishing approached and knelt beside Myx. "I know you can't forgive your mother for the Camp at the moment. But someday you'll see the wisdom in her decision. If we had left the planet's rule to you five weeks ago, everything we have worked towards would have fallen apart."

Naichom stroked Myx's cheek. "Look at you now. You're an intelligent, master manipulator. You can even defend yourself—somewhat. The Camp experiment was a success."

"I'll admit," Bishing added in his robotic tone, "we didn't think you'd do so well. Learning to absorb the life forces of the dead was never anything we imagined. It will serve you well in the coming years as you work to unite the Tarasi and Hathak under one government."

Myx blinked at them, retreating to a wall. "That's what this has all been about?" Even with tears stinging her eyes, it was still clear to see the wisps gravitating towards Naichom and her mysterious broach. She needed more time to figure out what was happening. "I've just been a pawn to you? A solution to all your problems?"

"We have been planning this for over two decades," Naichom explained, moving away from Myx. She glided across the room to the throne dais, her club still resting on her shoulder. "When Bishing and I first met, we were sick of all the animosity between our people. I wasn't President yet, but my parents had bred me to take on that role someday. Bish and I decided that any children we had would be the best factor to pulling both civilizations under a single ruler."

Bish stared after Naichom, a somber glare on his face. "Tell her the other thing."

"I know dearest. I was getting to that." Naichom placed herself on the right golden throne and crossed her legs. The thick ribbons of radiation circling the room seemed to seethe and rage around the hovering drones as Naichom took a deep breath. "Myx, this next part is going to be especially hard to hear. Despite how awful it sounds, know that your father and I truly do love you."

Bishing followed Naichom to the throne and sat on the left chair. "Although we care for each other very deeply, we both have a dark, competitive side. Being in power amplifies that side of our personalities ten-fold."

Myx kept fixating on the unnatural movement of the radiation in that room, trying to distract herself from her parents' narrative.

But her curiosity was intrigued by Bish's last comment. She wondered what could possibly be worse than what she had already heard. Myx calmed herself and slowly made her way to her parents at the raised throne dais.

Naichom sat straight on her throne, poised dramatically for the broadcast drones as she began her tale. "My beloved wanted to whisk me away to travel the galaxy. However, I had spent most of my life striving to earn the Presidency. So we compromised and began a game. If I won, Bishing and I would stay on this planet and continue ruling, accepting the challenges of keeping our love secret from the rest of the world. Except if Bish won, I would give it all up and go with him wherever he wanted."

The drones shifted in their formation. Several zoomed forward, getting a close-up of Myx's face. She punched one of the drones away, tired of the machines distracting her attention away from her parents. Myx used the wisdom of Alycee's life force to calm herself, determined to be in control of her emotions.

"As the years wore on," Bishing added, adjusting his gold crown, "Naichom and I kept each others' skills and abilities sharp through various challenges. It began with simple logic puzzles, but then quickly escalated to full-on assassination attempts. That was until—"

"That was until you came along, dearest," Naichom interrupted, glaring down at Myx. "I was living permanently in this Palace at the time, but only Bish and Kaefh knew my real name. And I wasn't elected President until several years later. But somehow, the assassins caught on that we were manipulating them to do our dirty work; they turned on us."

Bishing pulled up a broadcast screen from behind their thrones. The picture quality was a little dated, but Myx could clearly tell that the video was of Naichom winning her election.

In his robotic voice, Bish resumed the tale. "When your mother's parents rigged the election for her to win the Presidency, Naichom decided to take the position anyways. That's when I hired Kaefh to take you away and live in Capitaras. At that point, the assassination attempts had escalated to where I was fighting off two to three every week."

Naichom stiffened a moment before letting her shoulders relax. "Myx, you're smart enough now to realize that putting you and Bishing in the Camp was my way of trying to win our bet. I nearly did, but then your father went and faked his death."

"I did more than that, Naichom!" Bish laughed, the metallic tones echoing off the throne room walls. "I successfully abducted you from your own Estate. I won, and now we get to go on a very long trip." He stood and moved to her throne. The Emperor stroked the President's pale cheek. "You got to have your fun and play President for a dozen years; now I want to enjoy the rest of our lives together—just the two of us."

Myx shoved down all the disgust she felt at her despicable parents. Waves of radiation finally made their way to her, invigorating her with the strength to confront them. She stared deep into her father's smoky quartz eyes and she could tell that there was even more.

"You need to tell me all of it," Myx said as calmly as she could manage. "Or else I'm stealing a transport, leaving this Palace, and jetting off to the most distant planet I can find!"

Before Bishing could respond, Naichom said, "That's all you need to know for now."

At her words, the thick wisps seemed to be whipped up into a frenzy. The way they moved reminded Myx of the Radiation Storm.

"You will have to be satisfied with what we have told you so far."

"No." Myx shook her head, not going to let them hide anything from her anymore. "You're going to tell me everything."

Naichom descended the steps of the throne dais, raising her club. Radiation stirred around her in a cyclone. "We've been through this; Bishing and I were only going to tell you some things.

It would take us years to explain the rationalizations of every little detail of every little decision that led up to what has happened. You will just have to be satisfied with what has been revealed already and accept your new role as supreme monarch of this planet."

Chapter 52

The silver broach! Myx could see everything clearly now. The pin was the key to everything. If she could get her hands on it, she could take the wisps under her control.

"You're right," Myx sighed, letting tears fall down her cheeks. She reached forward, her hands outstretched as though she wanted a hug. "I should just be happy to know who I really am. Thank you, mother, for telling me."

As Naichom entered her embrace, Myx moved her hands to the broach. The grey figurine felt hot to the touch as she attempted to rip it from her mother.

"You didn't really think it'd be that easy?" Naichom clicked her tongue as she ran her thin fingers through loose strands of Myx's hair. "Bishing has been trying to take my broach ever since we first met. Honestly, I'm more surprised that you didn't try to take it sooner."

Myx released the silver pin and stepped away. "So you admit that it's the secret to your power?"

"One of many, my dear one." Naichom blew Bishing a kiss, a strange tenderness in her eyes before she turned away from him. "And now, thanks to your impetuous plan to steal from me, the whole planet knows that this broach is special." She turned to the swarm of broadcast drones. "You hear that, everyone? This is what you want—not me." The President removed the broach's backing and handed the pin to Myx. "It's now your responsibility to keep it safe. Congratulations!"

Something else was brewing below the surface of her words. One moment, Naichom was amused at her attempt to take the broach, and the next she was giving it to her?

Reaching forward, Myx used the pin of the broach to slice a gash in Naichom's out-stretched wrist. Blood dripped from the wound onto the tiled floor. Pressing her hand in the red mess, Myx clutched tightly at the broach and willed the wisps to shoot towards her.

Thick ribbons of radiation swarmed at her. Myx felt all her mother's memories at once. Naichom's early life and teen years seemed dark and full of conflict as she was groomed to be the next Tarasi President. However, her days seemed to grow brighter after the moment she met Bishing.

Myx pushed past the memories of the two of them together, but kept them tucked away in her mind to watch more closely later.

Instead, she focused on the scenes of the Emperor, the future President, and their child running through the Palace halls. The scene rushed forward and she was in Naichom's office, reading letters about Myx and staring at a photo album of her as a young daughter.

All the while, schemes of how to regain power in her relationship with Bishing exploded through Naichom's mind. Loneliness and paranoia appeared to be the guiding factors in most of her main decisions over the extensive, dark years.

The broach—Myx remembered that she needed to find the secrets of the broach before the blood-transfer wore off. Roughly a week had gone by since she had absorbed some of Bishing's memories back in the radiation chambers of the Camp. And now those were nothing more than fleeting, incomplete glimpses into his life.

Her visions became blurry, as though she was watching them on a screen that was shaking. And then the connection broke.

Calloused hands covered hers with a white fabric. Red bled through the material as it was absorbed away from Myx's skin. She blinked out of the memory to see Gotasun's frowning face looking down on her.

"Let go of me," Myx demanded, weakly squirming out of his reach.

He grabbed one of her ankles, stood, and dragged her to the throne dais. "You're still an idiot, aren't you, my pet?"

Myx kicked at Gotasun's hand with her free foot until he let go. She scrambled to her feet to see that Naichom's wound had already been treated and wrapped. How long had she been in the memory trance?

The President sat on her throne, her face a mixture of disappointment and amusement as she cradled her bandaged wrist. "Well done, Gotasun. As always, I am honored by your unceasing loyalty." She turned to her daughter. "Myx, I hope you're satisfied with your decision. The drones broadcasted most of your little stint before we were able to end the transmission. Now the planet's inhabitants think you're violent and insane. But I suppose that's not my problem anymore."

Bishing signed something with his hands, making Myx feel almost as though the War Declaration and Labor Camp had just been one long nightmare she was finally awakening from. But she hardened her heart and prepared for his next shocking revelation.

"Stop trying to make me feel sympathy for you!" Myx growled, running her hands up and down her messy braid. "What else do I need to know?"

"Nothing. We're done here." Naichom eased herself out of her throne and approached Bishing. She removed his crown and dumped it carelessly onto the tile. "You're the Queen now. Bish and I will search for our next season of happiness during our adventure in the stars."

Myx retrieved the crown, but didn't put it on. "No. There's something else that you've been side-stepping. Bishing keeps looking like he wants to confess something; he keeps opening and closing his mouth." She took a step forward, only to be blocked by Gotasun. "Move away from your Queen!"

"Your authority doesn't work like that, my pet." Gotasun removed a screen from his pants pocket and showed it to Myx. "According to this newly ratified ordinance, the Chief of Security can override an order from royalty should the monarch be in danger due to their own decision-making." He gave her a moment to read the file before lifting her chin. His grey hematite eyes bore into hers. "It means that I still get to be your Handler."

"No. You can't! I was supposed to—" Myx couldn't finish her sentence. The broach in her hand burned beneath her skin. Her head span and she couldn't get enough oxygen to get her brain to function properly. In a painful gasp, she released the pin and rubbed her aching hand across her chest.

Gotasun's calloused fingers caressed her cheek. "If you have a problem with it, take it up with the Governing Board. However, I think they're going to be a bit busy the next few months as they answer for their war crimes."

Myx turned to Bishing and tried to imagine him as the man who had befriended her—not as the father who consistently covered up the truth of their identities.

She suppressed a sob before demanding, "What else, Bish?"

Bishing sat along the edge of the dais and pressed his hands together in front of him. "I knew that Alycee had tried to assassinate you when you were a child; I feared that she was going to make another attempt on your life at the Camp." He took a breath, rubbing the temples of his forehead. "Although I eventually learned how terribly wrong I was about that, it doesn't change the fact that I hired Voumatir to kill Alycee." The Emperor met the new

Queen's gaze. "Everything I did was to keep my beloved daughter safe."

"You're sick! I don't want to have anything to do with you." Myx collected the broach from where she had dropped it. She trudged down the long throne room, feeling the Radiation Storm circulate the room as her temper flared. "I'm leaving! I don't want to be Empress or President or whatever destiny you imagined for me." She grasped a wide door handle and pulled; it didn't budge.

She could feel the cold-warm tingling of wisps passing through her skin as she stood there, yanking on handles until her palms felt raw.

Even as the radiation swirled under her control, Myx couldn't help feeling utterly powerless in her situation. Bishing was the ultimate mastermind behind Alycee's death—not Heikah, not Parnuss, not Voumatir. Alycee's murder had been what pushed Myx over the edge at the Camp. It was what led her and Rauno to experiment with combining radiation and ashes to fuse life forces. Every step Myx had taken in the past weeks had all been influenced by that one event.

And despite being the one who was chosen to unite the Tarasi and Hathak, she was still not trusted to make her own decisions. Gotasun was going to continue having a position of authority and power over her. Myx collapsed to the tiled floor of the throne room and ordered the wisps away with her mind.

Fingers ran up and down her shoulder. Myx shied away from the touch before realizing that her comforter was Rauno.

The ginger-haired researcher helped Myx to her feet. He let her lean on him as she led her back to the dais. "From the moment I met you, Myx, I knew there was something different about you. But who'd have thought that the kind, mousy woman I met all those weeks ago would turn out to be the Queen of the planet?"

Myx's head ached from all the memories that pressed against her skull. "Can we please not reminisce anymore? I'm not exactly excited about this. I don't understand why you're so chipper about it."

Tieg joined them at the dais and held up Bishing's crown. The soft glow from his white opal irises reflected off the gems in a spray of multi-colored light. "I've been given evidence of every past ruler's illegal activity to gain power, money, or knowledge. With it, we can help end the corruption of the government and finally unite the people of this planet! What's not to be excited about?"

Rauno nodded. "And with the animosity gone, Dolra and I can live in peace, enjoying our life in matrimonial bliss until—"

"But don't you feel disgusted at all the scheming and manipulation that has led us here?" Myx couldn't believe that she was the only one not enjoying herself at the Emperor's Palace. "Doesn't it upset you—even a little bit?"

The men shared a look that Myx couldn't quite understand.

Placing Bishing's crown on Myx's head, Tieg said, "We think you're old enough to understand that no situation in life is one-hundred percent ideal."

"All we can really do is handle our circumstances the best we can until something else changes." Rauno paused, scratching at his scraggly red beard. "For the moment, I'd be happy to live in this exquisite Palace with my beloved Dolra and all of our close friends." He made adjustments to the crown and gestured for her to ascend the dais.

The door behind the thrones opened and Gotasun strode back in. A thick blue cape with gold trimmings decorated his massive shoulders. "Alright, my pet. Your parents send their love and what-not." Gotasun tossed his cape's material over a shoulder as he plopped onto one of the thrones. He unhooked a simple silver halo from his belt loop and placed it on his head.

Myx gaped at him. "What are you doing on my throne?"

"You only get one, my pet." Gotasun lazily slouched over the golden chair's elaborately-carved arm. He pointed at the chair next to his. "That's yours. This is mine."

"But you're not the King," Myx replied, confused by what was happening. She studied the smirk on his smug face. Her cheeks warmed as she gasped, "Oh, please don't tell me that you're the King! I will take this broach and slice open my arteries before I let you be my husband."

Gotasun was quiet several moments, obviously enjoying Myx's anguish. But eventually he replied, "No, I'm not the King. I can be, though. I have the authority to make sure that you choose a suitable man as your husband. If you don't, I can announce myself as your groom." He let out a soft chuckle, his cold hematite eyes warming slightly in amusement. "Don't worry about that right now, my pet. You're still several years away from being trusted enough to court responsibly."

Myx ran her thumb up and down the length of her heirloom pin. From the life forces surging within her, she understood a number of places she could plunge the broach to give herself a quick death. And yet, suicide didn't feel like a viable option for her.

Letting out a sigh, Myx settled into her throne and secured the broach to the lapel of her shirt.

She barely flinched as the broadcast drones zoomed out of the walls once again.

Tieg stood between the thrones. He whispered, "The planet is waiting for an explanation of today's events. Shall I—"

"No," Myx interrupted, gathering her courage. "I'll do it."

All the lies were going to stop there. Even though she was being forced to rule, that didn't mean that she shouldn't put forth her best effort, ending the deceptions. Things were going to change between the Tarasi and Hathak—for the better.

Moving to the other side of Myx's throne, Rauno whispered, "Endure, my Queen. Adjust to your situation. We have a whole crypt of your ancestors to experiment with over the following months. I bet they have some rather interesting skills to pass on." Rauno had his "escape plan" face on as his green emerald eyes sparkled from the swirling radiation. He waved at the broadcast drones, hiding any signs that he was devising a scheme.

Tieg added his input. "Of course, you can count me in on any getaway attempts from the Palace—should you need my assistance in the future. In the meantime, I'll let you two handle the desecrating of corpses while I focus my energy on the diplomatic side of ruling. But for the time-being, I'll advise you to bide your time until our next scheme to secure your freedom."

Flashbacks of Myx's time at the Labor Camp surfaced in her mind. She had been through more abuse than she could have ever thought a person could experience. But she was still alive, stronger and wiser than her younger self.

Myx shook her head, realizing that she was done running for her destiny.

Although her situation wasn't exactly ideal, Myx now felt capable of bearing any surprises Gotasun or the others had to throw at her.

Stepping toward the drones, Myx activated her new ability, forcing the waves of radiation to obey her will. The colored ribbons danced around the ballroom in rhythmic pulses, giving the new Queen strength and fortitude as she addressed her subjects.

Thank you for reading!

If you'd like to learn about Amy Engle and her other works, visit **amyengle.com/BLOG.**

While you're there, don't forget to subscribe to Amy's Newsletter through the **contact** page.

Amy's other works:

- UNDOING LIFE
- IRIS
- REPS AND ROYALS

Other forthcoming books from Amy Engle:

- THE PEOPLE'S ORDER
- NOT SO ANONYMOUS
- THANKLESS CONTACT
- ALTERATION
- THE FANCIFUL UNION
- ENCHANTED RECKONING

CPSIA information can be obtained
at www.ICGtesting.com
Printed in the USA
FSHW04n0801030418
46365FS